ULTRAVIOLET

ULTRAVIOLET

SUZANNE MATSON

CATAPULT NEW YORK

Copyright © 2018 by Suzanne Matson
First published in the United States in 2018 by Catapult (catapult.co)
All rights reserved

ISBN: 978-1-936787-95-1

Catapult titles are distributed to the trade by Publishers Group West
Phone: 866-400-5351

Library of Congress Control Number: 2017964532

Printed in the United States of America

10 9 8 7 6 5 4 3 2 1

For Joe, Nic, Henry, and Teddy

CONTENTS

ULTRAVIOLET

CODA

Boston, 2015

On the fifteenth day, her mother's breathing comes in little fish gasps, mouth ajar. Samantha angles her toward the window to catch every flash of birdwing, every thin ray of winter light. She sits on the edge of the bed and holds her mother's hand, silky warm. The good eye is open its slit. Once in a while Samantha says something, some commentary on the still and unchanging world outside, or some encouragement that her mother can go when she is ready, follow whatever new thing is revealing

3

itself. She also says ordinary things like, the boys will be coming home from school now, they'll be letting the dog out.

Samantha rises to change position. When she turns back, her mother's face is dark, the gasping stopped. Samantha grabs her hand; after all these days it can't be only this, can it? But Kathryn's last breath, a breath not taken in but released, comes next: a large sigh, a letting-go, and with that something in the room—the spell, the cord knitting them together—is cut. Or no, that can't be right, either.

In the days to come, waiting to claim her mother's ashes, she sorts objects. She packs away the flowered housecoats Kathryn died in, one day at a time. Will keep the carved elephant from India. And the dentures: They were her mother's smile, her mother's bite. What, in the end, do you do with the teeth?

ULTRAVIOLET

Dehradun, India, 1930

R ahul, their regular driver, has a toothache. He always smiles
in his friendly way as he opens the door to the hired sedan.
He teases Kathryn in his half-English and half-Hindi, making her laugh. He drives purposefully but carefully down the mountains. Though swinging around the curves usually gives Elsie a sick
feeling, with Rahul at the wheel she can expect the least amount of
discomfort. But Rahul is looking after his tooth, so Manoj, their
houseman, accompanies them down the paths to the motor road
to confer with the replacement, a tall Sikh. Elsie hasn't seen him

before. But if Manoj thinks he is suitable, the arrangement will have to do. J.N. is still in the plains and not around to decide things.

Elsie, after three children, trouble with her circulation, and an ever-thickening waistline, is no longer a good walker in the hills, and on steep paths has to be borne in a dandie, a fact that perpetually embarrasses her. Kathryn skips along beside her sedan chair, nimble as a young goat. Manoj keeps Kathryn from straying too near the edge and also keeps an eye on the porter toting their lunch hamper. It is a cumbersome, hour-long procession, down three or four miles, and the lurching of the dandie makes Elsie irritable in her discomfited state.

After glancing once at their approach, the Sikh driver doesn't look at them again. He and Manoj stand off to the side and discuss arrangements in one of those mysterious Indian conferences that make Elsie feel passive and dependent. She is too far out of earshot to know if they are talking in Hindi, or Punjabi, or a mix. The number of languages in India, hundreds of them, is a fact perpetually astonishing to her. Her own children can rattle on in simple Hindi or fluent Chhattisgarhi, acquired without effort from their ayahs and their Indian playmates in Dhamtari.

Though she took some trouble to learn Hindi when they'd arrived years ago, sitting through her course at Landour and repeating the phrases with the rest, she never gained a secure hold on the language. She can say the necessary things to the cooks and knows how to tell the servants this and that about changing beds or washing floors. House Hindi, she thinks of it. But even half of that is gesture, not to mention English filtering in, since the servants seem to pick up her English much faster than she manages their Hindi. J.N. is fairly fluent, so matters outside the house have always been left to him.

But Manoj has been with them from the beginning and she trusts him implicitly. Finally, the Sikh inclines his head to show it is finished and all is understood. He stares neutrally into the middle distance as he holds the car door open and Manoj loads the hamper in the back between them. Kathryn bounces a little on the seat with excitement.

"All is settled, Memsahib," Manoj says, bending slightly to speak into their open door while the Sikh assumes his place behind the wheel.

"He knows we're to be at the doctor's by eleven thirty?"

"Yes, Memsahib."

"And he's familiar with the address in Dehradun?"

"Yes, Memsahib. This driver knows Dehradun very well."

"Does he speak any English, Manoj?"

Manoj angles his head toward the driver. *"Angrayzi?"*

The driver from his seat replies something without turning his head.

"He says a little, Memsahib. Do not worry. We will be awaiting your return here in the afternoon."

"Shukriya, Manoj."

She attempts no exchange with the driver as they set off; he's acknowledged nothing further about them, and his statue-like bearing makes her even shyer than usual. If it were Rahul, she would inquire after his family and make small talk in a mix of Hindi and English about the long stretch of hot days or the coming monsoons. He might remember that it had been Kathryn's birthday a week ago. His wife and daughter had come by to drop off some sewing, and they'd been offered leftover slices of cake. Kathryn and Vasati had eaten outside while playing jacks on the warm flagstones.

As the curves unspool, Elsie has the funny feeling that the brakes are out, not on the automobile but on the trip itself, and that she has no way to control it. Perhaps the tension of not knowing the driver is taking a worse-than-usual toll on her stomach. They swoop with the bends in the road, lurching a little with each downshift, and she glances over to see how Kathryn is taking it. Her daughter is turned away from her, chin tilted up to watch the passing of trees and sky out the window, her poor little arms swathed in bandages over the eczema. She seems to be fine, so Elsie thinks it unwise to mention her own distress lest she plant the seed in Kathryn's mind. The warm wind comes in through the driver's open windows, but even the fresh air isn't helping.

The more Elsie tries to repress the sick feeling, the more it wants to well up, until she doesn't know what to do. Ask the fellow to stop? But where? There are no pullouts, and even if she does get him to stop a minute, she is more afraid of resting at the side and being in the way of other autos barreling down the mountain than of simply proceeding. She tries to follow Kathryn's example and fixes her attention on the passing view. She hears her husband's pulpit voice: *He gives power to the faint; and to them that have no might He increases strength.*

"Look, Mamma, is it a hawk?" Kathryn points. The broad wings float over the empty space alongside the road drop.

"No, a vulture, I think," Elsie murmurs. Then the sulfurous smell from Kathryn's ointment seeping through the bandages coupled with a sudden vision of the vulture waiting for something beneath it to finish twitching and go limp—maybe a cow that had stumbled off the embankment—brings the bile up.

"Stop, please!"

Kathryn looks up in alarm. "What is it, Mamma?" Then, to the driver in her small clear voice, "Stop!"

He pulls over, not a good spot, not much room in the road, and Elsie wrenches open the door, bending her thumb awkwardly in the process. She leans as far out as she can manage, losing her breakfast: tea with milk and sugar, toast that had been spread with the preserves sent from her sister's farm in Illinois. Some of the mess gets on the running board, and even splashes a little across the lower portion of her white cotton lawn dress. She feels the Sikh's expressionless eyes upon her in the mirror as she fishes for her handkerchief to daub her face and mouth.

"Mamma, are you all right?" Kathryn's small hand is lightly

patting her shoulder over the hamper. It's the way Elsie pats her when she's not feeling well.

Embarrassment and the relief of emptying her stomach put her back in charge of herself. She closes the door firmly, nodding to the driver, who engages the gear and proceeds.

"I'm fine, Kathryn. Nothing but a stomach upset. It's better now." She takes a drink from her water flask but the acridness still burns in her throat. Several mouthfuls don't make it go away. She pours a small amount of water on the handkerchief and uses it to make herself and the spots on her dress as neat as she can; still she detects a smell and a stain. She tells herself it is no matter. God provides. She'll wash up at the doctor's office. There is no sin in getting sick, but there is glory in feeling the returning strength of the body, and she is already better. She hopes the same for Kathryn—that the treatments will finally begin to take hold, that she'll finally be able to do without the messy ointments and hot, bothersome bandages. That there will be no more itching, no more scabs. The hill climate will help; she knows that from experience. But the situation remains difficult and perplexing. One doctor said Kathryn must eat no eggs, another doctor said she must eat plenty of eggs. One doctor said no milk, another said milk three times a day. They must boil it first; Kathryn gags on the skin that floats on the top.

After a time, the curves widen and flatten and the buildings of Dehradun spread out before them. She has no idea how to direct the driver; Rahul knew all. But this driver, too, seems to know his way. He makes a few turns among the bungalows and government offices, and arrives in front of the two-story hospital where Dr. Withers sees patients. Here are the ultraviolet lamps.

Standing outside the car, she looks directly at the Sikh, which necessitates looking up at him, instead of levelly, as with most Hindu people. The Sikhs are a tall race. J.N. has always spoken highly of their discipline, their asceticism, but beyond that, she doesn't know what they stand for. She knows the men have uncut hair coiled underneath their turbans, but she doesn't know why. He probably doesn't know why she wears her net Mennonite cap; they are at a draw there.

"Here," she says, pointing to the ground beneath their feet. "One hour." She holds up one finger and then taps her wristwatch.

He inclines his head in the way people in this country do, which usually means yes. Sometimes it doesn't, she's found out, after she's expected a dinner to be ready at five, and it hasn't even been started yet. Sometimes she has the feeling it means, *I hear what you say and will take it under consideration.* His direct gaze is unsettling compared to Rahul's modest smile and eyes that flicker away. Kathryn is tugging at her hand.

"Let's go in, Mamma. I'm hot."

There is nothing to do but trust Providence that he understands what is required of him. Rahul would use the waiting time to clean the mess on the side of the car, finding a bucket of water and a rag. She thinks this fellow will probably consider the task beneath him. It is a perpetual puzzle—which servants think which tasks are suited to whom. Her brothers and sisters at the mission wouldn't say that any task is beneath any person since all is God's work. Though some things, building the school in Dhamtari, for instance, should absorb the missionaries' primary energies if there are others on hand to do the everyday chores. And servants abound here. J.N. says it is a kindness to hire them; in one's employ they eat better, provide for their families, get medicines when they need them, and are closer to the Word of God. This is how Elsie has come to be managing several natives to keep her household running, some of whom wouldn't dream of scrubbing the dirty floors, and some who are apparently fit for nothing else. In her frustration at keeping all their restrictions straight she'd almost rather mop and sweep herself. It is the kind of vigorous work she enjoys and is good for her. She blames her stoutness on having servants. The year she'd arrived to marry J.N. she was so slender that the other missionary women clucked their tongues and scooped extra rice onto her plate.

•

The hospital smells reassuringly of ammonia and other strict odors. English nurses bustle about in starched uniforms, and Indian nurses glide by in soft white salwars. White-painted signs with red lettering in Hindi and English point to Reception or X-ray or Laboratory. Elsie gives Kathryn's name at Reception, and settles her daughter in a rattan chair with a book they have brought with them. Then she goes to the washroom she knows is around the corner.

Elsie checks her face in the mirror for evidence of her sick episode, then splashes water on it and uses a clean corner of her handkerchief to pat it dry. The towel on the ring is grimed with use, even though the tile floor and porcelain are immaculate. Her cheeks have spots of high color. Blood pressure, nothing she can do for it except keep off the salt, which she does love. Despite the breezes from the open car, her hair is still tucked decently back in its bun under her cap, save one strand that she secures with a hairpin. Then she sees to the spots on her dress.

Nervous that they might be called, Elsie rushes, not caring if she splashes extra water on her dress and arms. It feels good, and it will dry. Back in the waiting area, a fan rotates too slowly overhead to be of use. Fly strips hang in the corners but are mysteriously bare, while several obviously vigorous flies buzz about in the still, warm air. But the heat is nothing compared to what they left behind three weeks before, on the plains where J.N. still labors. Time at the hill station is her favorite stretch out of the year, though she feels guilty for enjoying it so much. The children's health of course comes first, and as a mother it is her job to take them up to the cooler climate. But J.N. will stay trapped in the swelter for another two weeks, just as a great mass of Indian humanity is always trapped there, without relief.

They wait another ten minutes, Elsie listening to Kathryn read aloud, until an English nurse, one they've had before, calls them, and they follow her down a corridor to an outpatient examining room.

"How is Kathryn today?"

Kathryn looks at her shoes. Elsie nudges her.

"I'm fine," Kathryn says, looking up. "Except my arms." She says it with a degree of impertinence, as if the nurse should know very well how she is, since they have come for the express purpose of curing her. Elsie tries to give her a warning look, but Kathryn is still looking at the nurse, chin thrust up.

"Well, let's have a look, shall we?"

The nurse helps Kathryn step up to the examination table and Elsie seats herself in the chair. The ultraviolet apparatus has already been rolled in on its cart. Kathryn doesn't look at the lamp, though she's told Elsie before that the rays don't hurt. Gingerly the nurse unwraps each arm, then uses cotton balls to stroke away the salve.

"Looks better, would you say?" the nurse asks.

"Does it?" The possibility charges Elsie with hope. "I see it every day and find it hard to tell. I didn't think there was that much change."

"Hmm." The nurse looks at the chart, frowning. Elsie thinks she must be calculating, weighing the jottings from two weeks ago against what is presently before her eyes.

"Well, we'll just let the doctor have a look, then," the nurse concludes, and Elsie's hopefulness vanishes. The nurse has just been making pleasant talk.

They are alone in the room a few moments, and though none of the tongue depressors or syringes or other instruments in the glass cabinet are for Kathryn's ailment, they still have the power to intimidate. To distract her, Elsie asks, "Is that watercolor of the tiger new?"

"No, it was here last time," Kathryn says.

"Interesting that the artist gave it green eyes," says Elsie.

"They should have given it yellow, like the ones in the tiger Daddy shot."

The villagers were pleased with J.N. for protecting their livestock, and J.N. was extraordinarily pleased with himself. He offered the skin to the village elder, but didn't argue very hard—at all, in fact—when the elder insisted he keep it for himself.

In Dhamtari, Kathryn likes to stretch out and read on the tiger skin. She would know what color glass was in its eye sockets. Sometimes she and the tiger lie cheek to cheek.

Dr. Withers enters, a stoop-shouldered gentlemanly figure with a stethoscope looped around his neck. Elsie heard he's spent his whole career in India, and wonders why. Still, J.N. might do the same, without ever calculating that he intends to. Time floats by here, days drumming away in monsoons, then the heat of the plains settling one into a deep drowse. He pauses gravely to shake Kathryn's hand.

"How now, Miss Kathryn?"

"Fine, thank you."

"That's the stuff. Let's have a look at those arms."

He puts on the spectacles from his pocket and looks closely at the red, scaly welts snaking up each one.

"Much itching?"

"Yes." Kathryn makes a face.

"I haven't noticed quite as much, I don't think," Elsie interjects. "When she thinks about it and gets going, yes. But there are long stretches when she seems able to ignore it."

"Let's stick with this salve, then."

"It's smelly," Kathryn says.

"That it is," Dr. Withers agrees mildly. "But we do what we need to, to get well. Ready for the special goggles?"

Kathryn likes this part, Elsie knows. She puts on the smoked goggles Dr. Withers hands her and grins, her ears protruding under the elastic band that flattens her bob. She does look like a strange explorer in them, or like that female flier, Miss Earhart. Elsie puts on the pair the doctor hands her. He puts on a pair of his own as well.

"Aren't we a strange bunch, then?" the doctor asks. And surely they are.

Dr. Withers tinkers with the settings and directs Kathryn where to lay her arms.

"No looking directly at the light, remember," he says, "even with the goggles."

Then the room lights up with a bright glow that indirectly illuminates Kathryn's face, which is tilted toward the tiger. Elsie knows there is no pain involved, but she can't forget that the beams have a malicious power as well as a curative one. If they looked directly at the source, how damaged would their sight be? It feels like a sinful temptation, to look at what might hurt you. There is nothing to see but obliterating whiteness, but still it tempts.

As he dresses her arms with fresh salve and gauze, Dr. Withers asks Kathryn if she will be starting school at Woodstock this year, now that she's eight.

She nods silently, so that he has to look up to catch the answer.

"And won't that be fine, to be one of the big children?"

"I'd rather learn at home with Mamma, as I have been. I can already read fourth-form books. And I write stories in my notebooks."

"That's fine! But you'll learn even better at such a fine school."

Kathryn purses her lips and does not answer, and Elsie knows she is quitting her side of the discussion, seeing nothing to be gained.

"There we go," Dr. Withers says, patting her arm after the last neat twist and tuck. His professional competence puts Elsie's efforts to shame. White, clean arms like a cloth doll. Kathryn is her only daughter, her baby, and Elsie can't help holding her closer in certain respects. Russell is already in college back in America; Paul is having a career of his own at Woodstock—captain of this, president of that—and barely seems to need her. Elsie doesn't know if she is making KK more fragile by holding her close, or if she instinctively holds her closer because she was more fragile from the start. She is a chatterbox and cheerful when she's around those who are familiar, but slow to leave her mother's side when they are someplace new.

"How about we get rid of those bandages by fall, Kathryn? What do you say you go to school without them?"

Kathryn looks up, surprised. Elsie is surprised, too. By now she thinks of the bandages as part of her daughter.

"Really?" she asks, because Kathryn is silent. "You think so?"

"I see improvement. I think the light treatments are working. If you keep up the salve at home, we stand a good chance. And we'll see you back here in two weeks. Let's hope for the best."

Two weeks: J.N. will have joined them by then; they'll all go together. J.N. loves to drive, will find someone's car to borrow, and will make up a list of supplies he'll want to secure in Dehradun for his various tinkering projects. Or it might be more books, never enough for him.

They pay their bill and make the next appointment with the clerk at Reception. Outside, the sun feels at first like warm hands, a benediction. Then Elsie's body begins to sweat inside her clothes; a whiff of the sick smell rising up, despite her efforts to clean the dress.

The car isn't there. Sun spangles off the white hospital and the white, low, crowded buildings across the street. In front of the buildings, a vendor, sitting cross-legged, stares. He is selling fruit from a basket, his knobby ankles and long bare feet protruding darkly from the ends of his white pajama. Down the street a bony white cow is immobile, head lowered, lost in whatever thought it has. Lost to the white light.

"Can we have our lunch now, Mamma?"

"Yes, of course. When the driver comes back with our hamper." It is twelve thirty. She thinks of their jam sandwiches, thermoses of tea, tin of biscuits. Asha tucked in a bag of *jamun*, ripe from the tree.

But the car is not there. And after another minute it still isn't. Kathryn does an improvised hopscotch beside her, without the chalked lines. Like a bird with one leg folded up, she hops then bends down, balancing, and snatches a pebble. She hums to herself.

Elsie wonders if when she said "one hour" and held up one finger, the driver thought she meant "one o'clock." Very possible; she's learned to calculate that every communication between herself and a native has a fifty percent chance of going wrong. They should get themselves out of the heat and go sit in Reception again. She casts one final look up and down the street—surely he understood correctly and will arrive any second. But there is only the unmoving cow, the staring fruit wallah. What will they do if he never comes? No telephone back at the Landour villa. They'll have to use the phone at the hospital to call the office at Woodstock to send a runner to inform Manoj—and then what? When she works herself into this kind of state, J.N. reminds her that if she asks for God's assistance, He will provide it in all ways great and small.

I will lift up mine eyes to the hills; from whence cometh my help.

She does lift her eyes then, even turns her head so she is looking directly at the green hills, the direction of their trip home, their shaded villa, and Manoj and Asha, who will do what needs to be done, speak to the incomprehensible people in the language they can comprehend.

When she returns her gaze to the bleached light of street level, she sees the black car, approaching slowly, then coming to a dignified stop in front of them. Everything the Sikh does is slow and controlled. He unfolds himself from the driver's seat, stands erect as he holds open the door.

In her relief, Elsie gives free rein to her irritation. They were exposed to sun and strangers; he should have been waiting for them in advance of the time. She struggles to govern her feelings, put them away as J.N. always instructs her to. Anger is bad for her blood pressure. But her anger doesn't want to be put away; it spills to her husband, too. He knows she dislikes taking charge of excursions like this. Why isn't he here seeing to things? Why is his work always more important than his family?

"Where did you go?" Kathryn asks the driver. Elsie is taken aback then, as she often is, by Kathryn's matter-of-factness. India, Indians, the slowness, the heat, the mysteries—they are all she has ever known. She is, in fact, a native herself, born in Nainital. It occurs to her that Kathryn has not been at all afraid the driver would not come back for them. She sees the Sikh look down at her daughter, a flicker of a smile.

"*Gurudwara*," he says.

Elsie is instantly ashamed. His place of worship. They had passed one coming into town, the distinctive tall thin flagpoles, red against the pale stone of the building. J.N. is right about her quick blood, her jumping to conclusions. As she usually does several times during any given day, she asks God to make her better, more patient, less focused on her selfish needs.

It is probably a mistake to try to eat while bumping along on the road. Their tea will spill, their stomachs will be unsettled. If it were Rahul, he would ask her if she preferred to stop; he would know where, some place that was shady, a park here in town, perhaps. But the Sikh simply climbs back behind the wheel and begins driving this way and that through the streets of town, routing them back to the main road. She could speak up; she could insist. But something in the way he is calmly enclosed in his self, seemingly forgetful of them in the backseat, makes it too hard. In his presence she feels silenced. She has always been quite sure that she doesn't like being mistress to a house of servants, but she is also sure that she doesn't like this: being at the mercy of someone supposedly in her employ who shows utter indifference to her. Who even—she doesn't know how she knows it, for he has not been outwardly rude—clearly wishes she were not here, in his country. He radiates dismissal.

She opens the hamper, pours a half-cup of tea for Kathryn, and says in a brisk and cheerful voice, "We'll just eat as we go, that will be much easier. We'll get back to Landour sooner and you can play with your friends." Kathryn doesn't seem to think anything is amiss in this arrangement. She accepts her tea and tests the temperature. It will have cooled just to the point of warm by now. She drinks the half-cup down, not spilling any. Thirsty girl, Elsie thinks, taking the cup back and pouring her another. She is conscious of her own thirst now, but will help Kathryn through her food and drink first, for the sake of neatness.

"Mamma, do you think the doctor was just saying it to make me feel better?"

"Saying what, about the bandages coming off by fall?"

"Yes. How can he know?"

"Well, he can't, of course. But he's hopeful."

Kathryn considers this, taking the tea and half of a sandwich, placed on a napkin on her lap while she drinks with two hands.

"I wouldn't want them to come off if there are scars. I'd rather have the bandages."

Charm is deceitful, and beauty is vain, Elsie almost says to her, but doesn't. She wouldn't like to see Kathryn have to go to school with scars, either.

"We'll just have to see," she says. "Scars fade, you know. Maybe there won't be any if you don't scratch. And anyway, in the cool weather you'll have sleeves."

"Oh, yes," Kathryn says, her voice brightening. "I forgot about the sleeves."

Elsie takes pleasure in having said the comforting thing, rather than the Scripture. Which, she knows, is meant to comfort, but doesn't always. When her babies were laid in her arms, all she was conscious of was the overwhelming desire to be their refuge. Her mother had died when she was twelve, leaving her as the oldest child with a father who drank up any few dollars that came his way. After her mother's death, Elsie and the other children never had true security until she marched them in the cold, when they hadn't eaten for two days, to the Mennonite Home Mission on the south side of Chicago. I am here with my sisters and brother, Elsie told the woman with spectacles and a plain blue dress and net cap over her bun, because God has led us here, having no one in this world to turn to.

The woman nodded. You'll want a hot supper before anything else. There's a table for you by the stove.

The Mennonites became her family. Later, she made a new family with J.N., who could make her feel small sometimes, but always made her feel safe.

Elsie offers Kathryn another half-sandwich, but she shakes her head. She does take a biscuit. When she's all finished, Elsie packs away Kathryn's thermos and napkin, and thinks she has just time to nibble something before the car leaves these gentler curves and begins the serious business of climbing. She remembers the morning; she'll eat only enough to keep body and soul together until they arrive.

She has unscrewed her thermos and begun to pour when the car gives a sudden lurch, then pulls left to a patch of gravel at the lip of the embankment and stops. A warm stain of milky tea spreads across her lap. She leans forward.

"What is it?" she asks.

He shrugs.

Kathryn pipes up. "Is something wrong with the car?"

He tilts his head. Maybe yes.

But Elsie didn't feel the thump of a flat tire, didn't hear the flapping of a broken belt, or see a billow of steam from the radiator.

The Sikh turns his head only ten degrees in their direction. "One minute," he says in English.

He leaves the car and strides several yards ahead to a tea stall perched on the edge of the road. In front of the stall are three cane chairs and a low wood table. The proprietor must be inside, shadowed from Elsie's view. From here she can't tell if they exchange words.

"What's he doing, Mamma?"

"I don't know. Maybe he is asking about something." She keeps her voice relaxed for the sake of her child. If J.N. were here he would be out of the car and following the fellow, talking to him in English or Hindi, or even the few words of Punjabi he's managed to acquire. If there were something to find out, he'd want to know it, too. If there were something to fix, he'd want to watch and learn it, so he could do it himself the next time. But Elsie knows there is nothing to fix. And that if J.N. were here the Sikh would not have stopped without asking first.

She leans forward to get a breath of fresh air from the open windows and to hear whatever there might be to be heard. At the moment, a hush. Then, as if to answer the silence, the shrill ascending notes of the brain-fever bird, coming again and then again.

The Sikh turns his head in the direction of the sound. Walks across the road and waits. In a moment, a young boy scrambles down the hillside from a copse of trees, a Sikh child with a small twist of maroon turban. Elsie realizes that the notes were not from the bird; they were from the boy.

If he needed to stop, he should have asked her, or at least told her the purpose. She feels ashamed in an odd, oblique way for being taken advantage of in front of her child, for being treated as a person of no power or import.

Perhaps the driver is conferring over a family matter; maybe that is his nephew or even his son. Or it is a business transaction, and the boy is merely a courier. He is looking up, nodding intently, as if taking instructions. The Sikh is writing something down on a pad. This is not his son, not his kin, Elsie feels. The boy is to carry a note to someone—but to whom? She tries to quell the helplessness, and the fear—who else is up on the hillside, waiting to scramble down?—but gives in to a wave of homesickness, wanting to be free from all that is strange, from all she does not understand even after twenty years in India. She longs for her sisters, Lena and Emma, the kitchens of their farmhouses in Illinois, the communal rhythms of meals and chores and crops. How she loves to be there on their missionary furloughs—the last one five years ago—rolling out pie-crusts for the combined families and multiple field hands, beating the cake batter until it is velvet. Whenever she's afraid, she still clings to her sisters in her mind, ghosts from the time when they shared one bed and had no mother.

"What are they doing, Mamma?"

"I'm not sure, Kathryn. They seem to have some business, but the driver will be back in a minute."

"Can I get out?"

"No, you may not." Her voice sounds fluty and wrong. There is no other sound save the dry scraping of insects. They rest at the edge of nowhere—green terraced hills climbing above them and dropping beneath, hills that offer no outlet unless you know your way on foot.

What she has written in letters to America: the good that they do, the children they save, the eyes that they open. But India keeps reducing her to a person who knows nothing. The vast impassivity of it; its endlessness always poised to swallow up their carefully laid bricks and pews. Will they ever be allowed to stop building? And go home?

At long last—or maybe it was only a matter of five minutes—the driver returns, bows his head slightly to them, as if he can only now, his arrangements tended to, acknowledge the importunity.

Without a word of explanation, he starts the engine and sets off. The car begins winding up the hills again. The mystery of the Sikh's business is a thing they carry with them. Even Kathryn doesn't ask. Elsie has forgotten to eat, but her appetite is gone now so she packs up the hamper and stows it on the floor. Kathryn scoots over to lean into her side. Such a small weight a child is, but solid and real. It is only a few minutes before the afternoon heat and the rocking of the car cause her daughter to doze off, Elsie's arm around her.

With Kathryn sleeping, there is a new privacy between the Sikh and herself. Her mind keeps returning to the indignity of the stop, of not being informed. The man moves with so much dignity himself; what right has he to rob her of hers? All he had to do was ask and she would have said, *We don't mind at all. Perhaps we'll even stretch our legs.*

It's odd to bring it up this many minutes later, but it is odder still to let it hover in the air. If she doesn't speak, she knows it will remain painful evidence that she doesn't count; and if she doesn't count, except to her children, of course, what is she doing here?

"Was that your son back there?" she asks. She detests the slight tremolo in her voice. Perhaps he doesn't have enough English to understand the question.

He looks at her in the mirror, and does not seem startled to be spoken to.

"No. I have no son."

He adjusts his gaze back to the road, the hypnotic curves. The back of his neck is a warm brown. His dark blue turban is tightly, precisely wound; Elsie thinks of the doctor's professional wrap of Kathryn's linen bandages. She can just see the line of his black hair where it is swept up and under the turban. The sight of his hair uncoiled would seem unbearably personal after growing used to the turban—just as she would never remove her net cap and undo her own coiled bun outside of the house. Even her own children don't often see her with her hair down.

"I wondered why you stopped," she says. Her heart knocks wildly against her ribs at her own audacity, but after a few hard thumps it quiets again. She did wonder; it is an ordinary question. Although, she realizes, she didn't technically ask a question. He could leave it dangling.

He looks back again, his eyes somehow not so cold. He has, she realizes, expressive eyes, not like a statue at all.

"Just a message," he says. His English is very good. She wonders where he learned it. But she is disappointed by his answer. Does he think her a dolt? Obviously, a message. What else, if not a message?

"Business?" she asks. She would never pry at someone's reticence like this. She would consider it rude. But.

The Sikh's eyes, framed in a glance, seem exasperated. Then they disappear, because there is the increasingly steep road to attend to.

"Business, yes. The business of the Sikh people." A note of challenge in his voice.

She has heard this note before: It comes with talk of politics, which are at a low simmer everywhere in this country, a miasma you can't help but breathe.

She doesn't think there is an answer to his statement; what would it be? That God's business is all people, and all people's business is with God? She knows the Sikhs have a God, and unlike the Hindus they have just one. J.N. always says the missionaries will never make any inroads with the Sikhs. He says this cheerfully enough. He has pointed out the line waiting at the door of a *gurudwara*, where anyone, regardless of faith or caste, may come and receive a meal.

The business of the Sikh people. Elsie is not in possession of the nuances. Though the British are the ones now granting the mission its land leases, J.N. is convinced that the survival of their work will be dependent on the goodwill of the natives. She understands the issue in the main, of course, the part about white skin, the Britishers' and hers, too. But there is layer upon layer of complication, and that is where she gives up: too many factions here, Hindus, Moslems, Sikhs. The missionaries are not supposed to take sides about government, and Elsie has found it easier to be impartial if she is ignorant. They are here to nourish spirits, minds, and bellies—there is clarity for her in that. She looks away from politics like she looks away from the ultraviolet light. And they must stick with the British, at least for now, at least on paper, or all the walls they've raised and whitewashed could come tumbling down, the land beneath them pulled out like a tablecloth in a magician's trick. When Mahatma Gandhi came to speak to the farmers in their district and invited the Mennonites to tea,

Brother Lapp directed J.N. to write with their compliments and their regrets.

Look away and save your sight.

"Well, I'm glad you were able to see to it. Your business," she says, with a sudden feeling of generosity.

The eyes that flick to the mirror are amused. Then, after a few seconds, "You have been here for a long time?"

Elsie sees the steamer; the gangly young man with his perfectly white minister's collar waiting to escort her through the fetid air of the docks; the Mennonite brothers and sisters singing hymns at their wedding.

"Yes, a long time."

"And you like India?" This time the eyes have something else; an edge of hard mockery. Her usual answer is *Yes, very much.*

She hesitates. "Sometimes I miss where I come from."

"Then why not go back?"

"We will. My husband has helped build a school for Hindu children in the plains. It has been his life's work."

The eyes do not appear. But the turban nods slightly.

"I do like India," she says after a moment, as if he has been pressing her. "But I'd also like to go home."

The turban nods again, barely.

"Maybe when your husband's life work is finished." When he looks in the mirror, his eyes are kind.

Elsie's hand rises to her throat. "Oh, dear."

They laugh together.

Home is India, too, but broken in pieces. Home in Dhamtari, flat and hot, checking shoes in the morning for sleeping snakes. Home at the hill station in Landour, all of them together for the sweet season. J.N. will put down his burdens for a brief spell. There will be much baking, and the cooking of group suppers nearly every night. By day the mothers will knit, and make lists, and measure the children for clothing they will need during the school year. The children will catch beetles to race; Kathryn will frisk on the trails with the neighbor's dog. They will all sit outside after supper, prolonging their fellowship into the twilight. When darkness comes, the adults will allow a final game of flashlight tag—just squiggles of light instead of their children, shouts and laughter blurring in the night.

Kathryn stirs in her sleep and raises her face to look at her with half-dreaming eyes.

"Mamma?"

"*Shhh*, sweetheart. Not yet."

KK lowers her head again, flinging her white-linen arm across her mother's lap. Elsie would like to remain in this moment indefinitely; her daughter tucked against her as a mother and child are meant to be. She tries not to think ahead to September—*Take therefore no thought for the morrow: for the morrow shall take thought for the things of itself*—but cannot fend it off. She sees Kathryn lining up with the other Woodstock students as the mothers and fathers prepare for their descent to the road head at Kin Craig. Final kisses. Her daughter is stubborn and will stand still, not changing her face. Turning back to the path, the adults must concentrate on the uncertain ground beneath them as they pick their way.

But Elsie, carried on her infernal dandie, will not need to look down to watch her step. She'll see the dark-clothed backs of her fellow missionaries, bobbing in the dimness, all of them a herd of migrating animals obeying some unrelenting need to return to the plains. She'll wonder if it is better to glance back one final time at her daughter, who has never been away from her side, whom she will not see again until Christmas, or if it is better to remain facing front. She will not have solved this riddle by the time her bearers round the bend.

YOUR BEST YET

Chicago, 1942

Through the square of the train window Kathryn sees her father, whose tallness is strangely diminished on the platform. He is wearing his black overcoat over his black minister's clothing, but is bareheaded, so his shock of white hair and long pale face seem to float amid the dimness of the station. She gives a little wave, suddenly overcome with affection for him, but he seems unable to distinguish her from the faces at other windows. He smiles in a benedictory way at all of them, his hands clasped behind his back.

Suddenly they are moving, an effortless gliding without warning, but it turns out to be the train opposite them, a swimming sensation followed by the shock of still being in the same place after the other train slips away like a blur of silk. When she looks out her platform-side window, her father is still at attention. She doesn't try to wave again.

She hears the sounds of a late passenger coming up the aisle behind her seat, and can tell they are masculine sounds, the noise of someone taking up room in the world and not caring who knows it, a cheerful bumping along. The sounds stop just behind her, and she tenses a fraction.

"Is this seat taken?" The face that bends down to speak is about her age, friendly. He is in uniform.

"No, not at all." She hates how even simple phrases like this sound unnatural coming from her. She hates that her face is coloring, as she knows it is, a fanning of warmth.

The train lurches and he catches his balance. He does it easily, in the way of someone at home in a strong body. Then he hoists his suitcase up into the rack above them and flings himself into the seat.

"That was close."

He is saying something else about being late, but she must turn her back on him if she is to catch a last glimpse of her father. Craning her neck, she does, barely. Her father is waving, but at all the cars now; hers has already passed him by. She presses her fingertips to the window, just above the sill, watching until he's gone behind the posts.

"I'm sorry, what were you saying? I was just turning to see my father."

"Oh, sure. Came to see you off?"

"Yes."

"He'll miss you, wherever you're going."

Kathryn, who has up until this moment believed that he would not, or perhaps told herself this in order to be able to leave, suddenly knows that this is so.

"Where *are* you going? Wait, sorry. First things first. Mitch Myers." He extends a hand.

She shakes it, glad she has not yet removed her gloves. "Kathryn."

"Where are you headed, Kathryn?"

"Oregon."

He tilts his head at her, slack-jawed in mock astonishment. "Where they have Indians? Great Scott, I thought you were going to say Chicago, or maybe Milwaukee. What takes you all the way out there?"

She knows which Indians he is thinking of, though the fact that the word always means something different to her first is a perpetual gulf between herself and others. Even when she thinks she is all finished catching up.

"I'm going to visit my brother and his wife for a while." She doesn't add that she is going to find a job, live there on her own. Not even her brother Russell knows that. She's been working on the mental picture of herself doing this for over a year, so that the Kathryn off in Oregon seems almost like a separate being from her, someone established in the greater world. She is looking forward to joining up with that person.

He whistles. "Well, that's an adventure."

"Where are you off to?"

"Back to Fort Custer. I had a leave for my sister's wedding."

She could pursue the wedding conversation or the soldiering one. One direction might lead unnervingly back to neighbors, churches, schooling, friends in common.

"Have you been in the army long?"

"Just finished up my basic. Won't be long now before they ship me out."

His voice ends on a slightly mournful note. She reverses course, asks him about the wedding and he turns enthusiastic. He has a lot of sisters, three or four—she loses track when he is naming and describing them—and he is the baby, and, she gathers, the apple of various eyes, and he grew up on a farm, where they had the reception after the wedding, and yes, it does turn out that her aunt Lena and uncle Manny would probably know his parents as the farms aren't that far apart, but—thank lucky stars—they did go to separate high schools, Mitch in Peoria, Kathryn in East Peoria. She wouldn't have liked to have him slap his forehead in sudden recollection to say, *Of course I remember you!* She doesn't want to be remembered from then, spots on her chin and forehead, extra pounds from the ice cream shop where she scooped sundaes, almost mute that first year when she was around new people. The gulf between India and America was so wide she could scarcely see past it. She remembers staring at all the green and silver money, trying to do the math in rupees. The ice cream shop finally cured that; hitting the SALE button again and again on the cash register: Forty cents equaled one banana split. She began from there until she finally had an understanding of the worth of everything else. Then she'd sit down on her break, spooning up butter brickle, a textbook open in front of her as a decoy while she surreptitiously tried to acquire her fourth language, that of American teenagers speaking boisterously to one another.

But Mitch back then was at his own high school, carrying the football—she sees his head ducked in determination, ball tucked close as he sorts through the crush of opponents. His would have been one of the happy, loud voices in full possession of the currency and slang. There is the possibility that he could have sat at one of the crowded tables in her ice cream shop after a game. But she was invisible then, so she has no worries about him remembering that.

She is suddenly hot. She is not that girl with the ice cream scoop, has not been for several years now, but thinking of that girl has made her hot. She makes motions to shed her coat, a new one, an elegant shawl-collared wrap like you'd find in the movies she is not allowed to see. She bought it with her earnings as a schoolteacher, the one beautiful thing to come out of that unsuccessful year. It is not a schoolteacher's coat. It is not a Mennonite's coat.

"Here, let me help you with that."

She twists a little, rising from her seat as he expertly slides the coat from her shoulders. She sees him stroke the blond mohair as he says, "Very nice, we don't want that to get dirty."

He stands and flips it inside out at the shoulders, so only the lining shows and the coat is divided into a long third of itself, a column of caramel satin. Then he folds it in thirds again lengthwise, tucking the hem section up first so that when he finishes it is a compact, shimmering lozenge.

"I learned that in the army," Mitch says. "I'm just going to put it right here between our bags. That way it won't slide."

She wants to protest that now the lining, the part next to her skin, will be the side to get soiled, but she does see the logic of the inside-out move. Her father said nothing about the glamorous coat when she brought it home, except he hoped it was practical enough, being so light colored. She will not write and tell him that a soldier knew how to save its appearance.

"It's funny what they teach you," he said, settling in beside her again. "The first day was all about our things. We had to mark our initials on everything in a designated place for that particular article of clothing, then we had to roll each piece a certain way so that when you opened the drawer the same part was showing."

"My goodness. Did you do that when you went home on leave? Was your mother surprised?"

"Man, was she ever!" Mitch laughed to himself. "I wasn't exactly the tidiest one of her kids. She couldn't get over it. Kind of made her feel a little different about me being in the army."

Kathryn remembers how they were told to make their beds a certain way at boarding school in Landour. How they were shown the right method to put away their clothes. She was eight then; old enough, her father had said.

"Of course, she's still not crazy about it. But you know how mothers are. Your mother must be worried about you making this long trip on your own."

Kathryn by now has had almost three year's practice saying it. She knows how to modulate the sentence to impose the least amount of burden on the listener.

"Oh, geez. Gosh, I'm sorry," he says.

She is touched by the fact that Mitch looks not so much embarrassed as struck. Exactly as if someone had struck him physically. Part of her job now is to glance sympathetically at the nonplussed person, to console.

"Thank you," she tells him. After acknowledging the effort to comfort her, she must help him leave the painful subject. "She'd been ill for a few years."

"Oh, that's tough." But the words have had their magic effect. Something is relieved in him: that perhaps she'd had time to get used to it, that maybe it was for the best, to end her mother's suffering.

Her mother did suffer, no question. But she also had fun, right up to the final stroke that took her all at once. Kathryn would wheel her chair next to the kitchen counter, so she could supervise the making of a red devil's cake, always the kind that church committees demanded Elsie bring, the special recipe that had been adjusted in the margins for both Himalayan and Illinois altitudes. They would count the strokes of the spatula together as Kathryn worked the batter, Elsie's voice hoarse and the words slurred. They'd dissolve into fits of laughter, her mother's more of a croak, when they got lost in the counting, and finally would just agree when it looked right. Even though she wasn't supposed to have many sweets or fats in her condition, her mother would always taste whatever Kathryn made, working her mouth slowly, the good side chewing with judicious deliberation. Always the same slow and effortful pronouncement: "Your best yet." Kathryn was the only one who could understand every word—not always on the first try, but she wouldn't abandon any utterance her mother had worked so hard to make until she had turned it around from every angle and imagined her way so far into her mother's thoughts that it would suddenly appear before her, in plain, crisp English.

"Thank you," Kathryn says again. Now it is finished, and she is allowed to change the subject, which she does. She gets him going on the farm again, which he intends to return to after the war. As the only son, he will work with his father until it's his to run. His enthusiasm makes him easy to talk to. She lets his words run over her, only half-listening, because she can supply the correct questions at the correct intervals. She knows farming from her aunts and uncles and cousins on her mother's side. Her parents didn't farm, of course, though her father came from a long line of Old Order Mennonites in Pennsylvania who did. Her father is a modern sort, a kind of businessman for God. A minister, yes, but always also a treasurer or secretary general of this or that, running the business of the mission. When they came home from India he had his talks to give, raising funds for the school in Dhamtari, or some village relief plan, or a new church. He is on boards and committees, and was made a bishop. He wrote his memoirs and couldn't find a publisher but had them printed up, selling signed copies at his lectures. A celebrity of sorts. Her mother was just grateful to be home, reunited with her sisters, able to unpack once and for all. She'd been home just two years before the first stroke.

"That must have been quite a sight," Kathryn says, of the cow picked up by the tornado and placed back down in a neighbor's pasture. She is just marking her place in the conversation, but forgets herself, and says, "We missed that one. We weren't back yet in '33."

Then—drat it—she has to explain. Mitch, unfortunately, is not just wrapped up in himself; he's interested. Wants the details of their years in India. Can't believe she lived more than half her life there.

He gives a low whistle. "You don't look like a Mennonite," he whispers.

Kathryn giggles, and doesn't redden.

"That's the idea," she whispers back.

Oh, it is delicious, this riding on a train talking to a soldier. The fact of her new permanent wave, which for once got the bangs to curl just right, is delightful. As is the new coat, its soft nap staying spotless in the overhead rack. It strikes her that she is already acting more like the knowing and worldly woman she has conjured for herself waiting in Oregon, and less like the self-conscious, awkward girl left behind in East Peoria. Moreover, she is for the first time on her own in this interval, having left her father and not yet arrived at her brother. Even in college, there were housemothers watching on a daily basis, frowning over the dormitory sign-out log.

She lets Mitch talk himself out, which he finally does, pushing his cap forward over his eyes for a little rest. Soon he is snoring softly, and the sound both frightens and thrills her. She watches the farmland roll by, sere and stubbled after harvest. She can see a yellow bus making its way down one of the long, straight country roads. It's small from this distance, as she supposes her train appears to the students riding it. She can imagine the tumult and teasing going on inside. That was not a good mix, of her and school-children. She doesn't know what they'd wanted her to be like, but they soon found out that she was nervous, and somehow foreign, and they'd made sport of it.

When she confessed to her father that she'd lost control of her class, he had advised only that she rule them with a firmer hand, precisely what she lacked in the first place. It had been his idea that she leave college and take her emergency wartime teaching certificate, the requirements shortened to two years instead of the full baccalaureate degree. Since she'd been unable to study with any concentration since her mother's death, her grades had of course slipped drastically. *I'm not stupid*, she wanted to tell him. In fact, she loved reading, thought she might try to be a writer someday. But his general air of disappointment made it impossible to speak up for herself. First term, her marks had begun at the top of the class. She'd only been away nine weeks—had already joined the a cappella singers and begun performing with them—when she was summoned before bed to the telephone on her floor to hear her father say he was driving to get her in the morning. Even so, it had been too late to see her mother alive one final time. After that, yes, it was true: She'd been a failure as a student. She'd had no counter-argument when he directed her to shorten her schooling and begin teaching.

The train and the school bus are traveling roughly parallel, so that the students on their way to class look to be making little prog-ress. Now the bus stops at a crossroads and takes a right-angle turn away from her. It soon becomes as small as the toy Dinky truck wrapped in her luggage for her young nephew. Then it vanishes altogether.

Mitch sleeps all the way to Chicago. When the conductor passes through their car shouting, "Chicago! LaSalle Street Station!" he comes to with a start. He stares at her in a split second of wonder. Then he grins and says, "Already? Where was I?"

He hands down her suitcase and unfurls her coat, helping her on with it. The train is stopped at a switch and then jerks forward, bumping them into each other. He insists on carrying her bag along with his off the car.

This station is big and serious compared to the covered platform and small waiting room of the Rock Island Depot they left behind. Announcements crackle over an intercom; passengers getting off the *Peoria Rocket* are rushing through the doors, on to their cabs and Chicago destinations.

Mitch glances at the station clock. "Say, do you have any time before your next train?"

She has loads of time; it's not even ten in the morning and the *City of Portland* doesn't depart until six that evening. She had thought she'd check her bag and explore the stores in Chicago for a few hours. But now that she's here, even the station seems to engulf her.

Mitch has time, too, before his transport bus shows up late that afternoon. She agrees to have lunch, a walk. They check their bags and make their way through the bustle of the station.

The steep buildings lining either side of the street make her feel a little dizzy, as does the river of traffic, honking cars, and the press of pedestrians. One woman actually pushes Kathryn along with her balled fists, until a gap presents itself where the woman can pass. She doesn't even glance at Kathryn as she makes her determined way around her in a tweed business suit and a brimmed hat pulled low.

Ever since they left the station Mitch has been guiding her along by her elbow. He's kept hold of it, lightly, but Kathryn feels it as a glowing center of her whole being. At Goshen College, she'd been with boys in mixed groups. Maybe once in a while she'd been shoulder to shoulder with a fellow, squeezed into a restaurant booth. But she believes this to be the first instance that a man unrelated to her has held on to any part of her person with a particular claim. Even just this claim to be her protector in the crowd.

"Hungry?" he murmurs into her ear. She knows he's moving close to be heard, but the sensation of his breath on her skin makes her shudder.

"Not cold, are you?" he asks, before she can even answer the first question. "In this beautiful coat?" He moves his guiding arm briefly to her shoulder to stroke the mohair, then returns his cradling palm to her elbow.

"A little." It's true that the street's shadowy chill—she knows the sun is out, but it's somewhere behind these skyscrapers—suddenly grips her. "Cold, I mean, not hungry. Are you hungry?"

"Nah, not yet. My mother gave me the full farm treatment— eggs, bacon, pancakes, you name it."

At sunrise, her father had pressed Kathryn with oatmeal, eggs, stewed fruit. But she was unable to eat a thing. She still can't, now at mid-morning. It's as if her body can focus on only so many sensations at once.

"Hey, I've got an idea. How about a matinee if we can find one, then lunch after?"

She won't tell him that she's seen only one movie in her life, illicitly, with her friend Marlene from Goshen College. She'll say that sounds like a good idea.

They pause at a newsstand, where Mitch buys the *Tribune*. He thumbs through to find the listings.

"I'm sure you've seen the new one with Bing Crosby and Fred Astaire."

"No, I haven't." She's read all about it, though, surreptitiously at the drugstore—*Photoplay* and *Modern Screen* her secret vices, begun in the days of the ice cream shop when customers would leave the magazines behind on tables, and she'd hide them away in her binders until she could be alone with them.

"I have, but it's terrific, I'm glad to see it again." Mitch confers with the newsboy about the location of the Clark, then determines that they can walk. He glances down at her two-inch square heels. "Good girl, sensible shoes."

She is happy to walk. He takes a couple of extra steps to maneuver himself to the outside of the sidewalk, returns the guiding hand to her elbow. He walks like a soldier, or a farmer, miles to march or acres to cross. But she has no trouble keeping up; they are in step. How marvelous the day is turning out to be—an escort, a movie, a guide in the big city.

He pays for her ticket, insisting—"Who else am I going to spend this on now?"—and they enter what feels to Kathryn like a kind of temple, dark and gilded and velvety. They climb the carpeted stairs to the mezzanine, and find loge seats. It's like being underwater, this darkness, lit just enough from the petaled sconces and footlights along the aisles. Mitch glides the coat off her shoulders, folds it back along the top of the seat, and Kathryn settles in, surprised that the chair rocks slightly under her. He leaves his arm casually along the back of her seat, a protective gesture, not touching her, but enfolding her within his zone of soldierly protection. She feels it even without feeling it, and it absorbs her consciousness so powerfully, in a pleasant, disorienting way, that the images from the previews—Ingrid Bergman's soulfully lovely face, Bogart's slightly mocking one—don't quite penetrate. Then the movie comes on with the singing and dancing and gowns and cocktails and chiffon and sequins and fast, wise-cracking dialogue, and a plot that shows coupling and uncoupling that purports to be fated and yet seems so volatile and even random that Kathryn can't quite grasp it.

But it's mesmerizing nonetheless—the shining, beautiful excess. Everything is beginning for her right now at this very moment with a boy from home but still a stranger, beside her in this lush, embracing dark. Life, the bright spectacle in front of her. And then Bing is at the piano with a Christmas tree and a fire in the background and Mitch leans in and says, "Boy, I'll miss being home at Christmas," and she looks at him with such affection and sympathy that he holds her eyes a minute, receiving it, then leans over and kisses her very sweetly on the lips, then harder, with his arm crushing her to him in a way that doesn't hurt but startles her, until he releases her and they look at each other for a few seconds partly stunned and partly wondering what's next. Then she knows that it is she who must move back a few degrees, that he will take his signal from her, and though no one has ever told her how to let a boy know what to do, she does know how—by tucking herself back into herself, and letting something smooth fall across her expression.

He keeps his arm there, though, directly around her shoulders for the rest of the movie, the bargain they have arrived at. She is his girl, today. But she is a good girl, a girl from home, and he is a nice boy, and also a boy from home. She is a woman in the world in a coat that could be in this movie, and he is man in uniform who will be shipped to Europe soon, and for this reason, and the reason of her six o'clock train, she can afford him a certain amount of leeway, and he knows how much and will ask no more.

This is settled then, in the space of what they saw in each other's face after the kiss, and so she can relax into the movie in a new way, and lean against the warmth of his arm.

The daylight and city noise crash around them as they emerge from the theater. Mitch now gives himself permission to steer her in a variety of ways—by the elbow, as they hurry across the street, or with an arm around her waist, keeping her close against him from the noontime press of pedestrians. They pause to look at a menu taped to a restaurant window and agree that it will be perfect.

When she watches him talk as they eat their sandwiches—naming the guys in his unit, sketching the eccentricities of his commanding officers—she has time to study his features. They are all Illinois farm boy, a fullness of face that is guileless and friendly, sandy hair, eyes that don't register as any particular color unless you ask yourself, and then determine that they are blue. He could be one of her cousins. He is not, she realizes, the sort of man she could be in love with, though she has little notion what sort of man that might be. But she has a buzzing, almost flying feeling that she thinks must be like love—in this case, love of her circumstance, here in a steamy, clattering restaurant in a big city lunching with this soldier she has just kissed. Even her egg salad sandwich, with its little frill of parsley on the side, looks unfamiliarly glamorous, and her dewy glass of Coca-Cola, sitting on a scalloped paper coaster, decidedly so. She slips the coaster in her coat pocket when they stand to leave, and one of the folded paper menus from beside the cash register as well, feeling that her life from this moment forward must be documented; that things are about to happen to her that she will have to retain evidence of to believe.

By the time they begin their stroll back to LaSalle Street Station, the day is slanted toward afternoon. Everything is winding them in separate directions, the flags and war bond posters speaking straight to them. She is his girl, and this is measured in minutes. It's irrelevant now that she wouldn't want to be his girl for weeks or months or forever, because war hangs over him, and a train and transport are about to decide matters. For this reason and this alone, she is his girl more than ever, and they walk in the comfortable silence of lovers who have been together for a long time. There is nothing to say; he has kissed her in the dark and he is the first boy to ever do so. This marks him and this day and grants him rights. She allows her hand to be held, and she takes it for granted that he will pay for the taxi that carries them to the Chicago and Northwestern Terminal. It is his right and even his duty to pay for her; she is his girl. Because she is, she sits demurely beside him in the grand marble space of the waiting room, their luggage at their feet, while he clasps her hand and has a cigarette. She could scold him for this, it is her new right as his girl, but the war grants him privileges, too.

Time, when he is done, bears the press of urgency. He must get a cab back to LaSalle, where the transport will be, and he must do this within minutes. They scribble their addresses for each other, hers in care of her brother, his a series of army identifiers. "This will find me anywhere," he says. The prospect of her letter searching him out at an encampment somewhere—amid rockets, shells—of the army seeing to it, makes a profound impression on her, so much is she now a part of something large, a matter of grave consequence. She feels bonded to it, like a vow. Then he really does have to go, and he kisses her again and she is ready for it this time and tilts toward it, recoiling a little from something acrid, then realizes it is the trace of his cigarette. She leaves her suitcase by the wooden bench, a bit of a risk, she thinks, but risk now is necessary—needing to see him to the brink of it—and follows him to the line of Checker Cabs waiting in front of the station.

"Make sure you write," he says. "I don't want to lose track of you."

"I will."

They kiss once more and then wave until his cab has rounded the corner, and she is even fuller now, full of his absence. She must spool the day back to its beginning, to the first sound of him bumping along the aisle toward her on the train at Peoria. She must turn over every moment, until she has the shape of each one memorized.

Dear God in heaven, what if her bag is not at the bench—*that might serve her right*—but there it is. She vows to be responsible again, the girl with her feet on the ground. Though, finally, maybe, not so different anymore, no longer invisibly foreign in her own country. She could tell by the way Mitch looked at her that he saw an American girl, not a person awkwardly between worlds—India and Illinois, Mennonite and modern. The wooden bench is hard like a church pew, and she wraps her coat around herself and begins the pleasant task of waiting, situated where she can watch the black schedule board change, with the times and trains ticking past in black tiles. The coaster in her pocket is reassuringly tactile as she fingers the scalloped edge. She will begin a letter to him on the train. When her brother Russell sees her bent over an aerogram at the kitchen table in his house, he will wonder. A friend from Peoria, she will tell him, and it will be absolutely true.

After half an hour Kathryn needs to use the Ladies Lounge, and after another ten minutes quite desperately so, but there is again the question of the luggage, and no one reassuring nearby to watch it, just an older businessman on the next bench over. But she can't possibly wait the forty minutes until she boards the train. Must she carry the big bag all the way there and back? She could leave it for just the two minutes it would take; it was fine before, and this time the idea takes shape in her mind like a dare: How much can she get away with? She leaves the suitcase but has her handbag, of course, and wears her coat.

She hurries, even avoiding a glance in the mirror as she finishes by running a dash of water over her fingertips.

As she leaves the Ladies Lounge, she sees that a soldier has taken a seat in the middle of her bench. She's startled, because from the rear she thinks it's Mitch again—and why would he be back?—but, no, this uniform is taller, the shoulders narrower. In that second her gaze widens to take in the tableau of the whole waiting room: more than a dozen soldiers now, talking in clumps, dotted across the rows, standing in line to buy tobacco or magazines—how had she missed seeing so many? Or have they just arrived, a sudden influx? It's like in Landour, when you'd feel a rustle off in the pines beyond the path. When you stopped and stared into the green, a langur materialized, starkly silver. But then, all of a sudden, you saw not one, but three, seven, ten; it was the shift of vision that showed them to you.

Occasionally when she would walk to the bazaar down the steep turns of Tehri Road, a troop of rangy langur males would descend in a succession of lightning-quick swoops from the hillside to her right, swinging off branches with raspy barks that sounded like laughter, then leaping ten, twelve yards, to land on the road in front of her. They weren't coming for her, they were en route down the mountain, but when they saw her—upright, earthbound—they were ready to stop and take an interest. They'd spring up to the stone wall at the lip of the road and stare. The trick was not to look directly at them, but to stroll on exactly as you had been. Her mother never got over her terror of being taken by surprise, always stifling a scream, but even as a child Kathryn knew that these muscular, graceful beings were like gods, meant to be adored. And although you weren't supposed to meet their eyes—you might invite something you wouldn't want—she paid silent tribute to them as she went past, pretending to ignore them. When she could finally allow herself a backward glance she'd see that they'd all leaped off the stone wall down the slope, disappearing in the shadowed pines. She wanted nothing more than to fly after them, share the immense sport they made of freedom.

On her way to the bench she doesn't see her suitcase and makes a small bet with herself: If it is there, she is meant to do what she will do, without remorse. She is meant to leap into her life. If it is not, she will have learned her lesson, and will never be so reckless again.

But on the other side of the bench it squarely sits, dark marbled blue with white stitching, a going-away gift from her father. Unstolen. From it hangs the new leather luggage tag holding the identification card written three years ago with her mother's good hand. Even hampered by her paralysis, she'd wanted to help Kathryn get ready for college. Belatedly Kathryn realizes what she just offered up to chance by leaving the suitcase unattended—she could have borne all loss except that small card, her mother's determined act of rallying behind whatever journey she was undertaking.

Kathryn reclaims her seat, then after a few seconds, glances over to see the soldier's face. He is ready for that glance, already smiling in her direction, and says, pointing at the suitcase, "I kept an eye on it for you." Then he winks, removing a packet of cigarettes from his breast pocket and shaking it just enough so that one cigarette is loosed and leveled toward her, which she might, if she chooses, reach for. If she did that, she would hold it aloft in a moment of stillness while he fished for his lighter, then she would lean in to his flame and take the fire inside her. She has studied this ritual wherever she's seen it, and knows it exactly.

"Do you smoke?"

Though she has, just in this moment, decided that she does smoke, or, more precisely, will smoke—because she can picture it so clearly, and because she somehow knows that as a woman on her own she is going to sooner or later crave its bitter heat—she shakes her head, for now, no.

"Mind if I?" he asks, raising his amused dark eyebrows along with the pack.

"Not at all," she says, smiling back. "Please do."

PIE

Portland and Los Angeles, 1947

She is wiping the counter down for closing when he comes in and seats himself on a stool, asking for pie and coffee. There is nothing special about that, nothing special about him. He is in working clothes, a heavy cloth jacket, gray to begin with, but blackened now at the elbows and cuffs. He doesn't look especially clean, but what man does after manual work? He smiles at her, asking what's good.

"Pretty much all," she says. "The coconut cream is the freshest."

He takes coconut cream. She asks how he likes it, and he says *wonderful*, looking at her in such a way that she flushes. The pie and coffee come to a dollar. He leaves two.

When he comes in again a few days later, he's still dressed in work clothes, but his dark hair is neatly combed. There's the slightest bit of accent in his voice but she can't place it.

"What's good today?" he wants to know.

"They're all good, I told you that."

"Okay, what's freshest?"

She thinks; which had Helen brought out last? The lemon.

"Lemon," he agrees. "I'm going to come until I try them all."

Involuntarily, she glances at the pie case, counting. Six kinds, give or take. Sometimes Helen goes to town on it and there are more.

"And then," he adds, "I'll have them again."

She laughs. "You like pie."

"I didn't know I liked it so much."

He always comes toward the end of the day when she isn't busy. He'll take a second cup of coffee, black, and light a cigarette, smoking thoughtfully while she wipes the counters, tops up the salt and peppers, marries the ketchups. She gets used to his watching, so much so that one day when he doesn't come she feels off-balance and unmoored behind the counter.

Then he's back, ordering custard. She doesn't ask him where he was, because she thinks he might expect it. That particular day rain streaks the windows where *Charlie and Helen's* is painted in yellow, the letters appearing backward as you look out.

"Kay," he says. She still feels a strange sensation when he calls her that. She told him her name was Kathryn when he asked, and he nodded gravely, though when he stood up to leave that night he said, "Good night, Kay." And "Kay" is all he's called her since. It amazes her, how someone thinks he can rename you, just like that, though after the shock of it, she secretly agreed: Kay.

"I'd better give you a ride home tonight. Look at the rain."

"I have an umbrella. And it's just a few steps to the bus stop."

"But when you get off the bus—you'll have a walk then."

"Not a long one." But it's true that it's longer than she likes most evenings, especially in weather like this.

"I had better."

He's older than she is; she can't tell by how much. Helen noticed him one day and then the day after that and put two and two together. "He's handsome," she said. "But you'd better watch out."

Kathryn—Kay—who is she now?—was made uneasy by the remark. She'd been dating servicemen, so she knew lots of things to watch out for, but he wasn't fast-talking like a soldier on a twenty-four-hour leave. She was minding her own business carrying plates. And now she had better take a ride.

Kathryn goes back to the kitchen, where Charlie is wrapping the meat loaf in waxed paper.

"What's up, kiddo?" Charlie peers at her through thick glasses. He was sorry to sit out the war but they wouldn't take him.

"Charlie, do you think I should take a ride from Carl?"

"You mean the fellow who moons over you every night?"

"It's raining rivers out."

Charlie wipes his hands on his apron and goes out front. Kathryn follows, not knowing what she's set in motion.

"Name's Charlie." He extends his hand.

"Carl." They shake. "You have a fine place here."

"I see you've become a regular. Must have to do with something more than my wife's pie."

Carl is smoking his after-pie cigarette, which he always stubs out in the ashtray, not the saucer, like some customers do. "I won't deny it."

"You won't mind showing me your driver's license will you, Carl? If Kathryn here decides to take a ride with you?"

Carl reaches for his wallet, worn curved and shiny from the back pocket. His attitude is neither insulted nor cowed. "That's a good idea," he tells Charlie.

Charlie examines it like a cop. Helen will have a laugh over this tomorrow, Kathryn thinks.

"It's up to you, Kathryn," Charlie tells her. "I don't see the harm. It's a terrible night for the bus and I won't be out of here for another hour yet."

Kathryn unties her apron and hangs it up. She goes to the coat rack and gets her raincoat; she heard the forecast and left the mohair at home. She ties a kerchief around her hair, knotting it under her chin.

"Give me a ring when you're home, Kathryn." Charlie turns back to the kitchen.

"Nice to meet you," Carl calls after him.

She is used to him sitting down. He's taller than she thought, but not tall. She knows what he does for a living now. His sheet-metal trade takes him high on the girders; he crawls though ducts, the inner workings. During the war it was all shipyards. He missed the war, too, but he didn't say why.

He holds her umbrella over her as the rain slants around them. She's used to being steered by fellows now. Before coming to work at Charlie and Helen's, she had a job selling cigarettes in the nightclub of the Benson Hotel. She wore a white blouse and black skirt and carried a tray from a strap around her neck, weaving around the tables while the all-girl orchestra played. When customers needed her, they raised a finger. She had a little flashlight, but she never used it, making change in the dark. *Do your eyes bother you?* a sailor asked her. Puzzled, she shook her head. *Because they bother me*, he said. After the first time, she waited patiently for the punch line. Whenever she had nights off, soldiers booked them solid with dinner dates, movie dates, dancing dates. She had an address book with so many names that sometimes she stared at one and had no idea whose it was. A lot of what they wrote to her on thin aerogram paper had been blacked out. But what remained was this: They all needed to know that she missed them. After so many, she didn't, really. But she told them she did. It was the least she could do.

Now they are all somewhere besides the war, disguised as

civilians. They rushed home after V-J Day with their discharge papers and paired up with the girls who'd made promises. Even Kathryn had had one come back with a ring box but she shook him loose back to Pittsburgh; it had all seemed like make-believe and she hardly recognized him when he reappeared out of uniform. What seemed solid and strong in him before, now looked blocky and stubborn. He expected she'd turn Catholic, for one thing. She didn't think she was a Mennonite anymore, but she knew she wasn't a Catholic. And she knew she wasn't supposed to move back east with him to live above the family filling station, no matter how nicely his hair fell in waves across the back of his head.

Carl opens the door and keeps the umbrella over her until she's all the way in the passenger seat. He drives smoothly up Burnside to Twenty-sixth, wipers beating out time, and she tells him the turns and gives him the house number. Living at the Johnsons' is her other job, and all she has to do to earn her rent is a little morning babysitting between the time Mr. Johnson leaves for work and Mrs. Johnson gets home from her night shift as a nurse.

He doesn't say much as he drives, but she finds that restful. It takes only five minutes to arrive. The bus, when you count the waiting and the walking after, sometimes takes thirty.

"Thank you," she says. "It's nice to be dry."

"Anytime," he says. "I'll walk you up to your door."

"No need. Really. Thank you again."

She likes that he doesn't argue when she lets herself out with a little wave and walks herself up to the porch holding her umbrella. She likes that he stays put until she lets herself all the way inside.

After that, Carl times his visits so that she's always closing up, and she takes a ride nightly, even when it's nice out. The daylight is lasting into the evening hours now, and the nights are balmy. Carl is always pleasant and relaxed, but doesn't chat a lot, so she doesn't feel she has to either when she's tired after a day on her feet. She'll accept one of his Parliaments and he'll light it for her, and because they won't be done with their cigarettes by the time they get to the house, they'll sit a few minutes and finish, blowing smoke out the open windows. She gradually learns the particulars of his big Finnish family, most of them here in Oregon, an hour outside of Portland in a farming community called Mulino. He seems unfazed about things like Mennonites, and her minister father, and even the humdinger—her missionary upbringing in India. When she asks him about his church, he says he's been in one only a few times. He doesn't seem to have anything against religion, but he also doesn't seem to have a built-in place in his brain for it, like everyone she grew up with.

One Sunday afternoon in June he shows up at the Johnsons' door with the Sunday paper, a basket of strawberries, the field dust still on them, and a jar of thick cream. He chats cordially with Mrs. Johnson as he presents her with the fruit. "From my sister's farm," he says.

Kathryn slices the fruit in Mrs. Johnson's nurse-tidy kitchen, where soapy water as hot as you can stand it is used to wipe the counters, and the dishrags must be unfolded to dry thoroughly on the rack between uses. Though Kathryn has been brought up with similarly orderly habits, there is a modern, scientific gleam to Mrs. Johnson's housekeeping that Kathryn intends to emulate when she has her own home.

Every Sunday after that, he drops by with the paper and something from the farm. When the strawberries are done he brings raspberries, and sometimes a few eggs, brown and flecked with crumbs of straw from the roost. They remind her of eggs from her aunt Lena's farm in Lowpoint, Illinois. Curiously, he never asks her out to dinner. Never tries anything. Never touches her at all, in fact, except for the gentlemanly steering to his car. She's gotten used to him in the sitting room, and so has Mrs. Johnson, who greets him like an old friend and then tactfully disappears. Mr. Johnson, a mild accountant who had a desk job in the war, shakes hands and also disappears. Lucy is upstairs with her mother in the playroom.

Sometimes Willie comes in with toy cars to drive on the carpet. Carl talks to him levelly, man to man, never as if he is a five-year-old. One morning, he pulls out a rabbit's foot and gives it to him. Willie stares at it, his mouth slightly ajar.

"That one's straight from Montana, where I grew up. I trapped that rabbit myself, so even though the rabbit wasn't so lucky, it'll make you lucky."

Kathryn watches Willie's face, worried he might cry. He rubs his thumb over the end of it and says, "Claws!"

"Let me see," Kathryn says, and the boy comes over and leans against her side and gently rakes the foot down her arm. He's right; the foot has tiny curved claws beneath the velvety softness. She strokes its length in the direction that the claws don't hurt, its strange mix of bone and fur.

"What do you say?" she asks Willie.

They read the Sunday paper and smoke Parliaments. Kathryn's rule about smoking is that she never buys her own but takes one when it's offered, so she's tried a lot of brands. She likes these for their smoothness. After they make their way through the sections she goes into the little kitchen at the side of the house and makes sandwiches. Then he thanks her and leaves. Even though she's been wondering how she's going to let him know that he's too old for her, she's beginning to feel insulted that he's never once tried anything.

One morning, he turns the page in the features section and whistles.

"What?" she asks.

"Harry James at Jantzen Beach," he says. "Only tonight. How about it?"

She agrees, forgetting that she intended to discourage romantic ideas. She loves Jantzen Beach. She loves the swimming pools, the ballroom, the twinkling view of the city from the Ferris wheel—she even loves the roller coaster, which various soldiers have coaxed her onto. It was always during the dizzying descent, when someone other than herself seemed to be screaming and screaming, that she found herself embroiled in a tight embrace: with Private Lewis; with Corporal Maxwell; with Ensign Dougherty; with Staff Sergeant Wilkerson.

It's hot out, late July, and she decides to wear a sleeveless black shell rather than the portrait-collar blouse she usually pairs with her taffeta skirt for dancing. As usual, she gives her bare arms a critical inspection. Something about the climate in Oregon banished her childhood eczema for good. But when her arms tan, a faint fretwork of white marks rises to the surface in contrast. Kathryn tells herself only she can see this evidence of her bandaged past. She tucks the blouse in so that the patent leather belt will show, adding her costume pearls, but costume of a very good quality. It's hard to know the difference unless you rub one against your teeth, looking for the grit. The taffeta skirt was an indulgence bought from a women's shop on Broadway, but the saleslady assured her she would wear it over and over, and she was right. It's an elegant, shimmering plaid of black and silver and gray and white. Kathryn never gets tired of it, and she can pair it with any color.

She almost doesn't recognize him when she opens the door. His black hair gleams, combed back. His dark suit lies against his snowy, starched shirt. His tie, by sheer coincidence, glints with a silvery gray that matches her skirt. He doesn't seem to register the change he embodies; he stands loose-jointed, the same as always, not like some country boys she's known who become stiff as brooms when they cram themselves into Sunday clothes. He's as easy in his suit as he is in his cloth coat.

He gives a little whistle when he sees her. "Pretty nice," he says.

"Thank you," she says. "You, too."

Jantzen Beach is lit like a fairyland, but one for grown-ups, all the children home in bed. He doesn't suggest a walk around the amusement park, a late-night ride on the Ferris wheel, or a stroll over to see the pools reflecting moonlight. He seems all business, intent on getting to the ballroom. They hear the strains of the music before they arrive, coming out of the open doors and windows. The air is soft off of the Columbia, the heat of the day sifting through breezes that pleasantly rustle Kathryn's taffeta.

Inside, couples drift by to a slow number. The ballroom is at least twenty degrees hotter than outside, and Kathryn almost feels a reluctance to push into the wall of warmth, but the music is irresistible—she recognizes Helen Forrest's voice even before she sees her—*I had the craziest dream last night . . . about you.* Kathryn has the sheet music to that one, but no piano to play it on. They stand a moment on the fringe of the dancers as the song ends, joining in on the applause. The notes of the next song begin, and Carl says, "Okay," grabbing her hand. As he parts the middle, heading for a spot in front of the band, she sees the lean figure of Harry James himself, his trumpet to his mouth, leading off the intro. Carl swings her closer to him by her waist and begins a sedate foxtrot as she places one hand on his shoulder, the other clasped in his. Then she's taken over by something she can't quite describe. She's always thought herself a rather plodding dancer, something in her heavy with the prohibition of the church she was raised in. But in this moment, she's absolutely light, bobbing smoothly on the forefoot of her pumps, knowing when to sway left, when right, when to pivot in a sudden whirl. She's like a floating leaf.

It's him, of course. His face stays smooth, the merest smile hovering; it's something transmitted by the way he momentarily tightens and releases his grip around her waist, the way he pulls her into him so that they share the same center of gravity. When she realizes this, that she can transcend herself and her abilities if she gives herself up, she does. With this relinquishment, he increases the complication and subtlety of his movements and she ceases to have any notion of what comes next. Neither of them could have talked. Not him, especially, eyes a little lidded now with what he is summoning. Everything he has them do is one with the liquid wail of the horns. He doesn't hurry; he doesn't sweat. He doesn't seek attention in any way, yet Kathryn gradually becomes aware that there is a slightly larger space around them than around the other couples. Once she looks up and sees the eyes of Harry James himself watching them as he purses his lips into the trumpet, fingering the valves. She steps wrong then, and Carl somehow hesitates a quarter-second and brings her back around to sync with him before she even has time to smile apologetically.

Outside at intermission, they drink from his pocket flask, and he lights their cigarettes and blows his plume of smoke straight up at the night sky. "Not bad," he says. She has to agree; nothing—none of it—is bad: not the faint dust of stars almost drowned out by the amusement park lights, not the burn of the whiskey at the back of her throat, not their two small embers tracing conversational arcs in the silence, and not the two of them together a moment ago, stepping the steps.

***

She can think of a lot of good reasons not to go with him. She can think of a new one every few seconds, and she tells them all to him as they come to her. He doesn't try to shoot down a single one, even though she can also think of the ammunition he might fire back: She'll find another room later, another job. It isn't her brother's life to live, or her father's. If she wants to see California, live for three months in Los Angeles with him, why shouldn't she?

But all he says is "let me know," and that's infuriating. She's aware that she can't even deploy the biggest reason of all: that it's a sin. After the dancing they became a couple, and it was the dancing that showed her what, physically, a couple could be. He drove from Jantzen Beach to a small, neat-looking motel on the road back. He pulled into the lot, engaged the brake without turning off the motor, and asked, "How 'bout it?"

She was not wholly inexperienced. There were passes made by other men, and there were other flasks. What struck her was Carl's absolutely straightforward approach, compared to the wheedling and sulks of the soldiers. It was a real choice he was offering—after all, he hadn't cut the engine.

The whiskey made her feel loose and warm, but it didn't do the talking for her. So who was she when she answered yes? Kay, she supposed, who seemed daily to belong more and more to this man who one night determined that it was his job to keep her out of the rain, and one afternoon appeared to feed her ripe fruits almost still warm from the sun. A man who could make her so graceful that even Harry James had to take notice. Who christened her someone else, somebody freer. It's also true that the soldiers were back in their hometowns now, out of uniform so they couldn't be spotted, even the one whose engagement ring she wore for a month. There was no one to be loyal to except herself, and that elusive person didn't seem to be protesting.

Was it so much of a step, then, to move from Sunday nights of dancing and stopping off at the Columbia Motel (which smelled wholesomely of soap and crisply laundered sheets) to saying, yes, she'll go to Los Angeles while he works on a new bank tower? She very much wants to see Los Angeles and palm trees. She likes trailing her elbow out the window with a lit Parliament when he drives her places. She likes when he puts the receipt that says Mr. and Mrs. on the motel dresser. She likes, more than she thought she would, the press of his embrace, of being so urgently wanted. The bare skin of the encounter, the sharpness of smell, then the warm shower after, their clean clothes still clean on the chair. He takes care of her with his precautions, he takes care of her in all ways. Though he hasn't raised the topic of Mr. and Mrs., she supposes they would travel that way. And it is partly a relief, not to have to make a decision like that, but to try it out for a time.

So she never actually says yes but falls into talking about it first as a possibility. Then when he shifts the terms of the discussion to an actual plan, she doesn't correct him. The date approaches and she is all of a sudden packing and delivering notice at her rooming house and at the restaurant.

"A wedding?" Helen asks, her eyebrows raised in cautious surprise.

"Elopement," Kathryn says, telling Mrs. Johnson the same, which causes her to go up to her room and sob for a full hour one night, not because of telling the lie, but because of telling it to the two women who have taken a motherly interest in her. When she kisses Lucy's damp curls, getting her up on her last morning, the little girl points to her and says, "Bide." Bride. And Kathryn goes to her room and cries again, to the point where she needs to wear dark glasses, descending the stairs while Mr. Johnson follows with her suitcase and Carl with her trunk.

To her brothers in Oregon and Ohio, and her father in Illinois, she writes that she is taking a vacation with a friend, and might see what the jobs are like in California. In the course of telling five lies she snips the threads to all the people who keep track of her, making herself invisible to them—no forwarding address, no telephone number—and visible to only one man, whose apartment she has never seen, whose family she has never met, and whose history, though told to her, is uncorroborated.

They drive down the Oregon Coast, removing their shoes in the velvet sands at Seaside, eating corn dogs on the prom, buying a bag of saltwater taffy to keep on the seat between them in the car.

They lean against the cement wall at Coos Bay, feeling the sea spray in their faces and watching the boat traffic. Carl chases down Kay's kerchief when it blows away in the whipping wind, and when he returns it to her the wind comes between them and snatches it again. They watch it sail in corkscrews over the rocks before being abandoned by a sudden stillness. It floats down between some boulders below them where she thinks it might be claimed for a bright flowered layer in a gull's nest.

When they drive inland to the freeway there is the greenness of farmland, then the tawny stretches of ranch country, then the climb into mountains with thin, medicinal air, then down the other side into—suddenly—California.

She claps and lets out a little squeal, caught up by the glamour of change and migration, and the very word on the highway sign, *California*. He looks at her sideways and smiles at what he caused.

They stop for lunch at a diner, and he makes some calls. He still has buddies in San Francisco, and when he rejoins her in their booth he tells her they will see some of them at a party a friend is cooking up. By the time they reach the city it is evening, and the Golden Gate is all lit up. He tells her about the bridge men, who walked a mesh catwalk hundreds of feet above the water during construction. Then he takes her on a little sightseeing tour, winding up and down the hills.

Couples are arriving at the small bungalow at the same time they do, carrying bottles for the host, slapping Carl on the back. They shake hands with Kay and give her sizing-up smiles, particularly the women. For camouflage, Kay has been wearing a ring she bought herself when she first moved to Portland, gold-filled, with a paste emerald. The men take off their jackets, roll up the carpet from the living room, and stick it upright in a corner. Kay tries to help the women make the plates of sandwiches, but finds she is mostly in the way as they lean across her to chatter to one another. They keep stealing glances at her, and especially the emerald on her ring finger, as if they have a question they would like to ask, but never do. A heavy mix of perfumes hangs in the kitchen.

When she and Carl dance, everyone watches. One man jumps up after, saying, "Okay, clear the floor now. Peggy and I are going to show you how it's done," but he merely shuffles around, jerking his wife to and fro.

"Carl, where's your sax?" one of the men asks.

"Gone—a long time now," Carl said. "Sold it during the Depression."

"A shame," a woman said. "You were so good at it."

"You were?" Kay asks.

Carl shrugs, and Kay feels like she's seeing him brand-new

again through these people's eyes. He belonged to them, part of his long history without her.

After her second whiskey sour, Kay sits one out, perched on the arm of the divan. She blows smoke at the ceiling, toward the blue haze hanging there. She watches Carl twirl someone else's girl around and doesn't mind. It's all about the dancing for him, and she likes having this perspective on who he is. All the women want a turn with him, and he finds her eyes from time to time over their heads, looking to see if he should stop and come back. She feels as if she's the most attractive female in the room; she's undoubtedly the youngest, and her short, pin-curled waves are naturally dark, not like some of the bottle shades around her. Her waist, cinched in with her patent leather belt, is the smallest. She can afford to share.

In the wee hours, she dozes against his shoulder, listening to the men's political talk. The mayor fought off a recall election over cable car fares. They have no use for him—pro-business, all the way, always on the wrong side of any scrap. Remember '34, though? The pickets, the soapboxing, the feeling in the air then? Remember the meetings? Party's gone to hell; Stalin queered everything.

She listens through a veil of almost-sleep, half alarmed at the radical talk, half soothed by the joking, the low voices. Things are getting better; things are getting worse—she can't tell. She feels that these words, if she can just make them out properly, are the essence of the men, and Carl especially. There are stories he loves to trot out—about roaming the hills as a boy shooting rabbits with his dog, about learning how to go down in the mines with his father and older brothers. But she's beginning to figure out that the stories that matter most he doesn't tell. She has to piece them together by way of his reactions to things in the news, or here, by way of his membership in a group of men who think she's asleep and not listening. They are so different from her in their rough speaking and bare schooling and political anger. They're ready to kick over the traces. There's something brave about it to her, but also something boorish.

If her cousins, Lois and Boots, could see her now, would they think her bohemian, and therefore glamorous? Or would they think she had fallen among a low sort, and was fallen herself? As teen-agers, the three of them sequestered themselves after Sunday suppers to share giggling secrets, and to sing country music harmonies, dreaming of being on the radio. Boots left Illinois to work in the Foreign Service, and wrote in her letters that she liked traveling better than anything else. Lois taught school until her first baby was born, but plans on getting her master's degree when the children get older. They would understand, Kay thinks, that she's a modern woman collecting experiences.

"How old are you, really?" Kay asks Carl as they drive out of the city the next day. She feels unpleasantly smoky and stale. They slept on a pullout sofa and she dared only to give herself a sponge bath over the bathroom sink, knowing that the hosts and Carl all needed a turn in the lavatory.

He laughs, glancing over and grabbing her hand with his right one. He plies her fingers back and forth.

"I'm just right for you."

"But you're also a big liar."

He laughs again, seemingly delighted with this line of questioning.

"Do you blame me if I shaved off a couple of years, so I wouldn't scare you away?"

"So you're thirty-eight?"

"You got me."

"Older?"

"Now you're being mistrustful. Why are you suddenly so worried?"

"Because your friends are all as old as the hills."

He hoots. "We're not old. You're just a baby. And a mean one, too."

They motor down the Pacific Coast Highway, the curves and cliffs above the Pacific terrifying but also thrilling her. Even here he drives with one arm at the wheel and one arm out the window with his lit cigarette. He glances over from time to time, smiling when she gasps at the view or the drop.

"Don't watch me, watch the road!" she implores.

"But I like to see you see it."

"When we park somewhere you can see me see it. Oh my Lord, they're passing."

The convertible coming straight at them tucks in ahead of the sedan it is overtaking with only seconds to spare. She can see their fate unspool like a movie—the car tumbling off and somersaulting down the stone face into the surf. It will turn balletic loops on the way down. It will be beautiful and fatal, the orchestra delivering the horrified exclamation point.

***

Fruit ripens too quickly in its bowl on the table. Their small apartment in West Hollywood takes no more than an hour to clean, and she does this faithfully every day—runs her landlady's Hoover, scours the basin and bathtub after each use, wipes surfaces that show no dust. No one could make it cleaner. She buys a pair of small round sunglasses and spends a good part of each day walking, then uses up most afternoons in the cool of a matinee or reading books brought home from the library. She paints her mouth to look like the actresses, and once her fingernails, which was too much. But the mouth is wonderful, and she carefully creates it before going out—lining, powdering, coloring, blotting, coloring again. She hates to eat it off.

Carl makes terrific money. He comes home and washes up and they go out again, hardly ever cooking dinner in their cramped kitchen. Instead they spend his pay as fast as he makes it—eating steaks at Lindy's, or barbecue at Billy Berg's, or shish kebab at

Har-Omar. Since they go dancing nearly every night and she walks so much during the day, Kay eats as much as she wants and is still slimmer than before, even with the sweet cocktails she's grown fond of. They go to all the big ballrooms, but her favorite is the Palladium. It's a quarter-acre and can hold four thousand people at once on the dance floor. She likes the feeling of anonymity it gives her, being part of a big sea of people, even though Carl always leads them to the spot nearest the orchestra, and the space around him always widens, in tribute to him for being someone worth watching.

It's a dreamy kind of monotony, and nothing about it feels like real life. She thinks maybe she should get a job. Besides waitressing, she's been an elevator operator at Meier & Frank in Portland. They outfitted her in a smart blue shirtdress, very professional. She stepped out of the elevator at each floor to hold off the incoming riders; stepping back in, she'd take everyone's floors, rattling off the departments as they rose. When she was hired, she memorized the trainee card overnight, so from her first day of work she never had to look at the list. All the memorizing of Scripture in her childhood had given her a knack for that. She bought loads of new clothes, using her ten percent employee discount on top of markdowns. When she tells Carl her idea about the job, pointing out that with her pay she can buy some new gowns to wear dancing, he responds by fanning out bills from his wallet and apologizing for not thinking of that. How much does she need? he asks. Twenty? Forty?

Though he tells her to work if she wants to, he also lets her know that she doesn't have to. After all, they're just here for a few more weeks. Why not let it be a vacation? Perhaps it's indolence that seizes hold of her, or perhaps she just needs to be reassured that what he wants, in fact, is to take care of her. In any case, she lets the matter drop. She goes to Bullock's, but instead of taking the elevator to the personnel office, she gets off at Evening Wear, and spends hours mulling her options until she's satisfied that she's found the best values: a strapless peach organza and a cream off-the-shoulder in viscose, both with full skirts that will swirl around her. She has enough left over for new pumps.

Her father would say her soul is lost. His words come to her as if thundered from the pulpit: If she has no responsibilities, if she spends her days and nights watching movies and dancing and drinking cocktails, if she's living in sin with a man who buys her things, how can she be anything other than lost?

She should feel on fire with damnation. Instead she feels rather normal—part of a couple enjoying what Los Angeles has to offer, as everyone around them seems to be doing. The collective air of wartime sacrifice is over, and the national mood emphasizes enjoyment—every sign, every billboard, every advertisement encourages them to have fun. So she's having it, and understands this to be an interlude. As a teenager in her father's house she envied others their freedoms. But now if she wants rhinestones on her earlobes she puts them there, and no one prays over her lapse.

Carl's three-month job turns into four, then five. She eventually needs to write at least a few letters to her father and one to each of her brothers. The Kathryn who writes them has found secretarial work and lives with a female friend. She puts the correct return address on the envelopes so they can write her back, but lives in fear that her brother Russell and his wife, Bertha, will decide on a sudden trip down from Portland. Or that her father will instruct Russell to come check on her. But Russell has his job driving a bread delivery truck, and not a lot of spare money or time off. And he and Bertha have two children. The odds are on her side that they will never be able to manage it.

The replies are measured and brisk. Her brothers, both still Mennonites, have a way of sounding like her father, disapproving of all things. Almost a preemptive disapproval, in case she might be merely thinking of doing something wrong. Her sisters-in-law still coil their hair in a knot, covering it with a net cap. Kathryn—Kay—has long since cut hers, but in L.A. she no longer gives herself home permanents. She goes to a salon around the corner, where she sits under the large bubble dryer and reads film magazines. She makes appointments with the same beautician, Evelyn, who cheerfully combs and parts and trims, then rolls the permanent rods while itemizing her roster of unsatisfactory boyfriends, telling Kay she can't wait to be married and settled like she is.

To Helen and Mrs. Johnson, who think her departure with Carl was an elopement, Kay sends postcards of Bixby Bridge, of Sunset Strip at night. She's careful to say things that are true—*Carl's job working out well* or *Taking in the nightlife*, and the very truthfulness of those bulletins starts to convince her that she is, in fact, who she purports to be.

At Thanksgiving, they eat dinner with a fellow Carl works with and his pretty, round-featured wife, who is newly expecting. When the men talk about the job and the union over coffee and dessert, Millie shows Kay magazine clippings of the various improvements she plans for the baby's room. She's going to sew everything herself because they are saving for a down payment on a house, just a little two-bedroom bungalow to start with. And when do Kay and Carl plan to start, Millie wonders? And are they going to settle in L.A., and wouldn't it be fun if they had children around the same time?

Kay's been all along intending to let Carl know that their match can't last, that he's too old for her, that she pictured something different for herself. Though she has, in fact, pictured nothing specific, except, like Millie, interiors and children—a home she would shape and be mistress of, babies she would bear and raise. And here he, Carl, specifically is, and she finds herself taking more comfort in his solid know-how than she would have imagined. Nothing seems to alarm him, ever. Easygoing in a way that at first bewildered her, he judges no one except political figures. He has a sense of right from wrong, but it has to do with governments and greed, not sin and damnation. He seems to find nothing, whatsoever, wrong with her. He likes to see her have fun; she has the feeling that when she does, it's the cause of his fun.

Over the Christmas holidays Kay decides they will cook at

home, their facsimile of a home. They drive to Vons and load the basket with a turkey small enough to fit in their tiny oven, but large enough to have leftovers the next day. She buys cans of cranberry jelly, peas, and pumpkin, but they also have to buy all the spices and even the pie pans. It would have been much simpler and cheaper to go out, but Kay feels something important is on the line, and if they don't compose a scene of domesticity on Christmas, something crucial will have been surrendered by her, and could be hard to recover after that. When she moved west she brought her mother's Bible and handwritten recipe notebook containing dishes in no particular order, from Bombay Golden Cake of the missionary days to beefsteak pie for the Pleasant Hill church socials. Every recipe notes the giver, a genealogy of homemakers. Seeing the familiar handwriting—very like her own, in fact, blotched in some places by a drop of batter or a splash of water—shocks her, the juxtaposition of Elsie's industrious, communal kitchen (Mrs. Smucker's Fruit Cookies, Mrs. Ingelnook's Good Biscuits) and Kay's lone improvisations in West Hollywood.

Kay slips back to being Kathryn as she rolls out pie dough and mixes up the pumpkin with the cloves and cinnamon and nutmeg, cooking for all she's worth in their tiny alcove of a kitchen. They make do with paper napkins and place mats instead of linens. Earlier they debated a tree, but it seemed there'd be no good place to put it, so she bought candles and evergreen boughs. Bing Crosby sings on the radio as they eat seconds and she pours coffee. Carl is very pleased with their home dinner. He grabs her by the waist and sits her in his lap and tells her she's a wonderful cook. Kay knows he's used to rooming houses and transitory jobs, but the idea is growing in her that if they stop spending money like water, and if they make a down payment on a small house somewhere, she would know how to proceed with their lives. She could create what needs to be created.

January arrives, the last month of the bank tower construction. After that will come a crossroads. Sometimes during her idle daytime hours, she imagines that her mother arrives for a visit, and that Kathryn is making her a cup of tea with plenty of sugar and milk, and cutting her a slice of cake. Would she even have come west if her mother had lived? Undoubtedly not, but here she is, so she puts her mother in the California scene in a white cotton lawn dress, like one she'd wear at Dhamtari. Elsie would revel in the winter sunshine reminding her of India's, the flowers blooming in the darkest month—calla lilies, cyclamen, geraniums, and primroses. They'd have so much to catch up on that Elsie would never mention what God thought or what Daddy or her brothers Russell and Paul thought. She'd want to know what Kathryn thought, and what she's been doing, ever since she had to leave her when Kathryn was just nineteen.

Kay is rinsing her lunch plate before her afternoon walk. She's considering a new route; she already knows every garden and shop window on her usual loop. Maybe she'll put the map in her pocket for security and just follow her nose in a fresh direction. The radio finishes playing Dinah Shore when the announcer breaks in with a news bulletin. His voice is strangely excited, though you can tell that the excitement is about something bad.

A woman, a young woman—and as he gives the height, the weight, the hair color, Kay keeps noticing *my height, my weight, my color*—found dead in a vacant lot on South Norton Avenue. The details are just coming, but are said to be gruesome. He'll update listeners with additional information as he receives it.

Kay stands up, bolts the door. Carl leaves every day at just about dawn. She makes him his coffee and breakfast and smokes her first cigarette of the day while he eats his cereal and eggs, then she goes back to bed for another hour, getting up later for her own breakfast and to clean the apartment that doesn't need cleaning. She never before thought to lock the door after he left.

The man comes back on the air after a song by Sammy Kaye. The lushness of his low voice makes Kay think, *He's enjoying this*, though he uses words like *terrible* and *horrifying* and *twisted*.

The woman: no ordinary corpse. A body sawed cleanly in half. Drained of blood and apparently washed, so that no blood was at the scene of the discovery, just two marble-white halves that the housewife who found her thought at first were parts of a department store mannequin. The body mutilated with cuts in slashes and circles like some kind of code. The face, also mutilated—cuts made from the corners of the woman's mouth, three inches up on either side, to her ears, in what the reporters were calling a Cheshire Cat grin. More details would be released as they came from the medical examiner. No information yet on the woman's identity. Some kind of sex fiend, the announcer says in his low-keyed, excited way, warning the women of Los Angeles to stay indoors.

Carl calls on his lunch hour, in case she hasn't heard. He's glad she's staying in. He comes home that night with the *Examiner*'s extra edition. There's nothing in it that Kay hasn't already heard on the radio. She could leave the rooms, finally, since he is home to take her out, but she doesn't have any appetite for a restaurant and neither of them wants to dance.

The next morning, she walks out only to the corner box for the morning paper, and even then keeps looking over her shoulder, though it is absurd: Their street is bustling with life in the broad daylight.

Fiend Tortures, Kills Girl. The victim's identity is still not known. Kay spends another day caged indoors, starting letters and not finishing them, turning the pages of magazines she's already read. She naps, though it will ruin her sleep later, and keeps the radio on for company.

Then, on Friday morning, *Slain Girl Identified*, with a picture, and, yes, a slight resemblance between them—the dark waves of their hair, and their similar size, and Kay just two years older. As more details emerge, Kay keeps a kind of comparative ledger in her head: Elizabeth Short, a former resident of Hollywood (though lately of San Diego). Elizabeth Short, last seen at the Biltmore Hotel (where Kay and Carl have often gone dancing—a grand, refined place where for the price of cocktails you can feel you are far above the lowest common denominator in the city). Elizabeth Short, who dressed well, almost always in black, and whose last outfit had been a smart, fitted suit, and whose friends, after seeing the movie *Blue Dahlia*, had given Beth—Bette—Elizabeth (another woman whose name splinters into versions) a glamorous nickname: "The Black Dahlia."

The papers insinuate things, or say them outright: Bette Short was a lost soul, a drifter; she traded on her attractiveness to men; the suitors paid her rent, her meals, gave her pocket money. There was a name for that.

Kathryn lives with Carl. Who pays the rent, yes. Who buys her dresses and dinners and drinks, yes. But she cooked him a Christmas turkey and her mother's pie, despite the fact that her kitchen has only two burners and an oven the size of a breadbox. They taped the holiday greeting cards they received—six in all— to the cupboard.

"You need to get over your fear," Carl tells her one night, when she reports again that she didn't leave the apartment. "Just stick to the busy streets, the stores."

The next week the killer sends a packet of Bette's personal items to the newspaper, things from her pocketbook. He is taunting the police, letting them know he's still out there. The man on the radio continues to warn women to use special caution. Matinees are over for her; she can't sit in the dark alone. Nor can she be out there with him on the streets. She manages a trip to Evelyn's salon chair for a wash and set, and the Black Dahlia is all the women in the beauty parlor can talk about. The Cheshire Cat grin. The cigarette burns and careful, surgical dismemberment. He followed a plan, some internal instructions, and who knows how far they go, and what block he's on, and how he chooses? Evelyn says it's because of the way that woman lived, and Kay thinks about Evelyn's many boyfriends, but doesn't remark.

She has no appetite, so that she's down from her usual 115 pounds (the weight she and Bette shared), and smokes way beyond her usual six cigarettes a day. Her throat feels raw and scraped. She has to clear it repeatedly before coming out to the hall to take the telephone call her landlady tells her is waiting.

"Is it Carl?" she asks as she takes the receiver.

"A woman," her landlady says, hovering while Kay holds the receiver cupped in her hand. She waits for Mrs. Fitzpatrick to turn and finally shuffle back to her own door, taking her sweet time to close it.

"I am calling for Carl," the woman on the line announces. She has an accent of some sort, but not, Kay thinks, a Finnish one. But maybe; what does she know about Finnish?

"He's at work. May I take a message? Is this one of his sisters?"

The woman laughs, a bark really. "No, not a sister. Not a sister at all. And who are you?"

Kathryn stiffens. "I'm sorry. I didn't catch your name."

"This is Fanny. You've never heard of me, have you?"

"No."

"Tell Carl his wife called. And give him a message, no, two messages. One, Mamacita died. In Los Angeles. I thought he'd want to know. Maybe go see Gonzalo, pay his respects."

Kay clutches the phone. "I'm sorry, you're—"

"His wife, I just told you. The second message is that he should not bother to come home, if he ever intended to."

Kay is still standing stupefied with the receiver cradled to her cheek, the line at the other end dead, when she notices her land-lady's door showing an inch of light where she never closed it all the way. The biddy.

Then: the bastard. *The bastard, the bastard.* How could he? He knew who she was, what kind of a girl she was. This accompanied by a small misgiving: Was she? Still? Then: How dare he!

She goes to their apartment and shuts the door loudly so that Mrs. Fitzpatrick will know what a closed door sounds like. Sails into the bedroom and drags her suitcase out from under the bed.

She folds everything meticulously. Her mother's Bible on the bottom. Her handwritten *Tested and Tried Receipts*. The letters from soldiers that are tucked away in one of the suitcase's satin pockets. *The bastard, the bastard*, a kind of song in her head giving her movements a sick rhythm. Underwear and slips and stockings, blouses, pedal pushers, dresses, everything folded just so. The bathing suit she bought here—no, he bought it. She puts it back in the drawer. The plaid taffeta skirt, folded carefully. The peach organza and cream viscose, left on their hangers. There is the trunk, also under the bed, full of her winter things, including her mohair coat. She will have to write and ask him to send it. But no, it is January everywhere else. She kneels down to drag out the trunk with its film of dust—something that eluded her housekeeping—and pulls from it her best sweaters and a few woolen skirts and slacks and the mohair coat. She will wrap it around herself on the bus.

What else? She forces herself to slow down, think. She won't be back. She has her mother's things. Her letters. Everything else will arrive later or can be replaced. She has her savings from Portland. Just go.

She calls a cab from the hall, and sees Mrs. Fitzpatrick spying on her through the door's crack. She hauls her suitcase down the stairs and to the curb, and for a few minutes forgets about the Black Dahlia and about the packets sent to the newspaper with cut letters pasted to make the text. She forgets about the Dahlia's naked legs spread open, one foot just about touching the sidewalk, where the mother pushing the stroller came upon it in the clear morning. The torso half lay five inches over from the lower half, less visible in some higher weeds. The Black Dahlia grinned up at the uncracked sky.

The cabbie tries to make conversation about it. No one in Los Angeles can leave the story alone, stop prodding it. Perhaps her brothers and father have been following it in the papers. If they have, their letters demanding she leave town haven't arrived yet, though they'd never associate her with the kind of girl who wore lipstick and strapless dresses and spent evenings in cocktail lounges. Well, she is leaving and that should make them happy, if they care. Maybe she is going clear back to Illinois. It doesn't matter where, really; she'll decide on the destination when she gets to the station. She thinks of the bus as a clean arrow that could travel straight across the middle of the country, slicing through the heartland, back to the Mennonites and her father's house, and her stepmother the medical doctor, who was a missionary in Africa and who addresses her politely, as if she were not someone the doctor knows well. As if she were a patient, perhaps, needing diagnosis.

Kathryn now knows where she will go. To her aunt Lena, her mother's sister, and her uncle Manny. She will live on their farm and make herself useful. Maybe some soft summer evening shucking corn, Kathryn will tell her aunt the story of meeting this man, Carl. How he wasn't satisfied until he'd gone through all the kinds of pie. And Aunt Lena will listen sadly, and rub her shoulder in circles when her story is finished. She will pray with her, and Kathryn will feel her old life come back to her in the groove of the words— *The Lord is my shepherd, I shall not want*—and she will never be Kay again.

At the bus station, she stands in line to purchase her ticket. She doesn't know how many days and nights she will be on the bus before arriving. She will call her aunt and uncle from somewhere in the middle. It doesn't matter when she calls, or even if she does, Aunt Lena will open the door and gather her in her arms without amazement.

Someone touches her from behind and she recoils from a beery breath.

"Hi, doll. Where you off to?"

Kathryn stares straight ahead, her back rigid.

"Hey, don't be like that, all high and mighty when a guy's just trying to make conversation." His hand on her shoulder.

She jerks away as if it were fire. "Please don't touch me again."

"A live one!"

Kathryn is suffused with shame. Alone in a bus station, what does she expect? Her heart throbs in her throat. She casts around for escape, or rescue, and sees the blue uniform of a policeman by the wall. She doesn't know what she'd say to him. Maybe she won't say anything, just move closer for protection.

She leaves the line and carries her heavy suitcase toward the officer. The beery man sees where she is headed and mutters something. When she glances back, he's taken off in the opposite direction. Perhaps it's safe to go back to the line now, but then what? The whole trip by bus will expose her to this element. She needs to get another cab and make her way to the train station, where there is a better class of traveler. But first she needs to collect herself. She keeps moving toward the policeman as if to a beacon. She sits down on the bench nearest him, and is so relieved at the sight of his badge and gun and club that she has to wipe some tears away. He's young, younger than she is, but he has all those things: a badge, a gun, a club.

"What is it, miss?"

"Nothing, nothing at all. I'm sorry." She fishes for her handkerchief, ashamed. She is ashamed to be here, ashamed to cry, ashamed to have been accosted by the man slurring his words. She doesn't feel able to report him to the officer, because really, what is there to report? She would rather deny he existed, and that he picked her out as someone who might welcome his advances.

"No one here to see you off, miss?"

More shame. "No. My husband had to work."

She feels him glance toward her ring hand, but she has it buried in the twisted handkerchief.

"Where are you headed now, ma'am?"

"To visit relatives in Illinois. I have to buy my ticket. But I'm thinking—"

"Yes, ma'am?"

"Perhaps I'll take the train instead."

He stares at her quizzically. She must sound like she's raving.

"Do you know the schedule, ma'am?"

"I—no."

"Then you should telephone, save yourself a trip. I'm pretty sure both the *Golden State* and the *Chief* go out in the afternoon. You might have missed them for today."

"Yes, that's a good idea." She is relieved that he gave her a reason to move away and stop the conversation. There is a bank of phones ten yards down the wall; she can stay near him without having to answer any more questions.

Once she's lugged her bag over to the phones, she turns to survey the station. It's mostly men here; how could she have been so foolish? There are a few women dressed flashily; that's when she remembers that Bette Short came into L.A. from San Diego for the last time on the bus. Her trunk was discovered in checked luggage, almost all the clothes inside black. The press made it sound sinister, but Kathryn understands the value of black when you're poor. It doesn't show the dirt; it's elegant for any occasion; people won't remember if you wear the same thing more than once. Bette had been here, maybe been spoken to in the same way, by the same dissolute type of character. Had it bothered her? Or had she been exposed to so much insult that she was hardened, and had learned to brush off a drunk like a fly? Whatever armor she'd developed didn't do her any good. And there is surely no sense in Kathryn using her as an example of anything except how not to act, what not to become.

The officer is right. The trains have left for the day, or rather the last one is about to, impossible to make it to the station in time. That leaves the bus, going east to anywhere, or a hotel near Union Station while she waits for tomorrow's train. She still has all the savings she brought with her from Portland, and this is no time to pinch a penny. She'll go to a hotel, and a decent one.

"Kay!"

There he is, looking angry, looking hurt, hurrying toward her.

He clutches her elbow. "Don't ever do that again!" Angry now.

She shakes off his hand, glancing at the police officer, who is watching them keenly. If she needs him, he will come.

"I'll do as I please," she hisses at him. "Be careful. That policeman is watching you."

Carl doesn't look. "Fine, you'll do as you please, but don't scare me like that again. In this city! If Mrs. Fitzpatrick hadn't heard you tell the cab where you were going, I don't know what I would have done." Sorrowful now.

She doesn't believe his sorrow.

"Then Mrs. Fitzpatrick must have also told you that you had a phone call today."

"Yes. Who was it?" Wary now. She believes that.

"It was your wife, Carl, calling to tell you that someone's mother has died. 'Mamacita.' And that you shouldn't bother to come home, wherever that is."

His eyes change, first a kind of flinch at the word *wife*, then something else, a tenderness. "Okay. Let's go somewhere and talk."

"Talk about what? I don't want to talk about your wife. I want to go to a hotel tonight and get on a train tomorrow."

"I'll take you to a hotel. If you want me to leave after that, I will. But first we talk. Downstairs in the hotel lobby if you like. But we talk."

Who is he? No one she knows.

The policeman strolls over. He is a child, twenty-one or twenty-two.

"Ma'am, who is this?"

Carl barely bothers to look at the boy policeman. "I'm her husband."

"Ma'am?"

Kathryn stares at the man in front of her, trying to see him through the officer's eyes: a predator. When she does that, he becomes Carl again.

He'd wanted her straightforwardly, and such wanting was a distinct pleasure and also seemed as if it could not be refused.

Certainly, she was free to refuse it, but his single-minded focus had been at first, yes, a flattery, but then came to feel like an odd sort of destiny. He led. Quietly, without fanfare or ostentation, he led. She had allowed him to do that. But all along, she knew he had secrets. He was forty-two to her twenty-six, for one thing—not thirty-six or thirty-eight—she'd seen his driver's license. At her discovery he'd merely said, I didn't want to lose you. You wouldn't have gone for forty-two. And it was true, she wouldn't have, until forty-two became the same, after knowing him, as thirty-eight. And now this woman, this Fanny. Some part of her might have known that, too, if she'd added up the details of his odd courtship. She chose not to, and now she must make her final choosing here. He is wrong for her in so many ways. She would be settling, giving up on herself. But he wants her. Will anyone else, ever? She feels the policeman's gaze on her, waiting.

"He's my husband," Kay says.

**

It is an elegant pattern, sleekly tapered. Bertha covers the entire kitchen table with the crinkly tissue pieces, studying their fit, the arrows of grain. She never uses instructions. Kay has a trim waist; Bertha uses her piece of chalk to outline the body, so she knows how far to take things in. She wears glasses to see the tiny stitches, and purses her lips when threading the needle. They don't talk much. Kay dared to keep her lipstick on in her brother's house, subdued to a deep rose instead of red, but still carefully lined, blotted, applied again. It is her mouth. It is her wedding. She would have bought the dress herself, ready-made, but Bertha insisted.

Carl wears a white carnation in his lapel. It is his first wedding, his third so-called marriage—to that Fanny woman, and before that, an Ofelia—though no need for divorce. The other marriages were common law, he explained. Explained with a shrug.

After she recoiled, struggled, tried to take this in, it dawned on her that she didn't have to count those. If they weren't recorded, they weren't a fact, not in California with the first woman, and not in Oregon with the second. She had looked it all up. It actually made the whole thing better, and she closed the subject by saying, "Well, I'm not common, don't you think for one minute I am." So he bought the license and he wears the carnation. She carries orange blossoms. They look like the bride and groom they are. And it is all documented at the registry, and a minister says the words, and she is the first he makes actual vows to. It is understood that those others will never be mentioned again, because they don't—didn't ever—exist.

She had a Shakespeare teacher once at Goshen College, before her mother died and she dropped out. Comedies end in marriage, Mrs. Huntley lectured, and tragedies in death. It was, apparently, a kind of law. Mrs. Huntley never said what to call it if there were both a marriage and a death.

Kay can't help loving Bette Short, left out on the sidewalk, all broken in two. She loves her like a sister; she loves her like a secret, tragic, self. Though she knows she shouldn't, she loves her more than Bertha, who stayed up late out of duty and kindness, and who stitched the satin pieces into a whole. Bertha, who said not one word about the lipstick, but only scolded that Kathryn had better hold still, for mercy sake—she wouldn't like to see her stabbed with all these pins.

Gain a Child

Portland, 1953

They finally save enough to buy a two-bedroom house on Wygant Street on the northeast side of Portland. From there Carl can drive easily to the shipyards or a downtown building job, and Kay can walk to Eighty-second Street or Sandy Boulevard for a bus or electric car line. Their first married home was an upstairs apartment in a rambling old house in northwest; stepping outside, there was nothing but an alley and parking strip. Now they have a backyard, small but theirs. Kay sits on a chaise lounge in warm weather with her coffee, watching their cocker spaniel, Penny, run after robins and squirrels, or merely circle the territory, nose down and investigating. Most days her neighbor Dixie will appear at the fence with her own coffee cup and come in through the gate, her dog, Mugs, at her feet.

No Dixie so far today. Penny comes over to push her nose against her and Kay pats the chaise. She hops up, treading on Kay's thighs and belly, getting garden dirt on her housecoat.

"Oof, not there, you fat thing. I forgot how heavy you're getting."

They took her back to the breeder for a sire and now she is going to be a mamma. The breeder will help them find buyers. The puppies will bring in a little extra money, but Kay also wanted the fun of taking care of them for a few weeks.

Penny sits up, alert, her eyes intent on the side of the house. Then she hops down, barking excitedly.

"Hello there!" Dixie calls, appearing around the corner. Instead of a housecoat she wears pedal pushers and a sleeveless blouse. Mugs shoots in, a black Scottie, and Penny begins the chase—copper after coal until they stir the pot the other way, coal after copper. Kay privately thinks her dog is the beauty of the two—her silky ears and tail streaming back like a fleet little arrow. She told Carl that she worried Penny wouldn't slow down enough in her condition, but he said, "Nature will tell her what to do." He'd grown up around animals. He'd know.

"Where have you been already?" Kay asks, nodding at Dixie's clothes.

"Drove Jimmy to work. I need the car for a doctor's appointment later."

"Where's your coffee? I'll get you a cup."

Dixie wrinkles her nose, angling the second chaise closer and plopping down. "Makes me sick now." She takes out her pack of Kools and offers one to Kay, who shakes her head.

"I've had my second of the morning already."

"You're so disciplined. I don't know how you keep to only six. The doctor told me it would be fine if I held it to a pack—so that's my discipline!" She laughs, lighting her cigarette and blowing out a long stream of smoke. "Anything to help me keep my weight down. He said no more than fifteen pounds total and I've already gained three! Can you imagine? And I've got six blinkety-blank months left!"

Kathryn squints at her. "You don't look like you've gained."

Dixie settles back in the chaise, her eyes closed against the sun.

"All in my boobs so far. Jimmy thinks that's great. I certainly don't see how I could have gained even that since I can't keep a thing down."

"How about tea instead? Or lemonade?"

Without opening her eyes, Dixie raises her finger, as if Kay has made a good point.

"Lemonade, please. Anything lemony seems to help."

"Saltines?"

"Oh, yes, please. You're an angel, Kay."

Coming in from the sun to the dimness of the kitchen, Kay sees spots for a few seconds. She arranges Dixie's lemonade and crackers on a little round painted tray, a wedding present from one of Carl's cousins—people she couldn't even pick out of a crowd now. Someone made a record at their wedding reception, and half the messages wishing them well were spoken in Finnish. Only her brother Russell and his wife, Bertha, and their children represented her own family. Paul and Beulah couldn't afford the trip, and her father and stepmother were lecturing about their missionary years somewhere in Wisconsin at the time, going from church to church. Carl said it wasn't their fault if Kay had invited them only three weeks before the date. She conceded this to be true, but then kept forgetting it, holding their absence as evidence against them.

While inside, she takes a couple of aspirin for her toothache. She isn't eating much, either, because chewing is such an ordeal.

"Thank you, my dear." Dixie nibbles a saltine. She holds it up to show the little corner she's eaten. "So far, so good!" she says cheerfully. "But if I make a run for your bathroom, you'll know why."

"You poor thing. Isn't it supposed to get better anytime now?"

"Let's hope," Dixie says. "They say twelve weeks, and I've just cleared that."

Kay has never made it to the twelfth week of pregnancy; by the eighth or ninth she bleeds. She has a new prescription that's supposed to change that. The first few times she miscarried, they still lived in rented rooms in the northwest part of town. She thought the new house would change her luck, but it happened again, last winter. Dixie doesn't know her history. She would have preferred never talking about it, even to the doctor or Carl, just hugging it to herself as a private grief between her and her lost babies, extending to a line of five of them now.

"How about going out later?" Dixie is asking.

"What time?"

"Leave at eleven? We can shop after my appointment, and eat if either of us feels like it. Between my morning sickness and your toothache, we'll certainly be cheap lunch dates."

Dixie is waiting in the car in her driveway when Kay emerges from her house. It's good to have a reason to put on real clothes instead of housecoats or pedal pushers or shorts. They're both dressed in circle skirts they sewed together at Dixie's house. She has the bigger table to spread patterns on, and they take turns at her machine, sewing one thing or another almost every week. Together they puzzle over instructions for tricky pleats or notched collars, and they mark each other's hems and pin in adjustments to seams. While one of them stitches, the other one makes the tuna sandwiches, or changes the records, and they chatter about how they'll take turns minding each other's babies and how the kids will get on the school bus together. Kay lets Dixie take the lead in those discussions now. When Dixie presses to know when she and Carl are going to start a family so their children can be matched in age, Kay says they need to save a little more, get out of the financial hole of the last strike.

As Dixie backs out of the drive, Kay laughs, pointing. "There they are."

Penny and Mugs are framed by their respective living room windows, watching them leave. The two houses are identical in layout, Dixie and Jimmy's white with black trim, Kay and Carl's green with white. Every house on the street is of the same tiny cottage design—carport, two steps to the front door, living room window and a window from one of the bedrooms facing the street—though the various tree plantings and shrubbery are beginning to sprout up and change the pattern-book appearance. But Kay likes the general sameness. There's something reassuring about it, all the couples starting out together. There are babies everywhere Kay looks these days—in the advertisements, on the television programs. She and Carl and Dixie and Jimmy watched together—with all of America, it seemed—the night Lucy gave birth to Ricky Jr. in an episode last winter, the same night the real Lucille Ball was giving birth in a Los Angeles hospital. That was a pretty neat trick. They howled over Lucy standing there in her enormous maternity smock, moaning, "Ricky, this is it," sending Ricky and Fred and Ethel into panicked collisions and paroxysms and tangled telephone cords and suitcases springing open.

There is a rosy baby on the pamphlet for her desPLEX tablets, and a quote from a study that says, "under stilbestrol treatment the habitual aborter enjoys the same outlook for a living baby as does the average gravida." She has that sentence memorized, and has looked up *gravida*, which led her to *para*. She is a multigravida. And a nullipara. As soon as they have a baby, she and Carl will join the others on her block moving through the same milestones and sharing the same worries. They won't fall aside into some status that makes the others uncomfortable talking in front of them about Dr. Spock and growth charts and first steps. Sometimes on a Friday one of the neighbors will get on the telephone and invite the others over. They'll walk to the hosts' place with a bottle of wine, or a foil-covered tray of cocktail wieners, or a casserole. The babies will be parked in the living room and hall in their strollers and the toddlers will careen around the furniture grabbing on to skirts and trouser legs that might or might not belong to their parents, ashtrays being lifted above their heads.

Sometimes she thinks she can feel the desPLEX working inside her, because she is actually late on her period right now. She pictures her womb as a newly welcoming nest, fortified somehow by the drug. If they can't have a baby she won't be able to bear watching Dixie and the others raise theirs. They'll have to move from the Wygant Street house with small square rooms she and Carl painted themselves, the curtains she sewed and hung, the fence for Penny he built. But where would they move? The babies are everywhere.

***

"How long has it been bothering you?" the dentist asks her, peering in with his hand mirror and little hooked tool, his forehead momentarily blotting the bright overhead light from her eyes. He lifts his hands away so she can answer.

"Off and on for weeks." She is embarrassed to say months, but Carl's union was on walkout last winter, and the strike pay wouldn't have covered a visit to the dentist, especially since she knew what she was going to hear. She needs more work than a single extraction.

"Well, that molar is going to have to go. I see you've already lost one on the other side. There's a lot of decay back there and you'll need several visits and some restorative work."

"That will be expensive."

"Mmm." He pokes and prods some more. Nearly everywhere his instrument goes makes Kay wince. Her teeth have always been soft. Her mother blamed the lack of good dentistry in India for the many fillings she had to have when they returned to the States.

He positions her chair vertically and tilts the light away from her eyes. He has a kind face with rimless spectacles and close-cropped gray hair. She got his name from Dixie, who swears by him. "At the very least, Mrs. Anderson, I'd recommend two partial dentures. But I don't think that would be the end of your problems;

the upper anterior teeth show decay inside at the gum line, and if you lose one, you would need bridgework. You could save a considerable amount of money and future dental work by getting a full upper denture now. I think you can get along with a partial lower denture. The lower anterior teeth are intact." Kay can barely listen as he goes on detailing the options and cost. They don't have money for any of it. She does hear the price difference between the upper denture and the possibility of bridgework, though. She also hears him say that her new front teeth won't have the overbite that her natural teeth do, so she'll have an improved appearance. She doesn't smile a lot in photographs; her teeth make her self-conscious.

She can pay for the dentures over time. Or Carl's sister, Vera, would probably lend her the money if she asks; she made them the loan for the down payment on the house. Vera is widowed, and moved to Portland from Indianapolis, living on her own in a downtown apartment. Her husband had a flourishing trucking business, which Vera sold after his death, investing the proceeds. She tried to make them a gift of the Wygant house down payment, but Kay insisted on a repayment schedule, which she incorporated into her monthly budgeting. Now this. Dr. MacIntyre says she can pay twenty-two dollars a month over a year. If Carl works steadily, it can be done. Or if she miscarries again, she'll go back to work.

They discuss the timing. He knows from taking her health history that she is pregnant. She has not been back to Dr. Schirmer yet to confirm this, and has not even told Carl, for fear of getting his hopes up, but she is privately sure. She also has a nervous confidence that this baby might stay. Eight weeks and no cramping.

There are two ways of going about the dentures. The conventional way fits the dentures after the full mouth extractions have completely healed. The second method, the so-called immediate dentures, are manufactured while back extractions heal. Some weeks later, on the day of the front extractions, the denture is fitted and worn home.

"Definitely the second method," Kay says. "I won't be without teeth. I'll die first."

"Most women your age say that," he says. "With the immediate dentures, you might need several appointments to adjust the fit. Your bite might feel off at first until we can correct it. After full healing, you might need the denture plate relined when the mouth tissue is completely back to normal. Or you might even elect to make a new upper denture with a more precise fit, and keep the first pair as a backup, which eventually you'd probably want to have anyway."

Kay considers. Yes, absolutely a backup. If the denture breaks, is she to be toothless until a dentist can make her a new one? She'll pay the first one off then add payments for the second one with the precise fit. And never a day without her teeth. Perfect teeth. Film-star teeth.

They take a wax impression that very day. Then he numbs her and extracts her aching back tooth. She makes an appointment for the rest of the back extractions, and one after that, in another month, for her front extractions and dentures. She signs the contract for her installment plan.

"I think you've made the right decision, Mrs. Anderson. This whole process will be done before your pregnancy is well along. One less thing to worry about. And by the way, congratulations."

"Thank you." How strange that he is the first person beside herself to know. Easier that he's a stranger. If it doesn't last, she'll report later that it was all about nothing. "And you know what they say," he adds.

"No, what, Doctor?"

"Gain a child, lose a tooth." He laughs. "I think you should prepare for a big family."

***

They double-park outside Vera's downtown apartment to collect her for a Sunday drive to Celia and Matt's farm. Carl buzzes her intercom outside, and a couple of minutes later she emerges, letting herself into the backseat.

"It's a hot one!" she exclaims.

"Almost a record," Kay says. "Anyway, you look cool."

Vera is an impeccable dresser, and always in the latest store-bought goods. Today she wears a sleeveless blue gingham shirt-waist, a straw sunhat, and carries a woven wicker purse. While Ernie built his trucking business, she worked in various department stores, rising to managerial positions. Now she doesn't have to work, but has a part-time sales position at Meier & Frank, just to give herself something to do, she says.

"You, too," Vera says, craning forward to see over the backseat. "Is that a new skirt? What a pretty print."

"What's new, sis?" Carl asks, steering the car across the lanes one-handed, his other dangling a cigarette out the window. They have all the windows down because of the hot day.

"Is this too much air on you back there?" Kay asks.

"No, it feels good. Nothing new. I took on more hours last week because they were short-handed and the store is air-conditioned. I wanted to live there."

"Today's a good day to be in country," Kay says.

"Oh, I'm telling you. These sidewalks are baking downtown."

"You should get yourself one of those window units for your apartment," Carl says. "They've come way down in price."

"That's a thought."

"Let me know. I can pick it up for you and put it in."

Kay wonders how it would feel to buy anything you want, just like that, no calculating what's left in the monthly budget or what big expenses lie ahead. When Ernie was alive, he and Vera never bothered with a house, just rented an apartment in what-ever city they lived in—Detroit, then Indianapolis—but always, according to photos Kay had seen, a modern, spacious one. No children for some reason; Kay never felt she could pry and ask why. The two of them always had wonderful clothes and a new car. And now if Vera wants something like an air conditioner, presto.

They hum over the Hawthorne Bridge to the east side and out toward Clackamas. Carl and Vera trade family news—Matt's latest lung X-ray, summer plans of the teenage nieces and nephews—and Kay looks out the window, contributing a concerned or appreciative murmur here and there. They're not looking for her to join in. Gradually storefronts give way to open spaces—small farming plots and pastures where dairy cows graze. Celia and Matt live where Carl's parents had bought land after old Chris got out of mining. Kay is not unfamiliar with farming life; her aunt Lena married a farmer with a large parcel of acreage in Illinois. But she's come to understand what even a small piece of land means to Carl's family— the parents having come over from Finland, the men in the family making their start in copper or coal mines. It was their life dream to own a little piece of America and grow whatever they wanted on it.

Kay never knew Carl's mother, but she knew her father-in-law for a couple of years before he died. He had a bushy moustache and spoke little English but seemed to approve of her. After Celia and Matt bought the farm from him, he took turns living with all the children, preferring Carl and Kay's downtown apartment because it was a walk from the waterfront bars. More than once Carl had to go scoop him up off Skid Row and haul him home to the couch. Looking back, Kay doesn't know how she stayed so patient with it all, perhaps because he was such a novel contrast to her minister father. In her father's orbit, *she* was always the dark moon, the girl whom a man in the congregation once pronounced "unnatural," after she was caught singing a popular song into the microphone of her hand for the entertainment of her cousins in the church parking lot. But she felt old Chris's admiration for her neat housekeeping and trim appearance, and knew that he cared not a fig for her soul. When she refilled his coffee cup he'd level his hand in the air and say, "Dosh 'nuff," giving her a little wink, as if they shared some secret. She had the feeling that if she weren't his daughter-in-law he'd also be giving her a pat on the rump. But even that—if he ever did—she'd simply swat away with a finger scold. She understood that he thought Carl had made a catch, and that he appreciated her as a bringer of order and feminine influence. He found no faults and instead appeared hangdog before her in the morning, abashed at his own weakness. She held nothing against him.

She also liked his sober side, the essence of the man she guessed he'd been. He borrowed her typewriter and sat at her kitchen table with his reading glasses perched on his nose, tapping out two-fingered columns for the Finnish Socialist papers in Duluth and Astoria, adding in the umlauts with pencil. Carl told her that he signed himself "Old Man Mulino," after the hamlet his farm was in, so it wasn't much of an alias if federal agents wanted to track him down. She wanted to tell him that she, too, was a writer of sorts—just for herself so far, just scribbles on tablets and ideas for stories and articles, the thought that she might bring in a little money on the side—but they had no language in common, and her ideas were aimed at women's magazines, so she thought they'd be of little interest to him.

The roads to Celia and Matt's narrow until finally they turn in at the mailbox to a single dirt lane. They roll windows up against the dust and Carl bumps along slowly. First there are hugs to exchange, and Kay's cake to exclaim over, the brothers clapping each other on the shoulders though most of them have seen each other within the last two weeks. From here it looks as if they are—some dozen of them assembled—a big, happy family. And they are, her in-laws. She waits, almost counting down, for the English to slide into Finnish. For the glances during conversation to stop including her. For her sisters-in-law to start the kitchen work without assigning her a job, and when she asks for one, to watch their faces flash puzzlement as they wrest their tongues back to English—"Oh, no, you've made this beautiful cake! Have a seat outside and enjoy yourself." Outside the men are talking politics already, shouting at one another as if they are arguing, when in fact they're in fervent accord.

On the drives home she used to make Carl tell her what transpired so that next time she had at least an inkling of the current outrage. He didn't like to tell her much. It caused quarrels and coldness between them until finally he said one night in exasperation, "Don't you see that it's better *not* to know what we're saying? Then you can tell them, 'How should I know, they always talk in Finn!'"

"Who's *them*?" she retorted. "Who in the hell are *they*?"

He always wanted to drop it, but she'd gotten so angry at being kept out that she began to force herself to pay attention to things that had always bored her. She started reading what they wrote in the paper about the investigations of the House Un-American Activities Committee. The Carl she married was a Democrat and a Sheet Metal Local 16 man, but there was another Carl before that, and there were more to the activities of the family as a whole, and in their circles people had been interrogated, deported, blacklisted, jailed.

She grew to understand why it might be convenient to be left out of their politics. Carl's own nephew recently lost a job teaching high school in Washington State because he was a CPUSA sympathizer—a "fellow traveler"—who wouldn't name names. So it was just as well to be able to claim ignorance. That was one thing. But it was another to be excluded from women's talk about recipes and berry crops and sewing projects.

Kay, told to go enjoy herself, meaning not to trouble them with her English-only ears, wanders down to Milk Creek, picking her way around the rocks and young birches on the banks. She sits for a while on a boulder, watching the bullet streaks of small trout. Just after they were married, Carl would take these walks with her, ignoring the teasing of his brothers when he preferred being with her to their circle of politics and beer. He'd drop a line in the water and she'd pack the trout he caught in wet newspaper, and they'd stroll back to present them to Celia.

After a while, Kay leaves her boulder and walks back past the small fields with their neat rows of beans, spent strawberry plants, and the blueberries with netting over them to keep the birds off. She pauses to eat a few late-ripening raspberries off the bushes that have already been picked through. Sometimes she consciously pushes the length of these rambles until she knows they'll be sitting down to the outside meal so she can startle them with her reappearance in the yard—solitary and aloof. Carl might have begun looking around for her, but the others will have forgotten she exists, and she wants them to reckon with her apartness when she comes back. She means to cause the beat of awkwardness, and hopes they will take some blame upon themselves, though she has begun to think they are too simple for that. She believes they care nothing about their relationship to her, content to absolve any responsibility they have toward it by labeling her "strange" or "standoffish." She knows they knew Carl's women before her, probably liked them more, and who can say if some of the sisters might even keep in touch with that Fanny woman, who lives in Portland. She's gathered they had a spell of being angry with him for leaving Fanny the way he did and taking up with Kay. Since she's buried the whole episode of his deceit while courting her, forbidden him to mention the ex-"wives" (*common law*, she reminds herself), she has no way of finding out.

She plucks some sweet grass to take into the barn for the cow. She pats its head, holding the grass while its rubbery mouth munches it up. After she placates the mother she turns her attention to the calf, scratching its neck and delighting in its infant features. At Aunt Lena's farm, she and her cousins loved to loaf in the barn and trade confidences in the hayloft. Sometimes the girls would be called to the house to shell peas or shuck corn. In the kitchen, she'd find her mother, who would smooth her hair or give her a spatula to lick, and there would always be the weave of the women's voices to take her in. All she wants is that simple feeling of belonging.

The calf is so sweet on its little stick legs. It looks at her with immense liquid brown eyes. You and I, she thinks. Here alone, happy like this. On other days, she'd escaped to the barn to have a cry. But today she is serene. This must be what a card player feels like with a winning hand. She is certainly pregnant: twelve weeks now, and Dr. Schirmer confirmed it. There is a child within her that she knows in a wordless, animal way is going to stay. Her body is changing daily. Dr. Schirmer gave her a book about what is to come that she keeps underneath the Bible in her nightstand. Everything is happening to her exactly as it describes and exactly on schedule. This knowledge grants her a power and superiority over all of them back in the yard. Even Carl doesn't know yet, because she doesn't want him to tell his family without her, or in Finnish, which would be the same as without her. Perhaps she will announce it today when they are all together, cutting her cake. It is her fact, her choice when to share it, and they have no choice but to be spectators. Her child will be their kin, so its mother, whether they want it or not, will be, too, a fact they will have to swallow. Like Vera, Celia never had children. *They just never came*, Celia said once, looking away. These two sisters, the ones Carl is closest to, must now take her in.

Next summer she will be occupied wherever she goes with her baby—diapering it, feeding it. She will graciously accept help; she will freely allow her relatives to hold her infant. She knows that whenever—he? She pictures a boy—cries, her baby will be happy in no arms but hers. I'll take him back now, she'll say calmly, and the sisters will be forced to hand him over. And Kay will finally feel her center, her belonging. Already she's not lonely anymore. She doubts she will ever be lonely again.

***

On the first night with her new teeth, she wakes in the dark suffused with pain and the taste of blood and thinks, I'm losing it; the baby is leaving me. Then she wakes all the way and realizes that the pain and the blood are in her mouth. She was dreaming that she was climbing a stairway and at every landing, women were trying to thrust their babies into her arms. She kept pressing on, shaking her head, avoiding their gaze; the women were ugly and misshapen and she was afraid of them. She didn't want their babies. She was going to climb to the top and find her own.

It's too early to get up, only 4:30 by the nightstand clock with the green-glowing numbers. She'll do her first saline rinse in another hour. She's used to these from the back extractions a few weeks ago, used to her Cream of Wheat breakfasts and custard lunches and cream of tomato soup suppers. Now it's almost all done, just another few days until she is at least superficially healed, and the raw sockets can take their time beneath the denture to fill into solid gum.

When the dentist inserted her new denture for the first time yesterday, she had immediately admired her numb new smile, and when she got home, she couldn't stop checking her reflection in the mirror. She was without a doubt different; it definitely would become her to smile more now. When Carl got home and saw her, he kept looking, too, though the Novocaine was worn off by then and she felt less like smiling. The perfect regularity of her new teeth has taken the last vestige of Midwestern hayseed out of her. The fact that she has morning sickness and a swollen mouth and isn't eating makes her look pale, yes, but also very slim, willowy slim, and she admires her full-length reflection as well as her mouth. There is the slightest, slightest bump, but her weight loss makes it visible to no one but her, and to Carl if he runs his hand over her belly. He'll be fifty when his first child is born, and he tiptoes around her with amazed joy. She had asked him if there was ever a birth with those other ones, this was important information to know before she signed on to a life with him, and he said no, not a live birth. It was with the first one. A stillbirth. So that was that, and Dr. Schirmer will not let that happen to her.

"My doctor's threatening to put me in the hospital if I don't start eating," she tells Dixie on another of their mornings in the backyard.

"You will," Dixie says, "as soon as your mouth feels better. The nausea passes. Look at me, how I'm eating all the time now. I'm getting as big as a horse."

"You look beautiful," Kay says. "You're perfect."

Dixie rolls her eyes. "A perfect horse."

Dixie isn't in maternity clothes yet, but she has already sewed herself several smocks with broad collars. For now, she's still wearing Jimmy's shirts and an elastic extender placket in her pants.

"There's a nip in the air this morning," Kay says. "Pretty soon we'll need to sit inside."

Penny is curled up on her ankles, a warm weight on her skin beneath the hem of her capris. Mugs keeps circling hopefully, waiting for Penny to hop off and chase him.

"She's different today. Look, she has no interest in him at all. I think she's close," Kay says.

"Do you know what to do?"

"Carl says she'll know what to do. I just hope he's home when it happens."

But Penny begins acting restless that noon. She keeps circling the house, sniffing in corners. They set up a large box in the kitchen with old towels in it, the front of the box cut low enough for Penny to step in and out, but high enough to keep new puppies in. To keep her from settling in another room, Kay whistles her to the box and puts some tiny pieces of roast beef there on a saucer. Penny ignores them and steps out of the box again, nosing her way to the carpet in the living room, going behind the armchair, emerging to sniff between the sofa and the desk, circling back to the dining room under the table. Kay calls Dixie on the telephone. "I need you," she says.

Finally, Penny picks her spot, in the corner of the living room next to the bookcase. Kay drags the box there, and together she and Dixie scoot the bookcase a few inches toward it so the box fits snugly in the corner. Kay spreads an old blanket on the floor, tucking it under the edge of the box so no carpet is exposed.

"Who are we to tell her where to have them?" Kay asks.

"Well, they're not going to give *us* a choice," Dixie says.

"Anyway, I want to be dead asleep when it happens. When I wake up they can put the baby in my arms."

Penny curls up in her box, every once in a while standing up to circle in place and lie down again uneasily. Kay makes a fresh pot of coffee and she and Dixie leaf through magazines, chatting about the pictures. Kay has no concentration to read, and is on her tenth cigarette of the day.

Dixie rises and says, "I'm going to go home and put together a meat loaf; I'll make enough for you and Carl, too, so don't worry about your own dinner. I'll put it on a low oven and be back as soon as I can."

Kay sits and strokes Penny, who is shivering. Kay murmurs to her and tries to cover her, but Penny stands and shakes it off, nosing the towels in the box, pushing them into a nest the way she wants them. No sooner does she lie down again than she lets out a sharp cry, the kind she'd make if you accidentally stepped on her paw. She stands and turns a fretful circle, whining. Then she leaks fluid. She lies down again, whining and panting, still shivering.

"That's my girl. You can do it, that's my girl." Where is Dixie? Carl is still at least an hour from getting home. Then Kay sees the first puppy slide from her in its glistening sac, looking just like the picture in the pamphlet the vet gave them. It's not quite all the way out. Penny pants on her side, then lifts her head to regard it. She curls around to lick it, pulling at the sac with her teeth. She does know what to do. But the sac isn't coming apart. Should Kay help? She watches Penny lick and tug at the sack a few more seconds. What if the baby can't breathe? Gingerly she pinches at the sac herself, trying to tear it. Penny doesn't seem to mind her hand there. The membrane is tougher than it looks. Penny is the one who finally snags it with her teeth, licking at the pup's nose and mouth and clenched eyes.

It isn't moving at all. Penny shudders, expelling it all the way, and goes at the licking with more gusto, getting the sac off completely, cleaning the face roughly. The pup opens its mouth, eyes clamped shut. "Penny, you did it! What a good girl, such a good girl!" Finally, Penny bites at the umbilical cord, even lifting the puppy off the ground by it while she has the cord between her teeth. Kay cups her hand under the pup in case it falls. The lifting causes its limbs to splay and it opens and closes its mouth several times, emitting a little needlelike cry. Penny succeeds in severing the cord and the puppy drops into Kay's hand, wet and wriggling. It is fat and round with a snub face. The fiercely closed eyes make it seem as if it needs to keep the world at bay for the time being. It has a brown coat, lighter than Penny's. "What a good mamma you are." She places the puppy gently next to one of the teats. The baby burrows in and begins nursing. Penny gives it a couple more licks, then lays her head down.

They have a rest like that for about twenty minutes before Penny begins panting again. She wants to get up and turn around, so Kay pulls the puppy into the corner of the box and strokes it until Penny settles again. The second pup slides out all the way in one contraction, and Penny immediately begins licking it and tearing at its sac. She looks calm now, almost relaxed. Kay can see that Penny is in charge, so she merely tends the blind, clambering firstborn, keeping it out of the way while Penny goes about her business. Then two pups are both nestled in nursing, and Penny rests again. Dixie arrives. "Meat loaf in the oven and cornbread ready to put in! Later I'll just open a can of beans, and—oh, Lord! It's happened!"

"Happening. Two so far."

"If only we can be so good at it," Dixie says. "Look at those cuties!" When Penny begins panting again, Kay scoots the two puppies out of the way to the corner. Jimmy knocks and comes in, home from his job at the electric company. They watch the third puppy being born together, then Dixie says, "We'll go, and I'll put in the cornbread, and when Carl gets home we'll bring dinner over."

"You're an angel, Dixie, thanks so much."

They are a smoothly functioning team now, Kay and Penny, so when the fourth baby, the smallest so far, comes out of its sac, still and unbreathing, Kay is not worried. But Penny keeps licking and licking, and even when she bites through its umbilical cord, suspending it and giving it a little shake in the air first, the baby will not open its mouth. Kay massages its chest, she tries to pry open the mouth with her finger, and still nothing. She sees no mucus to clear from its nose. Finally, she has to acknowledge that no matter how much Penny licks and she massages, the tiny body is cooling off, not warming. Penny turns her head to lick the three that are squirming in to nurse. She is putting her energies with the living, resting up for the next wave. When the fifth one comes, robust and squirming, she has it all by herself, because Kay is on the edge of tears, still preoccupied with the stillborn. She's laid it outside the box on an old cloth napkin, one with a gravy stain. The hearty, greedy puppies look slightly monstrous to her now with their incessant hunger. The puppy that never moved is delicate, almost translucent.

Carl comes in and puts down his lunch bucket and crouches beside them. His scent, like always after work, is tarry and mineral, a mix of sweat and the smoky soldering. Usually she can't wait until he gets his work clothes off and himself into the shower, but today she leans against him and they sit like that for a while, his arm around her, his smell one with the pungent animal tang of the births. He gently wraps the cold puppy up in the napkin and places it out of the way. Kay can't help but turn her attention back to the overpowering draw of the live, clambering puppies. She and Carl laugh together at their blind maneuvering. She likes how he keeps repositioning the smaller ones so they get their share of the milk. His touch with the babies is so light that she suddenly knows he'll make a wonderful father.

Dixie's hot dinner arrives and is arranged on their table, and Carl and Jimmy slap each other on the back, fathers to be. The three remaining puppies arrived hale and hungry, all seven now crowding in to feed. Penny lies exhausted, stretched long on her side. After dinner Carl buries the stillborn in the yard under the lilac tree. Kay lines Penny's bed with fresh towels, and they move the whole operation to the bathroom, where there are no drafts and the door can keep them all in.

Kay has put the birthing towels to wash in hot water and Ivory Snow. She rinses her aching mouth in warm saline. She keeps her head down and the bathroom door locked as she scrubs her denture and partial with the special brush and paste, the puppies from their box piercing the air with their cries. She accidently looked once in the mirror at her reflection without teeth and will never, if she can help it, look again at the old woman's mouth waiting for her there, its gaping darkness. She slips her denture back in and lifts her face to the glass. There she is again, young and smooth-skinned, with her bright, regulation smile, her unassailable new teeth that will never decay.

Now to get busy. She has puppies to keep track of and raise and find homes for, liver to buy and cook for Penny to help her stay strong in the face of those voracious appetites. Maybe Kay will be healed enough to chew tomorrow; the thought of liver actually sounds good. She'll buy enough for the two of them, its bloody iron steeling them both for their maternity: the struggle, the holding on, the surrender.

EVERYDAY
HAPPINESS

For the annual Christmas-card photograph Stevie wears a striped jacket and a white shirt and a tie that Vera bought him from Meier & Frank. Kay arranges a bowl of pinecones on the dining room table, then frames it with two Fostoria glass candleholders her brother Paul and his wife, Beulah, sent them for a wedding present. She situates Stevie behind her display, deciding that he should kneel on the chair to put him at the right height. The long taper candles aren't lit yet; Stevie is so fidgety that that part worries her. He doesn't have much patience for this, she knows, but she has only twelve shots on her roll of film and wants to get it right.

Paul's two children are always posed in reverent positions on his Christmas cards, a Bible open before them or their hands folded and eyes lifted in prayer. They are dramatically lit. She shouldn't compare her efforts to her brother's; he runs a photography studio and his cards are professional. Her nieces on Carl's side are almost teenagers now, with waved hair and pretty sweater sets. They pose nicely in front of fireplaces or snowmen or piles of wrapped presents. Her cousins send photo cards of their children, as do her roommates from Goshen College, and she tapes each new one inside the front door. All these holiday children are scrubbed and neat and are meant to be representatives of the happy homes they live in.

Stevie is also scrubbed and neat and so handsome in his clipped-on bow tie and fresh haircut. How grown-up he looks—no longer her little toddler or preschooler, but a big boy. He is about to start kindergarten in the fall.

"Mamma!" he pleads.

"I'm ready now. You've done such a good job, Stevie. I'm so proud of you."

He beams at her, lifting his chin, and by chance his hands are spread on either side of the pinecone-and-candle arrangement, and though the candles aren't lit yet, she raises her camera and snaps three in a row. Then she lights the candles and tells him to stay back from them, and snaps a few more, though his eyes are now darting to the flames.

"Stevie, look at Mamma!" He does and she snaps and winds until the end of her roll. Fingers crossed.

"Can I play now?"

"Yes, after we hang up your clothes. We want them nice for Sunday school." They just started going this year, although she left the Mennonites years ago and Carl has no religious past. She chose First Baptist, downtown, a beautiful stone church where the pastor is an educated man and the choir is large, some of the singers members of the Portland Opera. Carl goes along willingly enough. He enjoys the socializing, and contributes a nice comment from time to time when they talk about the plight of the poor, or other social ills. He looks good in his suits, always wearing them so easily. They never go out dancing like they used to, so she knows he looks forward to Sundays for the dressing-up.

The prints that come back of Stevie in his striped jacket are mostly unusable—whether from Kay's thumb edging in, or Stevie moving a fraction and causing a blur. But the first one, the angelic smile he flashed when she told him how proud she was of him—that is perfect, except for the candles being unlit. She uses it anyway, having no other choice, and unable to afford another processing fee when she has holiday groceries and presents to shop for. She volunteered to host Christmas Eve for Carl's family again, and this weighs on her. Besides the cost, there is all the work. She wants everything to be perfect: linens starched and ironed, her house flawlessly clean, her kitchen filled with cookies and pies.

The relatives come with their bottles of brandy and wine, their own cookies and pies, an extra ham, some potatoes au gratin—the kitchen overflows. When she frets about the additions to her menu and where to put everything, Carl says to her, away from the others, "You gotta relax, Kay, no one cares if there are two potato dishes," and makes her a whiskey sour. She finally sits, exhausted, feeling like the drink is causing her to float above the mess of details. She even says it, raising her glass with a gay little trill—"I'm flying!"—causing everyone to laugh and congratulate her. Vera is there in a smart burgundy wool suit, along with Celia and Matt, who drove in from the farm, and Werner and Sylvia, who are only stopping in before going over to their grown children's family gathering, this year at Bill's house. Sylvia is the sister-in-law she fears, because her housekeeping is spotless, and she keeps an unforgiving eye out for other people's failings.

Hank, Carl's baby brother, is there, wearing a natty plaid sport coat. He is the only man in the family who doesn't work in the building trades—he teaches drama in high school and has lived for years with the same male roommate instead of getting married. Kay suspects Hank is a homosexual, but the family never discusses this. He is their baby brother and can do as he pleases. Kay likes him best, along with Vera. Those two—older sister and youngest brother—are the most worldly. They've been places and tell good stories. Hank has interesting hobbies like copper etching and calligraphy, and he gave Kay and Carl framed pieces of his artwork that she enjoys displaying in her home. He took in their cocker spaniel, Penny, when Stevie began crawling and the dog got too jealous, growling and baring her teeth at this new four-limbed animal sharing her floor. Now that Stevie is bigger, Hank brings Penny by for visits, and Kay sees that she's become Hank's child now, the way she was Kay and Carl's when they were trying for so long to have a baby.

Hank has never once talked Finnish over her head like the others. He seems in silent sympathy with her outsider status in the family, flashing her a kind smile when she's sitting through the clannish talk that so often excludes her, or rolling his eyes when Sylvia says in her clipped accent: "Did these cupcakes come from a mix? Sometimes a mix can be almost as good as from scratch."

There is no room at the dining room table for them all and the spread of dishes too, so they sit in the living room with the Christmas tree, pulling chairs in from other rooms and balancing plates on knees. The orchestration of the evening has gotten away from her, but it's fine. People are enjoying themselves, and she realizes she is, too. As her sisters-in-law help serve up dessert, Carl slips out to the garage to change into the Santa Claus suit he bought when Stevie was two. They didn't have the money for it, but he insisted on getting it, and he'd been right. Kay admits how much joy it's brought. He pulls the full white beard halfway up his face, and wears the Santa cap low, over his dark eyebrows. A pillow fills out the belly under the red jacket, and he wears round wire costume spectacles instead of his usual black horn-rims. They have no fire-place, so Stevie has been given to understand that in houses like theirs, Santa comes in through the front door.

Carl told Stevie that he had to do a quick errand at the store and would be right back.

"Don't miss him again, Dad!" Stevie said. He has his plate of cookies ready, and is anxiously bouncing from uncle to aunt, knee to knee, asking, "When do you think he'll come? Do you think he'll know how to find our house? Does he ever forget?" He is badgering Hank when there is a sudden jingling of sleigh bells at the door.

"Let's see who that is," Hank says.

"Wait!" Stevie darts to the coffee table for his plate of cookies. He carries them with a nervous little wobble to the door, slipping his free hand into his uncle Hank's.

Carl hams it up with his booming *ho ho hos*, and his gobbling of the cookies, crumbs lodging in the beard.

"These cookies are delicious! You're the nicest little boy I've met tonight!"

Stevie is wordless with stage fright. When Santa sits down and invites him onto his lap to discuss whether he's been good this year, he finds his tongue. Maybe it's because the lap feels nice and fa-miliar, but Stevie relaxes into it and tells how he helped his mother with the garden last summer, and how when she folds laundry he matches his own socks, and how when she needs him to play qui-etly because she has a headache, he makes the motor sounds for his Matchbox cars very softly.

Santa looks astonished at this paragon of virtue before him. "Is all this true, Mother?" he asks.

"Absolutely all of it, Santa," she says.

"Well, then! *Ho ho ho!*" Santa says, reaching for his pillowcase. Kay stocked it earlier with a couple of wrapped presents and some dime-store novelties.

"Can I open them now?"

Mother and Santa nod in unison, and Kay thinks, *whoops*, Santa just gave a very Dad-like nod, but Stevie doesn't notice and tears the paper off: a drum, a set of Lincoln Logs, and another Matchbox car.

"Mom, it matches ours!" Stevie cries, holding up the tiny Chevy Bel Air in their very own two-tone yellow and white.

"My goodness, Santa, how did you know?" she asks.

"I didn't!" Santa says, provoking a laugh from the family. "But those elves of mine, they pay attention to detail."

Santa has to go; he's got a lot of stops. When Carl steps back into the house as himself, Stevie flings himself into his father's arms. "Daddy, he came and you weren't here!" Stevie moans.

"Not again! Let's see what you've got there." They examine the presents, opening up the tin of Lincoln Logs and spilling them onto the floor to see what can be made. Kay is topping off the evening with an eggnog and brandy, and doesn't mind that the sisters are in her kitchen packaging the leftovers up, not knowing where anything goes. It doesn't bother her that the wrapping paper hasn't been picked up from the floor, or that there is a piece of pie crust under one of the chairs that will soon be ground under someone's heel.

She is enjoying watching her husband and son. This is Carl at his best. He is explaining to Stevie what makes a corner joint strong, and Stevie is hanging on his every word. She feels that because of Carl, the house around her will never fall. The physical house, that is; she's the one who gets them by week to week on his unsteady income. But when he comes home on a payday and tucks the bills from his cashed check under her dressing table lamp, she knows they'll be all right for the next little bit. Paydays are for celebrating. She'll be fresh out of a bath and changed into a nice blouse and slacks, unwinding her hair from the curlers and brushing it into a lovely dark cloud. When he is in the shower she'll reline her lipstick and have Stevie change into a fresh shirt and trousers. Over dinner at Waddles, with the lights of Jantzen Beach twinkling outside the window, they'll sip cocktails and Stevie a Roy Rogers while they look over the menus they know by heart.

At the end of the Christmas Eve party Carl carries Stevie to bed; they let him play until he conked out by his Lincoln Logs, the homey buzz of voices around him. In the morning, she'll watch them unwrap the father-son shirts she sewed in matching plaid flannel; maybe they'll wear them to Christmas dinner tomorrow at her brother Russell's.

"I think you need to carry me to bed too," Kay says sleepily.

"I can do that, ma'am," Carl says, and bends down to lift her off the couch.

"No, just kidding!" she says, kicking her feet. "You'll hurt your back, and we can't afford to have you out of work!"

That moment is punctured, but he jollies her along, and she is still a little tipsy, and he maneuvers her to bed and pulls off her shoes, and begins removing other things, and she lets him go ahead.

"Remember," she warns. She has told him no more children. She thought she'd want three or four until she had such a long spell of baby blues after Stevie was born, and lots of time when she never thought she'd make it through the sleepless nights and the circled days when the bills were due. She thinks she has enough spunk to do right by this one boy. She wouldn't be able to stand herself if she only did half-right by two.

He is trying to get romantic—kissing her neck, her ear—but she's really sleepy and would rather just drift off. She'll let him do what he wants, but she's inside her own thoughts. Everything went so well tonight. The family really enjoyed themselves and were, she has to admit, very nice to her, very warm.

He's pushed in, is moving inside her, but she can't remember him pausing first—"Did you get one?" she asks.

"We're out of them, don't worry, I'll take care of it," and she tenses at this and feels his tempo quicken and then begins to feel alert in a cold, scared way, because he's going too fast, and she says "Stop now?" and he grimaces in agreement but then bucks and groans, and by the time he leaves her body it's already happened.

•

Dr. Schirmer recommends she take the desPLEX tablets again, and Kay takes the prescription from her and tucks it in her purse, not sure if she'll fill it. What if she lets nature decide? There would be no sin in that, would there? Her existence four weeks earlier, that seemed so handicapped by need and want, now seems a faraway dream of stability and ease. She remembers the deals she made with God last time, and the way she put each desPLEX tablet to her lips as if it were a Communion wafer, her overwhelming gratitude and relief when the pregnancy lasted. But she didn't ask for this baby; she doesn't want it.

When Dixie still lived next door, she and Kay would put Stevie and Rose together on a blanket at one of their houses, and it was lovely to let the babies kick and wriggle and scooch around side by side while Kay and Dixie smoked an afternoon cigarette and had a cup of coffee together, comparing notes about everything. They pushed their strollers side by side in the neighborhood as the seasons went by, and sat in their lawn chairs with iced tea in the summer, watching Stevie and Rose toddle in the kiddie pool, scooping and pouring buckets of water. Dixie had two more babies in quick succession, and Kay helped out by taking Rose as much as she could. She saw how hard it was on her friend, even with Jimmy earning a good living and getting a promotion. She made Carl keep using the prophylactics, and the more time that went by, the more certain she became; after all, Carl was already fifty-three. If they could barely keep up now, what would things be like when he was too old to work?

Kay will be thirty-seven when this baby is born, and has nothing to show for her life except her son. When Stevie goes to kindergarten in the fall she was going to take a correspondence course in writing newspaper and magazine features. She's clipped out the advertisement for it. She feels sure that, given some training, she could sell pieces. What heaven that would be, to work from her home, be published, get paid for it, and still be a good mother.

Now she'll be sleepless, exhausted, and taken up every minute of every day with laundry and baby care until she falls into bed at night. And Dixie and Jimmy moved to a large house in Beaverton;

there's no sisterly friend next door to buck her up, and there will be no money for the correspondence course—all her savings for that going now to pay the bills for the doctor and hospital. She'd like to make the most of this time with Stevie while she has it, but she's too sick to her stomach now to even do that, to take him on bus trips downtown to the zoo, or to walk in the neighborhood while he tricycles beside her.

She feels herself slipping into the dark place where people seem to be living their lives on the other side of a glass wall that separates her from everyday forms of happiness. Carl is being as considerate as he can be—taking Stevie to parks and Celia's farm on Saturdays so she can lie home in bed—but she is angry with him for the selfishness of what he did, and has to bite back accusing words whenever the panic and sick feeling rise up in her, and he knows it and seems glad to get away from her.

Kay can barely rise from bed on the weekdays when Stevie is there for her to take care of, and it is he who ends up taking care of her, bringing her saltines and 7-Up. He plays quietly in her room or watches Lamb Chop or Captain Kangaroo on television. She tells herself it is the morning sickness keeping her down, but it is also this blackness covering her, a lead apron of despair. So far, they have told Stevie only that Mamma has the flu, and it is making her feel sick to her stomach.

Four weeks slip by and it is time for her to go to her second doctor's visit. Stevie bounces with excitement as they wait for the blue bus they'll ride downtown. It's a damp day at the end of February and they still wear gloves and hats and their heavy woolen coats, but the strip of garden behind the bus stop already shows the tips of crocuses poking up. Downtown they'll head to Auntie Vera's apartment building, where Stevie will stay for lunch and play with the cars he brought while Kay walks the few blocks to the Stevens Medical Building. She wonders what she'll answer if Dr. Schirmer asks her if she's taking the desPLEX tablets. It's not that she decided *not* to take them; she just never got around to filling the prescription.

She asks herself what her mother would say about the tablets. Her mother would only be joyful at the prospect of taking another baby into her arms. Her mother would praise God; her faith would light the path in front of Kay. But her mother is not here.

"Well, my dear, you're looking fine," Dr. Schirmer says, when Kay has gotten dressed again. Kay sits in the chair in the examining room and Dr. Schirmer on her rolling stool. "Let's continue with the desPLEX tablets. You might keep this pregnancy without them, but better safe than sorry. And you're moving into your second trimester, so the morning sickness should resolve very soon."

Kay opens her mouth to confess that she hasn't been taking the tablets, closes it when she realizes that she doesn't have to confess, and then dissolves into tears that prevent her from saying anything at all.

"There, there, my dear," Dr. Schirmer says, rolling closer on the stool and patting her shoulder. She peers with concern at Kay through her glasses. "What's upsetting you? It's an emotional time, I know. Hormones are wreaking havoc."

Kay pours out everything—her confusion, her guilt at not taking the desPLEX after she was so happy to have it before, the doubts she has about her ability to cope with another child, and the darkness that she moves through daily.

Dr. Schirmer takes this all in, her hands calmly folded in her lap. "I'm so glad you told me this. You have a lot to carry right now."

She puts her finger to her mouth, tapping thoughtfully. "The most recent diethylstilbestrol data hasn't been as convincing as we thought that it prevents miscarriage."

"You mean—"

Dr. Schirmer nods. "You might have carried your last child to term with or without the desPLEX; we can't say definitively. So I'll leave it entirely up to you whether or not you take it. And you certainly mustn't feel guilty if you don't. At least I can relieve you on that point."

Kay nods.

"And if you're feeling worry over the bill, I want to assure you that you can pay my fee over time. You have only to make an arrangement with Jane as you leave."

Kay nods again. "Thank you, Doctor."

"Thirdly, you must continue to tell me how you're feeling emotionally. You shouldn't hold it against yourself that you're ambivalent. For one thing, your hormones *are* all in flux. But for another, let me assure you you're not the first mother who doesn't think she'll have the strength or room in her heart for a second baby. I've seen it many times. And in the great majority of cases, all doubts dissolve when the baby arrives. But not always. If the second outcome is the case with you, there are things we can prescribe to help. Do you have family nearby?"

Tears threaten again as Kay thinks of her Illinois aunts and cousins, and her mother, gone now nearly twenty years. But six blocks away is Vera, feeding Stevie cookies and root beer this very minute. "Yes," she says.

"Well, use them, now and later. There's no shame in asking for help to carry out the largest job God ever created for anyone."

Kay nods, feeling overwhelmed by the doctor's kindness. This brilliant, professional woman who, she's gathered, never married, saying that mothering is the biggest job of all.

"One more thing, Kay. Contraception after this baby. If you remain certain that you want no more children, I recommend that your husband get a vasectomy. Don't look so startled. It's a surgical procedure, yes, but a very simple surgery that has only one long-term effect: permanent sterilization. It's a much easier surgery for men than a tubal ligation is for women. We can view this as a matter of your future health. Will he say yes?"

Kay blows her nose and laughs faintly. "Right now? I think so. He's afraid of me, I've been so mad at him."

"So think about the timing. You may wish to wait until this child is born to make sure you're absolutely certain. But if there's no doubt in your mind, have him do it while you're still pregnant, before it becomes an issue again."

•

In another couple of months, when the sickness has cleared up and Kay is beginning to show, they tell Stevie. He can't believe his luck. He tells everyone he meets he is going to be a brother, and regards it now as the central fact of his identity, the thing that suddenly makes him who he is. Kay catches a little of his excitement; if she can't be eager for this new child's arrival for her own sake, the least she can do is look forward to it on behalf of her little boy. The baby kicks and she puts his hand on the spot on her belly, and he feels the little nudge and runs shouting to Carl, and then the two of them sit still with their palms down and wait. The baby, maybe sensing an audience, does a little dance number for them, and Kay looks at their delight, and her husband's tender expression, and lays down her weapons.

Early in the summer, Dixie and Jimmy have them over to the new house for a cookout, and Stevie and Rose run off together on important big-kid business in Rose's room while Jeffy and Patrick, Dixie's little ones, painstakingly transport shovels of sand from the sandbox to Kay's feet.

"Mountain," Jeffy informs her. "Mownun," Patrick confirms. They head off for another load.

"You've inspired them, Kay," Dixie says. "When they grow up to be engineers making dams I'm going to chalk it up to this day and your magnetic presence that brought out the earth movers in them."

"You're welcome," Kay says, shaking some sand out of her flats.

"My goodness, I wish we were still next door to each other."

"Please, don't even say it. I'm going to start bawling like I did the day your moving truck left."

"Buy a house somewhere around here," Dixie urges.

"Beaverton's a little rich for our blood," Kay says. Then she looks around and says, "You have such a lovely yard. Room for a swing set and everything."

"You're going to have to size up eventually for the new baby," Dixie presses. "The four of you can't live in two small bedrooms forever."

Kay has thought of this, and has been checking listings to see where there might be bargains to be had in neighborhoods farther out. When she feels too panicky at the thought that they'll need a bigger house and never be able to afford one, the Psalm comes to her, unbidden: *Those who seek the Lord lack no good thing.* She guesses she can still qualify as a seeker, at least; hadn't she gotten them—mostly for Stevie's sake—to a church?

"Have you thought about looking out Division and Powell way in the Centennial district?" Jimmy asks. "I'm part of a utility planning group for that area. It's still mostly berry farms and dairies out there, but take my word for it, you're going to see a lot of new neighborhoods. And the house lots will be big. Plenty of room for swing sets."

"Stop, Jimmy!" Dixie scolds. "That's even farther from Beaverton than they are now! Kay and I would never see each other!" She rises. "Anyway, let's get those burgers on. The kids are going to realize any minute that they're hungry, and you ain't seen nothin' until you've seen the triple tantrums that can break out around here. By the way, that little Stevie is the most adorable creature ever. I hope you realize, Kay, that I'm already planning his wedding with Rose."

In early August, Kay sees the ad she's been waiting for. Not a brand-new house, but one built only five years ago in a ranch development in the district Jimmy told them about.

"Already?" Carl asks. "Don't we have enough on our hands?"

"You're working now, so this is the time to get a loan. And I'll be too exhausted to house-hunt when the baby comes."

So they take a spin down Division Street, Stevie on his knees between them on the front seat. After 122nd, they pass pastureland interspersed with pleasant residential blocks. They follow the Realtor's directions to a street with ranches that already have their

own identities, with mature rhododendrons and dogwoods and dif-
fering paint colors and trims. The house in the listing is on a corner
lot, has an attached garage, and rooms that are all double the size
of the ones on Wygant. The dining room opens to the back with a
sliding glass door. Light pours in. Beyond the backyard fence are
tall fir trees. And there are three bedrooms, so the baby won't wake
Stevie in the middle of the night.

It's the backyard that clinches it. "I could put a patio right here,"
Carl says, spreading his hands to indicate the space beyond the slider.

"And a clothesline there." Kay points. "And that side for the
swing set."

Kay feels as if she can breathe out here. They're a short drive from
the interstate, which would take Carl to the shipyards and into town
for jobs in that direction, and out to the Columbia Gorge, Rooster
Rock, Crown Point, Benson Lake, and Multnomah Falls in the other.

It's madness, but they make a bid on the house that gets ac-
cepted and put their own on the market that weekend. The Wygant
cottage sells quickly, bought by newlyweds. Carl's sisters and nieces
help Kay paint the rooms of the new house. Vera keeps Stevie with
her at her downtown apartment for a few days, and he reports to
them on the phone every night about the restaurant meals, the
new toys, and the television shows he watches from the hideaway
bed. Everyone makes Kay sit down and rest—the baby is due in a
month—but she has mysterious fires of energy. She has no time to
fuss over herself like she had with the first pregnancy, when she
and Dixie pored over layette patterns and sewed themselves cute
tented blouses and set each other's pin curls. Finally, they borrow a
truck from Carl's genial nephew Elmer, a contractor, and move the
furniture over Labor Day weekend, and the enormous task is done.

Stevie begins kindergarten right away at Lynch Wood
Elementary, and Kay waits with him at the bus stop in the mornings. The other women on her street are pleasant and invite her to
coffee, though she feels desperate to use these hours to advantage
while Stevie is at school. She lines the bureau drawers and cupboard

shelves. She sews new curtains for all the rooms. She organizes their clothing and hangs the pictures.

At first, she meets the bus at the end of the day, too. But a couple of boys in Stevie's class live on their street and the bunch of them are already a trio. His friends' mothers don't meet the bus and, after a week, he asks if he can walk himself from now on, even in the morning. The teachers call him "Steve," not "Stevie," and he thinks that's okay. He tells her he'll be Steve now, at school and in front of his friends.

Most afternoons, as soon as he's burst in the door to drop his lunchbox and grab the snack she has ready, he asks to be off with Danny and Frank, playing in one of their backyards. Frank has a tree house, and in Danny's yard they can get to the forest through an opening in the fence, and they catch salamanders and frogs there and bring them home in jars. After the first salamander dies, Kay persuades Stevie to release the others, so before bedtime they go out into the cool grass of their backyard, the crickets chirping and strange things rustling beyond in the trees, and Stevie sends his latest captives off into the dark with his blessing.

She barely has time to miss her little boy, now growing so independent. Carl has assembled the crib and set up a cot for Vera, who moves into the baby's room. She'll get Stevie off to school while Kay is in the hospital. Not long after Vera's been with them, Kay's water breaks at four a.m., a few days before the due date. The contractions are manageable while she gets up and dressed. Carl takes her bag out and idles the car in the driveway, headlights shining against the white garage door, while Kay lets Vera know they're leaving. Then Kay goes in to whisper to Stevie to have a good day and to give him a kiss on his forehead while he sleeps on. She won't wake him; he needs his energy for school. Every night when she's been tucking him in this week she's been talking about what will happen, how Daddy will take her to the hospital, half an hour away, and how if he wakes up one of these mornings without them in the house, that's the day his baby brother or sister will be arriving.

•

It's a sister. They tell Kay this as she wakes up from the general anesthetic in the recovery room, queasy and flattened with exhaustion. They wheel her into her room, where she has no roommate yet. The nurse raises the back of the bed, causing pressure to shift to her lower region, which suddenly feels loose and wobbly and pinched by the stiches. After the nurse does some further arranging of her bed table and water pitcher, she exits, and Carl is allowed in, who says he saw the baby through the glass in the nursery, and that she's beautiful. "You still like the name Samantha?" he asks.

"Yes," Kay says. She is so tired, and so sick-feeling from the anesthetic, that she can't imagine how she ever had the kind of energy that got her through a house move just a few weeks ago. She does like the name Samantha. It was her college roommate's name, and she liked that girl for her wit and her generosity. It's a different sort of name from all the Marys and Sues and Debbies.

The nurse comes back and says, "Dad, you can come back in a few minutes. Your little one is going to get her first feeding from Mom."

Dr. Schirmer recommended that Kay nurse this baby. "It's so convenient," she said. You won't have to worry about sterilizing bottles, and it will help your body feel normal sooner, and mother's milk is the best nutrition there is. It will also help you bond."

Kay hangs on to Dr. Schirmer's every word of advice. If she thinks Kay should nurse, Kay will nurse, although privately she prefers the idea of the glass bottles lined up in her refrigerator, ready to heat, and doesn't much like the thought of exposing her breast all the time, even with those drapes and shawls.

So now the nurse gives Kay some cotton balls dipped in antiseptic to wipe her hands. She raises the back of the bed a little higher, then pulls back the coverlet, exposing the clean side of the top sheet. Then she disappears for a few moments and reappears with Kay's daughter, a compact swaddled pod, with a pink face screwed tightly closed in a deep sleep. This is her daughter. She feels nothing.

"Why wake her up?" Kay asks. "She looks so peaceful." Kay knows that when the little mouth opens, the cries will demand, demand, demand.

"Oh, you'll want to get her on a schedule," the nurse says. "Ever nursed before?"

Kay shakes her head.

The nurse explains about the latching-on process, and maneuvers the baby into place as she talks. Her daughter's mouth opens, and Kay feels a tingling sensation, then a needlelike pain.

"Oh!" she cries.

The baby's eyes open. She stares fixedly at Kay, her mouth ajar.

"Well, that got her attention. Was it hurting you? It shouldn't hurt. It will take a while for both of you to get the hang of it. Let's try it again."

This time goes no better. Kay sucks in her breath and the baby stops cold.

"It hurts like the blazes!" Kay said.

"Well, I used bottles myself, because of my work schedule, but I've seen a lot of women nurse, and it doesn't hurt, once they're used to it. They even seem to enjoy it. It's a question of technique. Keep at it, just the way I showed you. I'm going to check on another patient and be right back."

The nurse leaves them to each other. Kathryn and the baby—Samantha—gaze at each other.

"Are you ready?" Kay asks. "Okay, here goes." She cups her breast, bringing Samantha up to it, the way the nurse did. The baby's mouth opens, and Kay gets the nipple in, but the baby's mouth won't close around it. When it finally does, the sensation is the same, sharp and painful. Kay holds her cry in, but tenses, not breathing while the baby's mouth works. Her daughter stares up at her, then opens her mouth, releasing the breast.

"Oh, you poor thing. I can't do it right, can I?" Kay asks her, the tears threatening to come. "I'll do it this time. Come on, let's try again."

They go through the same maneuverings, but always with the same result: a pain that makes Kay flinch, and it's the flinching that makes the baby give up. Then Samantha stops trying to latch on. Her daughter is only hours old, but it's as if she's already tuned herself to her mother's feelings, and refuses to hurt her.

The nurse comes back again, and Kay confesses that they never got going, and that it hurt the whole time.

"Well, maybe that's enough for the first effort. We'll try again on the other side in four hours."

"Do I have to?"

The nurse regards her over her half-glasses. "The doctor wrote on your chart that you wanted to."

"I did, but I don't think she's interested."

"Well, you haven't given it much of a try."

"I bottle-fed my son, and he's perfectly healthy, so I'll just do what I'm used to."

"It's certainly up to you. We'll get her going on formula in the nursery."

"Can you leave her with me a few more minutes?"

"Of course, I'll be back shortly."

Kay covers herself up, and feels immediately more whole and in control. Her arms make a circle around her girl. "I'll make you very good bottles," she tells Samantha. "We'll rock in the rocking chair while you drink them."

Samantha looks pensive. Her eyebrows dance up.

"And your brother, Stevie, can give you a bottle sometimes. And your Daddy."

Samantha's mouth opens, a tiny O.

"They're going to be delicious. And I can tell you're going to be a very good girl. You're already a good girl. So considerate of your mamma's feelings. Such a perfect angel."

FLEXIBLE FLYER

Timberline, 1959

They go super fast, he and Mom, on the Flexible Flyer he got for Christmas. At the top, Mom plants her boots on either side of the sled while he sits crisscross in front, then she brings her legs around so he's snug in the warm cave of her, then she gets them going with a little forward jerk. Both of them like to go straight down. Steve gets blinded, so he shuts his eyes against the white blur and lets the wind and ice crystals and belly drop happen to him. The steel runners hiss through the snow. Sometimes he feels the ground drop away when his eyes are closed, then it comes back with a hard bump and that's scary, but fun-scary. Mom is steering and Mom is not blind in her dark glasses. Other sledders' cries have nothing to do with them; the mountain is theirs. Snow comes in at the wrists and neck of his snowsuit when they tip over, but they don't tip over much. Dad went on the sled with him, too, earlier, but Mom likes it better, and fits better on the sled with him, and Dad seems to like it fine sitting in the lodge drinking coffee. They left his baby sister, Samantha, at home with Auntie Vera, even though Steve thought she'd like the sledding too. She can't crawl or walk yet, but you don't need to do those things to be held on the sled. Steve would put his arms and legs around her carefully, the way Mom does for him.

Up they trudge again and again, snow coming in over the top of the boots no matter how much his mother tightens the string at the bottom of his snowsuit. He doesn't care. Mom usually says things like "just two more times" or "let's take a little break," but today she wants to stay in motion the whole time like he does, in fact she almost runs up the hill, and he pants a little to keep up behind her. Always the tippy feeling getting on the sled, like he doesn't know if it will take off without them, or take off with just him on it, or take off before Mom has her legs and arms completely wrapped around. But each time they manage it, and each ride straight down the hill is as fast as it can be, and when they fly over the bumps they both cry out, but Mom doesn't try to avoid them. He can't think of any other mother who would go as fast as his.

Now there is Dad at the bottom of the hill with a big smile for him as they coast to a stop on the level stretch. He looks at his watch. "Let's get going, Kay," he says. "It's late."

"Not yet. Come on, Stevie, race you!"

So Steve races her up the hill, and wins by a single boot, and she says "Attaboy!" and holds the sled while he arranges himself. Before they take off he waves to Dad, whose arms are folded across his parka, and he thinks this will be the last ride, because Dad won't go back in the lodge with the light purple and dim like this, and if he doesn't go back in the lodge, Mom will give in.

But at the bottom, Mom surprises him by ignoring Dad again, whose voice now has gone soft, saying, "Kay, you're overdoing it. It's getting dark."

"We're having fun! The lights are up, it's no problem."

The lights make bright circles on the sledding hill, while the fir trees on either side gather the dark and grow taller and thicker, no space in between.

"You want to, right, Stevie?" she asks.

"Sure!" he says.

So Dad stays at the bottom like a small plastic soldier, straight and unmoving, and Mom whoops on every bump, though a tiny worry has begun to nibble at Steve, silencing him. The white carpet where the lights shine is a different world now, and he's stuck between wanting to stay forever in the speed and the shining and his mother's laugh, and wanting to go to the warm car because the black fir trees are leaning in and his father is by himself at the bottom of the hill.

Dad doesn't speak now when they come down, watching with his arms still folded, and Mom just grabs Steve's hand and keeps moving, not asking if he wants to go again. Now his legs are heavy and he notices that his feet are cold and he has to pee, and that they are among the last to be sledding, just one other family who came later, a mom and a dad and three big kids all laughing together, each on his own sled. As they begin the walk up, Steve looks back over his shoulder at his father and, as if in answer, his father shouts at his mother's back, "I'll be warming up the car."

Steve says, "Mom, can I go to the bathroom after this ride?"

She looks down at him, her dark glasses zipped away now in her pocket, and seems almost surprised to see him there. "Of course, honey. Of course you can."

So at the bottom they get off the sled and Mom pulls it behind her to the curb where Dad has their Chevy idling, and without a word he puts it in the trunk, and Mom tells him Stevie has to go to the bathroom, so Dad takes him into the lodge to the men's room, and when they come out he sees the sharp lines of his mother's face looking straight ahead in the dark like the silhouettes they cut out at school, featureless and black.

The heat in the car feels good. Dad helps him tug off both boots and both wet socks, then he rubs each of Steve's feet briskly, long enough for some of the warmth to transfer from Dad's hands. Then Dad rummages in their bag and finds his wool socks and Steve puts them on.

"Better?"

"Thanks, Dad."

Mom glances back to flash him a smile, then returns her gaze to the front.

"Gonna catch some shut-eye?" Dad asks. Earlier, Mom put a blanket and a pillow in the backseat for the ride home.

"I want to watch for a while."

"Okey-dokey, pardner."

The chains make their thumping noise as Dad noses carefully out of the parking lot. Steve sits on his knees in the backseat so he has the view between his parents' heads. It's started to snow lightly, and when the windshield gets ruffled with flakes, Dad sweeps things clean again with one flap of the wipers. Mom rummages in the sack at her feet and twists around to offer him a peanut butter and jelly sandwich wrapped in wax paper. He takes a bite and finds out he's starving. Mom hands him oatmeal cookies in another package, and a thermos.

"Hot chocolate?" he asks hopefully.

"No, we finished that at lunch. This is water. Don't make your cup too full."

The laughter is gone from Mom's voice, like it's all dried up.

"Does Dad want a sandwich?" Steve asks.

Mom says nothing.

Dad glances back at him. "That's okay, pardner. I ate mine in the lodge."

They thump along. Steve finishes all of his sandwich but the crusts, which he wraps back up and hands to his mother, then he starts on his cookies. He's started to get mesmerized by the narrow white road unspooling through the dark and the forest. No headlights coming toward them, but pinpricks of red taillights in front. He's warm and cozy, and starting to think about his pillow and quilts.

"Next time let's bring Sammy," he says, leaning in against the front seat. "I could hold her on the sled." His baby sister has just learned how to laugh, and Steve can make her do it anytime he wants by razzing her stomach, or making a face, or popping out from behind something. The sound she makes is loud and wild, little screams of happiness, and if they took her sledding he's sure she'd do it all the way down the hill.

Mom doesn't answer, so Dad says, "She's still kind of little. We wouldn't want her to get any bumps."

"Next time after next time?"

"Sure," Mom says. "That will be when she's your age at the rate we get up here."

Steve is silenced. Does she mean it? Will they have to wait that long?

Dad lets out a breath like all the air is coming out of him at once. Mom pounces like she's waiting for it. "Did I say something wrong?" she asks him. "I'm sorry. I forgot that you're always so willing to get off your ass and do something with us."

"Kay," Dad says, his voice sharp.

Steve leans away from the front seat, sitting back on his heels. He hates it when the voices get like this. He doesn't understand how Mom can sound so happy one minute and then be completely mad the next. It's like she's been mad all along and then suddenly shows it to you.

"*Kay*," Mom repeats, her voice mean. "*Kay*." She's mocking, doing what she tells Steve never to do.

"What do you want from me? We were here today."

"Yes, today."

"Didn't you have a good time?"

"I had a wonderful time. *Wonderful.* That's the whole damn point."

"Stop it!"

"The language? Well, who the hell taught it to me?"

"It doesn't matter who taught it to you. Who's using it now? In front of Stevie?"

At the mention of his name, Steve wants to say that it's okay, it's fine, they can talk with any words they want as long as they don't use the angry voices. He's wide awake now, and chilly. He pulls one of the blankets up around him. Dad has the wipers fully on, because the snow is falling harder. They drive a few minutes in silence, just the *whap whap* of the wipers and thumping of the chains, and Steve begins to think it's over, though he's still shivery and braced and alert. It must have been his fault, because everything was quiet until he said the part about wanting Sammy along.

When his mother starts up again, he burrows deeper in his quilt.

"I'm fed up living like this. Diapers, cooking, cleaning. That's all I have. Can you blame me for wanting to do things on the weekend?"

"We are! We did!"

"Because I nagged you into it! Made you call your sister to babysit!"

"Well, it's a long day for her."

"Yes, let's worry more about her! Poor Vera, with all her thousands in the bank."

"Drop it."

"No, I have a better idea. Drop me! Right now, right here! I'd rather walk back to Portland than sit beside you another minute of my life."

Steve sits up straight at this. He sees Dad flinch as if against a blow, though he keeps his hands on either side of the wheel, facing only forward. The wipers beat time, making short spaces of clear viewing. They have come up behind a plow that scrapes the road in front of them, shoving snow to the right. Usually Steve loves the plows. Now he's frightened. What if his mother gets out of the car and a plow comes and scoops her up?

"Why aren't you stopping? Stop the car!"

"You're acting crazy."

"Because I *am* crazy! Are you just now seeing how crazy you've made me? All around us, families having fun together. While you sit in the lodge. How many brandies did you have?"

His father is quiet, driving slowly while looking through the white window, then the clear window. Steve wants to remind his mother that they only have one sled, so of course they had to take turns. And Mom likes sledding better than Dad, so that's why he gave his turns to her. He wants to explain it to her, but he's afraid of his mother turning her mad voice around to him, and he's also trying to sort through too many things at once: Is something wrong with their family compared to other families? And is his mother really crazy? They both said it, but maybe they didn't mean it?

"How many?"

"I didn't have any goddamn brandies."

"Oh, ho—language! The halo slips. And you're a liar. I smell it on you."

He looks at her, and the look is savage. "I had *one*, early in the afternoon before the driving. I work hard all week and I don't have to apologize."

"Who's asking you to apologize? Just let me the hell out of the car."

Dad keeps driving. That's what Steve wants him to do. If Mom is crazy, then the two of them have to take care of her, keep her out of the snow and away from the plows.

"*Now-ow!*" she shrieks in a long wail. It's a terrifying noise, like a wolf whose leg has been caught in a trap. He's heard wolves crying on the westerns he and Dad watch together—*Gunsmoke, The Rifleman.*

Abruptly, Dad signals—they're at the turnoff to Government Camp, where they stopped on the way up the mountain for gas—and pulls over. Mom flings the car door open, then slams it behind her and walks ahead. She's going fast: One second she is right in front of their headlights, her dark hair shining in the flurry, and the next, she's striding stiffly in the distance, the beam barely reaching her white parka, her legs in black stretch pants disappearing into the night.

"Daddy, don't let her go!" Steve cries.

"Don't worry. She's just letting off steam."

"Why?"

"I don't know, Stevie." Dad rubs his eyes behind his glasses. "Even I don't really get it."

When Mom begins to vanish, their beams picking up only the swirl of snow, Dad puts the car in gear and creeps forward along the side of the road, his blinker still ticking. There isn't much space because of all the snow piled up there. Sometimes a car starts up outside a restaurant and pulls in front of them. The car's brake lights flash and then swerve around a darkness that must be Mom. Then Steve sees her again, a figure smaller than you'd think a grown-up should be. One car pulls up beside her and a head comes out of the passenger-side window. Dad sucks his breath in at this, but Mom shakes her head and the car drives off.

Government Camp, with its gas station and short strip of buildings, is almost over; they can see the highway ahead of her, completely dark. She is headed for it.

Dad leans over to roll down the passenger-side window, then drives forward to catch up. When he's even with her, he stays at her speed. "Kay, please get in." Steve is glad Dad keeps his voice quiet. He feels like his mother might startle and bound off at any loud noise. She would go lose herself in the black woods, and they'd never find her again.

She walks on, not looking at them.

"Please, Mommy," Steve says from the backseat. He doesn't think he is crying, but finds out he is.

His mother looks back. When she sees his face, hers crumples in her hands. "Oh, God," she says, standing still, so that Dad suddenly has to brake. His father leans over to open the door and she slides in. After she closes it, Dad picks up speed smoothly before she can change her mind. When the wind starts rushing through the open window Mom cranks it up, though she is still crying, still whispering, "God, God."

Steve holds back his own crying for her sake. He leans up against the front seat on his knees and pats her shoulder from behind. "It's okay, Mommy."

Mom blows her nose and reaches around to squeeze Steve's hand with her icy cold one. She doesn't look at him, but says "I'm sorry" at the same time she squeezes, so he knows the words are meant for him alone, though he wishes they were for both him and Dad.

Dad drives steadily down the mountain and doesn't say anything more. Finally, Steve settles back into his bed of blankets and pulls them around him, tucking his own self in. Usually they stop somewhere to take off the chains, but this time Dad drives on them all the way home, and Steve likes their predictable thumping, even when it gets loud on the asphalt. When his eyes begin to close, he makes them open up again. Once he sits up so that he won't feel so sleepy, and presses his cheek against the cold glass. He needs to stay ready the entire trip, just in case Mom needs to hear his voice again to make her stay. He doesn't know how he got this power to pull her back. But it's a thing he will carry, with concentration and both arms around it, the way he learned to carry their new baby, because Mom said the baby was depending on him. And he guesses that just about everyone is now—something could break if he lets go. He doesn't know what, exactly, and he doesn't know why. But he knows it's up to him.

THE FLIGHT OF IVY

Portland, 1963

Lessons are in her brother Steve's room, using his blackboard when he's at school, and it's nice, just the two of them, Samantha and her mother. Samantha can't wait until she's old enough to be at school, too, so her mother started the lessons. The lessons are serious time, her brother's delicate model planes shivering on their threads above them. The chalk taps while Samantha sounds out *cat* and *bat* and *that*. "T" and "h" march together, best friends. Silent "e" is lazy: He's along for the ride and does nothing himself, but he makes the others behave differently, *hat* to *hate*. Her mother erases and gives her more words and she gets them all, and her mother shakes her head and says, *Look at you, so smart.*

Her mother drinks coffee in the morning and writes things that aren't for Samantha, sitting in her special armchair with her feet up. She writes pages full of inky lines and crosses them out and writes something else and then, when she has enough pages, she types her words with the heavy black typewriter that she unpacks from its case and sets up on the dining room table. Sometimes she lets Samantha have a sheet of scrap paper and type whatever letters she wants. Samantha likes to makes lists of the words she knows how to spell, and the lists get longer every day. Her mother showed her how to change to the red part of the ribbon, so sometimes she makes red lists.

Her mother says her pages are stories, but she never reads them to Samantha. She says, "Maybe one day when you're a big girl you can read them yourself. Maybe they'll be in a magazine and you can read them there."

"What are they about?" Samantha wants to know. She hopes they are about cats like their cat Smoke, or fairies, or maybe elephants in India or children going *nanga punga* there, like her mother told her. They say *nanga punga* in India, and it means nudie, like you are when you come out of the tub and your mother wraps you in a towel with a hug. Samantha likes the towel hug and she likes to hear her mother say *nanga punga*, and she likes to say it, too. Her mother says the stories aren't about *nanga punga* or elephants. She says they are about Life As We Live It. Samantha thinks this might still allow for a story about Smoke, who is alive and her best friend besides her mother. Her mother puts the stories in large envelopes and hands them directly to the mailman when he drives up to their mailbox in his truck. She always crosses her fingers on both hands when the truck drives away, so Samantha does, too. She knows her mother wants her stories to Produce an Income, which is something she needs to Get Free, but free of what? When she asked once, her mother said, "Never mind."

For a few days after she sends away an envelope, her mother practices shorthand on her tablet, which she told Samantha was a kind of shortcut, so Samantha sits on the couch and writes things on a tablet too, in a series of looped "o"s that come as close as she can to what her mother is doing. Sometimes stories and sometimes shortcut. Shortcut can Produce an Income, too. They do their writing while they are still in pajamas and it's nice that way.

Her mother gets busy after tablet time. She jumps up from the armchair and changes into pedal pushers and rushes to do the breakfast dishes. She makes Samantha dress in a hurry, too. "It would be just like them," she says.

"Who, Mamma?"

"Your aunts. Just like them to drop in before I was dressed." Aunt Celia and Auntie Vera never drop in, but they might. Samantha understands that you never can tell, and she and her mother must not be caught lazing about with tablets while there are breakfast dishes in the sink. Her mother's tennis shoes go *slap slap slap* back and forth to the garage, where the washer and dryer are, or she'll clatter the glass grapes down on the coffee table after dusting. Then Samantha wishes Steve would get home, or her father, to play Go Fish. In the afternoon, she is allowed to turn on the television and watch cartoons, but her mother tells her to keep it low, so she sits cross-legged in front of the screen, with Smoke in her lap, close enough so they can hear.

Her mother and father are talking in the living room, which is unusual because it's Strike time, and her mother is always mad at her father during Strike time, and they don't talk much. Samantha doesn't like the not talking, but otherwise she likes Strike time because sometimes her dad is home during the day to play Go Fish, or he'll take her out on errands and let her pick coins from the little rubber change holder that is round like a turtle until he squeezes it from the ends and it opens up. She puts nickels in the vending machines at the supermarket, hoping that the twists of the knob will give her exactly the plastic cat or bracelet she has her eye on, but it never does.

She listens to her parents from her favorite corner by the bookshelf, which has a table beside her mother's armchair on one side, and the end of the couch on the other, so it almost makes a little cubby for her. She likes figuring out the titles on every straight soldier of her mother's books, wedged together on the shelf. A few are too hard, but not *The Good Earth* or *All the King's Men*—those are easy.

"I'll just have to do it," her mother says. "Six months, or maybe eight."

"Who will watch her?"

"Mrs. Miller down the street said she could."

"You belong home with the children."

"What do you think I want?"

"It'll get better."

"It won't, it never does. Even when you go back to work, we'll still be in the hole." Her mother's voice is cold. Then, scary: "I'm *so sick* of it."

When the lamp crashes down by her, the one her mother picked out for herself for a Mother's Day present, the white glass shade breaks into two neat halves. At first Samantha thinks the lamp must have jumped by itself, but then she sees the cord is wrapped around her fingers. She stays still and small and ready for a storm. But her mother only comes over to silently regard the broken pieces. "You didn't mean it." And when Samantha still doesn't speak, "Look, we can glue it. Don't worry about Mrs. Miller. It will only be for a little while."

Mrs. Miller is just down the street. Her mother says she is nice, but then cries the first morning she takes her there. Samantha decides that Mrs. Miller is neither nice nor not nice. She's old and fat and sighs every time she heaves herself out of a chair. She gives Samantha a peanut butter sandwich and a glass of milk at lunchtime. She's out of jelly and says she'll get some, but always for-gets. There are no other kids there, and no toys, so Samantha brings her own bag of Barbies and coloring books and easy readers. She's not allowed to bring Smoke, because her mother says Mrs. Miller wouldn't like it, and Smoke might run away and be too far down the street to know which way was home. Those days pass in gray, with the voices in the other room from Mrs. Miller's television stories jumping loud and then dangerously silky and soft. The grown-ups in the stories are always mad at each other like her mom is at her dad, but they do it with slamming doors and music that makes you feel like monsters are coming.

She likes it better when it turns into summer and the new babysitter is a high school girl named Gladys who comes to the house. Gladys teaches Samantha how to play solitaire and to shuf-fle, and plays Go Fish as long as Samantha wants to. Every morning after her mother leaves for work, Gladys faces the mirror over the couch to put on makeup, her knees digging into the cushions, and Samantha watches from the arm of the couch: first the brush that draws color across the eyelids, then the tiny comb that blackens the eyelashes. She finishes by dipping a finger in the little pot of pink gloss for the lips. Gladys always puts some on Samantha's lips; it tastes like strawberry.

Her brother is old enough to play in the neighborhood, so it's mostly just Samantha and Gladys all day. Gladys squirts her with the hose in the backyard, or they lie in the sun on towels and listen to the transistor radio Gladys produces from her big bag. Princess, the miniature poodle next door, yaps away at them on the other side of the Driscolls' fence, but Gladys isn't bothered. Not like Samantha's mother, who always shouts "Be quiet" to Princess, which only makes her bark more. Her mother has gotten into an argument with Mrs. Driscoll over it. She says she can't hear herself think with that dog. She says Mrs. Driscoll is a Fake, and that her fake niceness means nothing, because she'll just smile to her face but still let Princess bark. Her mother wouldn't be surprised if she even wants Princess to do it. Then she tells Samantha about her neighbor on Wygant Street who was the real-thing nice, and her name was Dixie, and she had an adorable dog. But Samantha has never been to Wygant Street. Her brother likes the kids on the street they have now. Samantha isn't allowed to play with them yet, because there are none her age.

Her mother asks her questions when she comes home: Did Gladys have any friends over? Did she talk on the phone a lot? Sometimes Gladys does both of these things, but Samantha wants her mother to like Gladys, so she says no. Still, her mother finds things to frown over, like Gladys's long hairs on the furniture where she sits and brushes it, or gum wrappers left here and there, or milk glasses in the sink not even rinsed, so there are little white moons on the bottom. When Gladys has a cigarette, she smokes it in the backyard, and buries the butt in the dirt by the shed where Samantha's mother doesn't have flowers. Samantha told Gladys it was okay, her mother used to smoke too, though that was before she saw Samantha puffing on her pencil during morning tablet time. After that she didn't.

Her mother takes a picture of her in the front yard on the first day of kindergarten. Samantha holds a plaid lunchbox that matches her plaid dress, and has to squint because she's looking into the sun. Everything about going to school turns out to be nice. Her brother walks her every day and isn't allowed to leave her until she's inside the primary wing. He's in the upper wing, starting fifth. Even if his friends from the neighborhood join up with them on the walk, he holds her hand on every cross. She has her own desk with her name on a strip of paper taped to it. Six girls can crowd around the wide-angle spray of the big curved sink in the lavatory. You press a ring on the floor with your foot to make the water come on. The warm water on her fingers makes her dreamy, and she is always the last one to dry her hands. At noon she lines up to pay her nickel and take a carton of cold milk from the crate that Mr. McNeil wheels in. You can ask for chocolate or regular and she'd like chocolate but her mother tells her to take regular, so she does. She unlatches her lunchbox and compares sandwiches with Sandra and Carolyn. They listen to Mrs. Field read a chapter of *Charlotte's Web* while they eat. After recess, they go back to workbooks or reading group and Samantha collects more stars.

Her across-the-street neighbor, Mary Ann, got a spider monkey for her birthday.

Samantha's mother says Mary Ann gets anything she wants, and that monkeys belong free in jungles like they were when she was a girl in India, and that the mother, Pauline, keeps a filthy house, and that all she does is watch soap operas the whole day and smoke. But Mary Ann's mother is always nice to Samantha, even if Mary Ann herself is not. Mary Ann is two grades older and not only has a monkey, but also a built-in swimming pool with a diving board. Mary Ann invites certain children in the neighborhood to swim, and the ones who aren't invited are allowed to stand outside the chain-link fence separating the front yard from the back and watch. Once Mary Ann said Samantha could come into the pool and Samantha ran home to put on her suit, but Samantha's mother saw that there were no adults watching and told Samantha she could not.

The monkey is tiny, with a heart-shaped white face and dark eyes. Her name is Ivy. Mary Ann's father built Ivy a pen in the basement with a swinging hammock and a platform and some toys. Ivy spends all her time jumping from the floor to the platform and back down again. Mary Ann sometimes takes Ivy for a walk in the neighborhood on a leash, but then has to scoop her up and carry her, because Ivy doesn't seem to know what to do on the ground.

Mary Ann's parents, Pauline and Zeb, sit up at night by the pool, drinking beer and smoking. They have a sliding glass door off their bedroom so they can walk barefoot to the patio from the bed anytime they want to. You can see through the open drapes of the sliding glass door that they have a color television in the bedroom, and also a wide bed, a giant one, not like Samantha's parents with two single beds and a nightstand between. On the nightstand rest her mother's *Guidepost* magazines and a box of tissues, one always pulled up like a little white flag.

Waves of laughter come from Mary Ann's house. Sometimes there is shouting, too, or the sound of glass breaking—you can hear it when the slider isn't closed—but the shouting comes in bursts and then it isn't too long before everyone is sitting around the pool again, laughing. When there is shouting at Samantha's house, it's usually her mother shouting at her father, and then, finally, her father shouting back for her mother to *shaddup*, which only makes Samantha's mother shout more. Then her mother goes quiet, which should be a relief, but isn't. Sometimes she stays quiet for days, and though she talks to Samantha and Steve, it's only enough to feed them and do what needs to be done. The quiet in the house feels like a new, fifth person has moved in, and that person has no name and no shape and no face, but lives in every room and makes them all act stiff and speak in low voices and feel like they are the ones that don't belong.

One day Mary Ann invites Samantha to go with her to the Dairy Queen, which Samantha is not allowed to do because it means crossing the four lanes of Division Street. Samantha doesn't have any money for a cone, but Mary Ann says she'll pay for hers, and since Samantha really wants ice cream, she goes. When the light changes against them in the intersection, Mary Ann says "Shit!" and "Run!" and Samantha does. The car that is turning stops in front of her and blares her heart out with its horn. But Mary Ann is true to her word and buys Samantha a kiddie cone, and herself a Dilly Bar. Going back, Mary Ann says, "Let's cross in the middle this time, because at the corners all the cars are doing everything at once." But then, halfway down the block on the way to a good crossing spot, she says, "I guess I'm going to go over to Denise's house now, I'll see you later," and dashes off down a side street, leaving Samantha standing on the wrong side of Division. Samantha takes a few uncertain steps down the street Mary Ann has taken, but it's clear Mary Ann didn't mean for Samantha to come. Denise is almost certainly in second grade, like Mary Ann. Samantha is still in kindergarten; Mary Ann won't be happy with her if she tries to follow.

Traffic streams by in both directions. Samantha stands still because the cars keep coming and coming. Then they stop, held back on the right side by a red light, while on the left they are still distant. She begins to cross, but then stops in confusion in the middle turning lane. Some cars have begun coming again from the right, turning from the intersection. Drivers' faces look at her as they blur past. She hears honks. One car pulls over to the curb and a man starts to get out. She can't go back because the cars on the left that were distant are now coming to the light, lining up behind her. Samantha sees that the turners have stopped and that the cars that have been held back are beginning to roll forward. Before they can get to her, she runs across the remaining two lanes, dropping the last half of her cone, cutting through the parking lot of Albertson's so that the man who got out of his car can't come and scold her as she thinks he is going to. Then she runs across the lot of John and Mary's hamburger stand and turns right at the flying heart sign of the Douglas gas station, which marks the way home. Even on that street, not her street, but the street on the way to her street, back among the houses whose colors she knows by heart from seeing them on drives home, she doesn't quit running until she passes the turnoff to her school. Then she goes right at the corner house where the old man yells at kids for crossing his lawn, the greenest in the neighborhood, and then, finally, left at the chain-link fence of Mary Ann's pool, and across the street to her own house with its gauzy living room curtains and venetian blinds, and the tall rhododendron that is blooming pink right now in front of Samantha's bedroom window.

This is the first secret Samantha keeps from her mother, though she doesn't think of it as a secret, just something she hasn't told her yet. After that, Mary Ann allows her more visits to the basement to see Ivy, though still not to hold her. Ivy has learned to ride around on Mary Ann's shoulders, peeking out of the limp curtain of Mary Ann's blond hair. Samantha has never wanted anything more in her life than she wants a monkey of her own to ride on her shoulder and clutch at her with tiny leather hands.

One evening Mary Ann rings their doorbell in tears. "Ivy's gone, have you seen her?" Soon Mary Ann's whole family, including her older brother and sister, are out with flashlights, and all the neighborhood kids, too, including Samantha with Steve, calling, "Here, Ivy!" "Treat, Ivy!"

Ivy is spotted the next day, high on a power line. Mary Ann, crying, shouts up to Ivy that she'll give her a whole peanut butter sandwich with jelly, a package of Oreos, fries from McDonalds. Ivy stares down. A bowl of Cap'n Crunch. Red Vines. Fritos. Someone rushes into Mary Ann's house to get the treats, and someone else runs home to call the fire department. Mary Ann stays in place pleading with her pet. Before there is time for Oreos or sirens, Ivy tilts her head at them, as if she has a question they're not answering, then flashes away into the tips of the firs in a couple of springing vaults, and no one will ever see her again.

A Century of
Progress

Portland, 1970

Samantha comes from the suburbs to sleep over at Vera's place once a year. It happens like an eclipse, an event that temporarily alters the balance between light and shadow, the texture and grain of the world. The visits started with Stevie, Vera's offer to help when Carl and Kay were moving house. Then she'd take him for a day or two whenever Kay was especially frazzled with the new baby. When he outgrew coming, and Samantha was old enough, it was her niece's turn. The children have always seemed eager to come. Favorite Auntie, her brother Carl dubbed her, and she tries not to disappoint.

The morning comes, and very early, Carl dropping his daughter on the way to work, but Vera is up, she has her coffee percolating and her old, sticking window cracked to hear the city birds, and the snap shade raised to see the sky outside, still gray with dawn.

Carl refuses coffee, has his thermos in the car, left it double-parked, must beat the worst of the traffic to Swan Island and the shipyards. When the door closes after him and it's just the two of them, Vera experiences a seismic shift in the day, now a day tilted toward taking care of another, when she's lived all these years since Ernie's death as a person who looks after only herself.

The bag is placed beside the sofa, where Samantha will sleep in the hideaway bed. Carl is several blocks away by now, his new Volkswagen—a car Vera can't seem to fit into properly—darting in and out of the morning rush hour, heading toward the great skeletons of ships he will solder and bolt.

"Have you eaten, dear?" She has to relearn mothering each time, but feeding, she knows, is basic. Vera brings out the white bread and the sugary cereal bought for this visit, knows better than to suggest *filia*. The girl got a whiff of its sharp sourness a long time ago and has not considered it since. Vera's *filia* comes from a very old starter; every time she makes a new batch she removes a small amount to stay warm in the rear corner of her cupboard. The starter might actually go back to the one her mother brought over from Finland. Is that possible? Probably not. She remembers the voyage, or has made up or been told what she doesn't remember, but cannot place the jar of starter in the scene, though of course her mother would have packed it in a trunk, swaddled from breakage until it arrived in the new world.

Anyway, it's an old starter, and Vera likes to think it came directly from Lehtimäki, an unbroken line of nourishment that began with milk cultured from a cow chewing grass growing in that faraway loamy soil, and why not, it could be true. A starter doesn't die if you're careful, if you keep it warm enough. Like a child, it becomes hardy.

Samantha chooses toast, and Vera did buy a small jar of Welch's grape jelly especially for her. For herself, Vera puts a cinnamon husk by the side of her coffee cup, and spoons out a dish of *filia*, to drizzle with honey and top with a few berries. The mistake was in letting the child smell it before she tasted it—a smell full of death and life rolled up together.

Vera washes up their few dishes and Samantha dries. She pours herself more coffee. They have chatted about her niece's family news: Her big brother, Steve—still Stevie, in Vera's mind—off to camp this week, this time as a junior counselor; and the fact that her mother will now allow her to take her bike across 182nd Avenue this summer if she walks it in the crosswalk.

"I'm trying to picture where," Vera says. The trouble, she thinks, with numbers instead of names. The outskirts where the family lives consist of miles and miles of numbered streets.

"It's the big busy road that crosses with Division and runs by the high school. You know, Rockwood Plaza, where there's Kienows and Rexall and Grants? It's not *that* busy. It was stupid that I couldn't go alone before now.

"It's funny how almost *all* my friends live across 182nd," Samantha continues. Vera detects a whiff of complaint accompanying this information. As her niece continues talking about the houses of her friends, she intuits that they are of a different standard than the one Samantha and her family live in—of a bigger, more luxurious type, with rooms that have names denoting their special functions: sewing room, rumpus room, den. Carl and Kay own a ranch on a street of ranches. To put their mark on the property they planted their own boxwood hedge and pair of spruces on either side of the picture window. Vera remembers being shown these improvements and more: the patio her brother poured, the redwood picnic table they acquired to place on it along with a matched set of webbed folding chairs, the shed he built to house the mower and shovels. It's twice as big as their Wygant Street house was, and there is nothing in the world wrong with it, if you like living that far out, but Vera understands that they are on the wrong side of 182nd, and that Samantha has recently discovered this. Their house has a kitchen, a dining room, a living room, a bathroom, and three bedrooms. Not one room requiring a special name.

Vera likes the image of Samantha walking her Schwinn across the busy street, mixing in with rumpus rooms and their self-satisfied inhabitants. Vera was just sixteen when she went door-to-door in Hi Bug—the fancy part of Red Lodge—volunteering with her wartime conservation pledge cards. She never once went there as a hired girl, always knocked at the front entrance. At all times she wore her white gloves and fox stole, bought on employee discount from the Grove, her first job.

"They sound like lovely friends," Vera says, removing her dish-washing gloves and draping them over the drainer. "Just be on the lookout, won't you, when you cross."

***

They have time to kill before the stores open. They sit on the couch together, Vera with the newspaper her brother brought upstairs for her, Samantha curled up with her book. The paper is full of ugliness, as usual. Vera has never seen a year of such bad news. More and more student strikes since last month's shootings in Ohio. Terrible thing—soldiers shooting at young people just marching. But Vera's seen it all before: seen strikes, seen soldiers shooting at the marchers.

Samantha makes a sudden sound of impatience, startling Vera out of her reading. She was just about to turn to the lighter pages, garden hints and fashion sightings. Her niece plucks her glasses from her face, the new wire-rimmed frames that were so argued over with her mother for months, so begged for, and thrusts them away from her. They teeter on the edge of the coffee table where she precariously placed them, then drop soundlessly to the carpet. This is what Kay had been afraid of: rough treatment. The old plastic frames were so much sturdier. Vera saw Kay's point, and yet she certainly sympathized with Samantha's wish to choose her own frames, keep up with fashion. But she stayed neutral at the Sunday dinner when she was polled; she has learned better than to get in the middle of controversies between Kay and her daughter, or Kay and anyone, for that matter. Her sister-in-law retreats so easily and stubbornly into hurt feelings, silent grievances.

"Is there something the matter with them, dear?" Vera asks.

Samantha is rubbing her face in exasperation, muttering something about the glasses. The basic text is that she hates them and that they are stupid. The girl has barely arrived and is already unhappy, the reason for it not completely clear. But here she is, curled on the sofa, disconsolate, her face hidden. She was rousted out of bed very early; that might have something to do with it. But the glasses are somehow the culprit. Or maybe it's just being on the verge of eleven. Not so much a child, yet not the next thing, either.

Vera gives her a pat on the arm that's meant to be comforting. Seeing her hand next to her niece's young skin reminds Vera that she's old. She knows she is, but the contrast is quite shocking. She was the second-oldest girl in their brood, and Carl is a decade younger than she. He started on children when he was nearly fifty, almost no business doing so then. Better late than never, she supposes. Nevertheless, this all makes her the age of a grandmother to Samantha, not an aunt. Her veins stand up on the back of her hands like a system of plumbing; her tapered nails underneath the clear lacquer have a yellow cast; her skin is spotted. It is a crone's claw and she withdraws it from the plump young arm because it looks so defiling there.

Vera has become bored with her niece's moodiness, thinks the problem with children now is how the fits are indulged, examined, made to seem important. Her mother and father certainly had nothing to do with such behavior. You'd be out in the snow before you knew what was what, a shovel in your hand to clear the path, even if it didn't need clearing. An hour of that would clear up a snit.

After a while she announces that it's time for a walk, raising the window higher to check the summer temperature. Portland washes itself regularly in sweet, mild rain, the air scrubbed perpetually by the river and pines. Vera's lived in several places and could recognize them all by the air alone, eyes shut. There was the alpine tang of their little outpost of Scotch Coulee, Montana—mineral with cold in winter, pungent with sage and juniper in the warmer months. The hot breath of the coal mine there, where sometimes she let a boy walk her down the slope after a dance, just for a little kiss. The acrid smell of Detroit. The grassy tang of Indianapolis. She can't recall the scent of Lehtimäki, but thinks if she breathed it again she would know it. Actually, she does know: birch sap, sweet and minty, and charcoal. And in winter the zero smell of snow, a kind of cold that scours out all else.

This morning they are going first to Meier & Frank, and Samantha is watching the sidewalk, with its embedded particles of glitter. She knows that Vera doesn't have the answer about those particles; they have wondered about them together before. Vera guessed mica, or glass, but it's almost better not knowing. The sidewalks take on a different sheen depending on the light. There are only certain blocks on Broadway that have them.

They used to hold hands, Samantha's little sticky one in Vera's gloved hand, but not, of course, for a few years now. With her niece recently shot up to almost Vera's height, there is a definite shift in the balance of things. Vera feels that if she stumbles, or is taken by the wave of dizziness that comes upon her now and then, she would reach for Samantha's arm to steady herself. Just last year, that wouldn't have been the case. Now there is this tall person, who is definitely slowing her steps on Vera's behalf, on whom she could lean.

Her niece stops in front of an optician's window to stare at the display of quarter-sized contact lenses. Vera is confused until she realizes they are that large for display purposes only. They come in oddly vivid colors—lavender, imagine—and are disconcertingly plastic.

"You don't mean you want those in your eyes?"

Samantha nods vigorously.

"I'm getting them when I'm thirteen."

This is still some time away, so Vera doesn't ask whether this is a decision Samantha has privately taken on her own, or one she has already wheedled her mother into accepting. She decides it's safer not to investigate.

The walk to the center of downtown is ever so slightly downhill and adds to the optimistic feeling one has when going there. Vera feels a certain strengthening in her person when she approaches a department store, any department store, the way a doctor must feel when stepping inside a hospital. She knows the workings. Her retail career was in other cities, but when she first moved to Portland, widowed, she worked in Meier & Frank part-time to keep herself occupied. If she wanted, she could step in and learn the inventory procedures in an hour; could carry on a brisk conversation with the buyers; train the floor help, write an advertisement, dress a window. She doesn't want to do any of these things now, but feels, none-theless, a more important person when setting foot on the marble floors, the ceiling above high enough to permit a soaring feeling, an elixir of scents rushing to meet her from the cosmetics counters, the voices low and courteous and elegant.

She wonders suddenly if the girl is too old for the toy depart-ment. It is their long-standing tradition, a toy and an outfit that they will pick out over the course of a morning's shopping. As they step on the escalator, she thinks perhaps that for the first time they should proceed simply to the clothing section.

But Samantha turns left, to toys. It shouldn't matter to Vera, but she is relieved. Some things are still the same. Next year, in all probability, they won't be. Maybe the girl will even decide it's time to stop coming to visit. It's a thought she should tuck away, be ready for, just in case.

Vera had expected the toy department to be tedious, but it feels suddenly precious. She will find a chair to sit in and watch her niece move up and down the aisles, surveying merchandise on every shelf, even the items meant for boys, and the ones for younger children. Samantha asks politely, as she is trained to ask at home, about limits. Vera doesn't think there is anything here she can't afford, certainly not as Favorite Auntie, and the pleasure of dismissing the question as unimportant, as having no particular answer, is worth whatever risk might be attached to it.

Samantha pulls a stuffed dog—she chooses the middle-sized, not the enormous one—and a Barbie doll off the shelf and deposits them in Vera's lap while she continues her survey. These are two of the finalists. Vera could buy her both, but while she enjoys setting no limit on price, she thinks it would be a mistake to bestow more than one thing. Years from now, when Samantha is remembering her—for this is what it is all for, isn't it? To live on in the mind of her niece, carried forward into a future she won't live to see and has no child of her own to see for her?—when this time is being remembered, it will be the doll or the stuffed dog that will be the image of it. If it were to be the two together, Vera senses some subtle risk of blurring, or dilution. That is the trouble with everyone these days having enough and more than enough. Nothing about more than enough is worth remembering.

What it means to have one thing: your first fine pocketbook, say, maroon alligator in a loaf shape with a gleaming brass clasp that snaps shut with authority. An equilibrium to it that feels both weightless in the crook of your arm and also as if it has the power to ground you. This was her first purchase in Detroit, as a bride, freshly removed from Red Lodge. The ceremony of watching it wrapped in tissue, slipped into a stiff bag emblazoned with the Klines name. Vera had wrapped countless objects in the same kind of tissue at the Grove back in Red Lodge, and followed the salesgirl's fingers with critical attention as they centered, folded, tucked. Yes, that was the way.

One fine handbag, not a dozen cheap ones. And not even, when Ernie's trucking business had begun to flourish, not even five fine handbags. One at a time, or two—one for evening, one for day. When the corners finally roughened, when the satin lining frayed, the clasp developed a gap, you considered carefully whether it should be mended, refurbished, or pressed into service for another day. If the answer was no, you found someone younger, poorer, maybe the girl who took out your washing or the one who greeted you in the bakery where you bought your *pulla*. Then you presented the used handbag, still perfectly serviceable, much more than the bakery girl or the laundry girl could afford, distinguished enough to go well with any dress or suit, even a working girl's poplin or serge. You presented it in saved tissue, folded nicely, in a saved store bag, so they could have a way to carry it home, their own moment of unwrapping.

This was the way to give a gift, and anything could be a gift if it suited, if it was carefully matched to the recipient. It didn't have to be new, and if it was new, it didn't have to be expensive. But it had to be allowed its due. And the way, now, to do that, is to have the girl choose just one item, and not two.

Vera grows drowsy. The toy department is quiet on a summer weekday morning. Her upholstered chair is comfortable. The stuffed dog occupies one side of her lap; the Barbie in the box, the other. Samantha winds up and down the aisles methodically. She brings over some kind of kit in a box with a photograph of a crocheted purse on the cover.

"Maybe this," Samantha says.

Vera studies the picture of the small square pocket on a strap, a simple button-and-loop closure. "We don't need the kit, Samantha. I can make you one of these in an afternoon. I'll teach you."

"Really? You can just look at the picture and do it?"

Vera nods. "This is very easy. You can make them for your friends."

Samantha returns the box to the shelf and glides by the baby dolls without a glance. Just last year she had picked one with jewel-blue eyes that blinked shut and opened wide again. Her niece had had a long run with baby dolls, even going so far as to buy them real bibs and rattles from the drugstore. She always liked everything to be authentic, the better to pretend.

Vera had never played with dolls. As one of the older children in a brood of nine, ten if you counted the one born blue, she'd had plenty of babies to help mind, all too real. Diapering, rocking, soothing, spooning, bandaging—she'd had it all to do as a girl, and as a bride wanted none of it. Ernie said wasn't he the luckiest bastard on earth to have a gal who wanted to have a little fun first in the big city—this was Detroit—before they started all that family stuff. The thing was, even when they threw the precautions away, nothing happened. She went on working at Kresge's, they went on dancing at the Boblo, going to Belle Island, taking in baseball, motoring to Niagara or on visits home to Montana, then Oregon when her family moved. They went on with their card games with friends and their drinking, first the bootleg Ernie trucked in, and then, when it was legal again, the stuff they bought from the corner package store. They lived their lives, Vera turning twenty-five, then thirty, the years ticking by one after another in suddenly accelerated fashion because she had started paying attention. And no babies, ever. And none for her sister, Celia, and none for her brother Walter, and none for Hank, though he didn't really count insofar as he had never married.

Vera wondered, in recent years when people started talking about poisons in the water and soil, about DDT, if it was something in the Scotch Coulee dirt where they'd had their cottage near the mines, between Bearcreek and Red Lodge. If the slack piles that drifted in the breeze had somehow sifted into her cells, or nestled in her womb, the way the cinders settled in the corners of all the dwelling places of her childhood. It was true that some of her other brothers and sisters had had children, her younger brother

Carl having Samantha at the age of fifty-four—who was still, if you could believe it, trailing her fingers down the rows of stuffed animals.

But the fact of Walter, herself, and Celia childless, all of them teenagers during the same period, all of them crossing Washoe Hill near the mine to go to high school, then Walter dropping out to work full-time underground. She had fully expected, after having a carefree spell with her husband, after working and earning and knowing she could do that, to have a child. She wanted one. But the child never came and Vera's mind now went back to the slack, the soot, the blackness that must have slipped in through their very pores.

Her niece has completed her inventory and returns to her side, silently stroking first the dog's fur, then critically examining Barbie's long straight hair, her flowered bell-bottom pants and sleeveless top.

The dog, the Barbie: One she will fuss over, feed, protect; the other she will—what? *Be?* Imagine herself as that rigid and perfectly smooth body? The child has a Barbie at home from a few Christmases ago, with a platinum bubble hairdo and several sheath dresses. That one seems much more sophisticated, a small painted smile, hardly a smile, really, just a moue playing about her lips. Heavy-lidded eyes. But this one grins wolfishly, eyes wide open, seems ready to try anything. Spirit of the times. When she used to babysit out at the house, Vera loved hanging the tiny clothes on the hangers in the wardrobe box, helping Samantha find both shoes to a pair and lining them up. There were tiny pearls and tiny clutches and lovely silk pillbox hats. The two of them dressed and undressed Barbie for hours. The boyfriend, Ken, always lay somewhere off on his side, of little interest to anyone.

Vera hears her niece's unspoken wish to have both the dog and the Barbie, to have everything, but on this Auntie will stand firm. The girl reads the price tags, but Vera tells her again not to think about that. To get what she wants. But she will not offer both.

***

They have their rituals, up the escalator and now down, the toy dog in its tissue swaddling, the new outfit from the Junior Miss department folded in its separate bag. Across the marble floor with the attractive array of chiffon scarves and out again into the suddenly cloudy afternoon. She has no umbrella, but the sky is merely white, as if padded with cotton. Not a rain sky. Lunch next, at Manning's with the steam table where they point to what they want, and the case of desserts. Samantha will always choose breaded chicken patty with green beans and finish with a chocolate ice cream sundae in a stainless-steel dish. The chicken and beans are just about the extent of the real food she will eat. Vera thinks the trouble with picky children is that they have never been truly hungry. If they had been, then any cooking smell, any offering, would tempt. But people who have never been hungry crave only sweets, and the girl would eat sweets the whole day long if permitted.

They take their seats at a table near the window where they like to be. Vera considers the turkey slices, gravy, and stuffing in front of her. Perhaps a little heavy for a June day, but it's what appeals, and when you reach a certain age Vera believes in having exactly what you want. What her niece wants is to go straight to the ice cream machine, but Vera insists on lunch first. The girl eats her buttered roll, drinks her milk, nibbles at the chicken and beans. Says she's full. Vera tells her to eat a little more. Samantha pushes the food around, darting glances at the big silver ice cream machine and the silver dishes waiting upside down on a tray with a cloth napkin.

Go ahead, Vera tells her, knowing that Carl and Kay often do the same, and wonders why her own mother and father were so capable of not allowing things, so happy to squelch a desire. What is it about this age, especially this decade, that makes it suddenly so much easier to say, *Go ahead*.

She watches her niece make a careful swirl of ice cream from the machine, top it with an equally meticulous spiral of chocolate sauce. They share the same instinct for doing things properly. Vera will have only coffee for dessert, a saccharin tablet stirred in from her enameled pillbox. Her niece returns with the sundae, fetches her the coffee, doesn't spill any on the saucer as she walks. They watch the men hurrying by in business suits, secretaries in skirts and heels on their lunch break, shoppers more casually dressed. Vera always enjoyed being employed, never found it odd that she should be, even when Ernie was earning enough, and then more than enough. It all depended on your perspective. The women that she had waited on in the Grove, back in Red Lodge, lived mostly in Hi Bug: Their standard was to run a home with servants, mostly Finnish or Irish girls, and never dirty their hands. Their notion of working hard was to chair a Women's Club meeting, or finish an embroidery project, or supervise a child's piano practice.

Vera's father's socialism had been a thorn in her side, always marking her family out as suspect, but she'd grown up taking it for granted that a woman had rights and responsibilities like everyone else, that a woman would cast a vote, as they already did in Finland, and get a job. Now the times are catching up; you can't watch the evening news without women marching over something or other, waving placards. But, of course, the poor women of the world always worked, then and now. The marchers today are the Hi Bug descendants, who've grown bored with, or been made crazy by, their embroidery.

Samantha spoons up the ice cream with devotion. She used to be the slightest bit chubby, at least by today's standards, the magazine pictures of females of all ages always showing toothpick arms and legs. But with her new height she's stretched out and become slim; she should try to stay that way. Vera's own youth had coincided with rounder times; she was lucky in that regard. She wants to suggest that Samantha forgo the last of the ice cream, but she will not. She will leave that to the parents, though she knows what they would say: *Go ahead.*

***

As they head up Jefferson they pass a shaggy young man coming toward them with a large drum strapped to his back, another hugged to his chest. They are long, tapered, foreign-looking instruments made of wood and hide, nothing you'd see in a regular band. She's seen this particular person before, circling the neighborhood, looking, presumably, for a place to plant his instruments and himself. He's typical of the sort milling around the Park Blocks these days, kids spilling down from Portland State, all of them dressed somehow like people from another country: ponchos, caftans, tunics, sandals or bare feet—rough, woven fabrics that you'd never find in a department store. Just as they seem out of place, they seem also out of time—almost biblical in their long hair and beards. This boy, scruffy but too young for a real beard, doesn't seem to recognize her—why would he?—though he himself is unmistakable with his drum baggage. His territory must be close to her own because of her frequent glimpses of him. Vera has nothing against these peaceniks, if that's what he is. She is, in fact, in sympathy—doesn't trust Nixon, doesn't understand this war, came from a family that always went against the grain. But a simple bath, that seems basic. And all that drug business causes an alarm to go off in the back of her brain when she sees a face on the street that's too dreamy, or eyes that are too sharp and darting. She feels Samantha staring, and instinctively puts a protective arm on the girl's shoulder until the sidewalk is clear sailing again.

After the morning exertions, she's glad to get home; she's always happy with the sight of her stone-fronted apartment building, though the businesses on her block have gone downhill since she's lived here. There used to be a millinery shop, a bakery, and a supper club. The millinery shop became a dry cleaner. The bakery is now a greasy Chinese takeout, which Vera sometimes patronizes if she's feeling lazy. The supper club on the corner was razed to be a pay parking lot. But her building stands, stalwart as ever.

The smell greets them like a doorman—a little cabbagey today, her niece is wrinkling her nose. The dingy wallpaper above the row of metal mailboxes is adorned with carriages and ladies with Marie Antoinette hair. It's only when she has a visitor, like today, that she notices the general grime. The wire-webbed glass in the front door has triangles of soot in the corners. The brass sunburst on the square of marble floor is so dull it's almost black. People's hands and sleeves have grayed the wallpaper near the banister.

Vera lets Samantha open the mailbox—no letters, just an advertising circular for a rug store. She has enough rugs. The light dims as they climb up, no easy feat for her these days, though she makes herself go out every day despite the effort. The day she allows herself to refuse the stairs, she'll become a prisoner, and she knows it. Her brother has already been after her to move somewhere—he means a rest home—where things will be easier, food on the premises, an elevator.

She will not tell him about stopping to catch her breath on each landing, and makes herself forgo the few seconds of rest now so her niece will not tell him, either. The price of this is the flare of an angina pain as she climbs the final flight, but she will slip a nitro tablet under her tongue when she reaches the top. Samantha has scampered ahead with the key and swings the door wide for them, the milky half-light filtering out to the landing. Vera intends to die in this apartment. She is not afraid of it happening when she is alone, the likeliest scenario.

***

General Hospital is the one story she won't miss. Samantha knows that. They efficiently assume their positions: Vera in the easy chair, stockinged feet on the hassock, a cup of Sanka in her lap, what she drinks in the afternoon. Her niece is stretched out on the couch, sharing one end with the stuffed dog. She has picked her library book up from the table and is already immersed in it, oblivious to the serious conversation of the doctors on the screen pronouncing on their patients' fates.

One morning Ernie sat with her at the kitchen table drinking coffee and eating toast. He had a big contract to sign that day with a grocery wholesaler and was studying the documents with his reading glasses down on his nose, his white shirtsleeves customarily rolled up to the elbows though he hadn't left the house yet. Every time he removed his jacket he rolled them up in three swift practiced motions on each side. Then every time he was ready to put his jacket on he did the same in reverse. He couldn't stand to have his shirtsleeves all the way down, even in cooler weather, nor did he like the short-sleeved shirts Vera had brought him home from Block's, where she became a floor manager when they moved to Indianapolis. Her shift that day didn't begin until ten, so she was still in her dressing gown. They each had half a grapefruit in front of them, but Ernie didn't eat his, something she didn't notice until after he left. She finished it. She didn't wonder at his lack of appetite.

His departure that day—of course she went back to it obsessively. He'd complained of the heat, patted his brow with his clean cotton handkerchief, which he then stuffed back in his trouser pocket. One handkerchief out of sight to use, and one in his jacket pocket for show that Vera folded to a point for him. He carried his leather portfolio case under his arm—had never liked the kind with handles, didn't want people to think he was a lawyer.

His kiss before leaving: dry, brisk, marital. Perfectly satisfactory, she'd thought at the time. Who needed more than that on a hot, sticky morning?

Their Indianapolis apartment remained cool through much of the summer, but by late August the thick stone walls and sidewalks never quite cooled off at night. That day the windows were flung open to catch any hope of a morning breeze; it was already humid and still. She had chosen a beige sleeveless linen shirtwaist to wear to work, though she would need a cardigan inside the store.

Vera had just finished her morning floor walk, making sure all cashier stations were properly opened and manned, that merchandise was perfectly arranged, and that employees were at their positions looking groomed and welcoming. The store was crisp from the air-conditioning, one of the few buildings in town to have it then. When she entered the steel-and-glass doors of the polished black marble building on sticky days, she felt as if she were stepping into a sanctuary.

The phone rang for her at 11:00 a.m., the precise moment when Vera had signed the log signifying that all was in order. She remembers the sober look of the young salesgirl who summoned her to the telephone to take the call telling her her husband had suffered a massive heart attack at his desk.

They kept Ernie on a breathing tube for a day while she waited by his bedside in the hospital for something to happen. The hospital, like Block's, was cool and she huddled there in her sweater, not bothering to take it off when she stepped out for a cigarette, though the sidewalks by that afternoon could have fried an egg. They kept his heart beating. He never saw her. He might have heard her. She whispered things to him, all the important things she could think to say, before she allowed them to remove the tubes they said could do him no good.

**

Her niece snaps her library book shut with a force that Vera can't interpret: Is it pleasure, or irritation?

"Can we switch channels, Auntie?"

Vera's shows are over and she was just thinking about rising to turn it off. On her own, the next hour or two would drift by easily: She'd scrutinize a bill, or wash out some stockings; if she were feeling lazy she'd leave the television on and see who Mike Douglas had for a guest. But now she's aware of time in the self-conscious way of the impoverished hostess: What in the world to offer?

"Of course, anything you like."

Samantha gets on her knees on the rug to click the channel dial, makes a complete revolution, then clicks through more slowly till she chooses a stopping place, sitting back on her heels to appraise it. An unnaturally happy grown man with a shock of reddish hair, someone announcing himself as Ramblin' Rod, has filled up the screen. Apparently, he is an impresario of cartoons. The camera pans to bleacher seats full of children. He brings his microphone over and asks the ones in the front row their names and ages. Some are struck dumb by the fact of Ramblin' Rod's too-happy face, and mumble downcast, incoherent replies to his interrogations. Vera wonders how many bladders have failed in his studio audience.

"Isn't this a little kids' show?" Vera finally asks. She doesn't mean to sound critical. But the children are all six or seven years old.

"I still like cartoons," Samantha says simply. "I was on here once."

"You were?" Vera asks. "Did I know that?"

Samantha shrugs. "It was my Bluebird troop. We wore our uniforms."

Why wouldn't Kay have told her something so important? She's quite sure she never heard about Samantha's television appearance. Vera remembers meeting Kay in Meier & Frank to acquire the pieces of the Bluebird uniform—navy skirt and white blouse and red vest, beanie and neckerchief. There were white socks with bluebirds and a small enameled Bluebird pin. Vera had insisted on buying the uniform; it was entirely her pleasure. She'd been entranced by the fact of the club for little girls, with perfectly conceived uniforms, and the pledge or motto that had to do, she remembered, with "having fun" and "making things." Kay let her pay, but also let her know by the set of her mouth that permitting this was not something she enjoyed.

Vera doesn't know why Kay still can't accept her money as the simple gift it is. Hasn't it ever occurred to her that she is trying to make up for Carl's deficiencies as a wage earner, his lack of initiative? If Kay could look at it that way, she could place the debt on the other side of the ledger: Vera trying to straighten accounts. Her little brother is charming, handsome, and kind. Good qualities, but not much for moving a man ahead in the world. How Ernie loved presiding over his little fleet, signing invoices and bills of lading, barking orders at a secretary, banging down the phone. His name, Killorn, in five-foot-high letters across the sides of his trucks.

"How is your mother doing?" Vera asks.

"The same."

Samantha leans forward on her knees to fiddle with the color knobs; at home, Vera knows, she only has black-and-white. First she makes the faces of Ramblin' Rod and his young guests go bright red like people suffering from extreme sunburn; then she twists them the other way until they're lime with seasickness. The girl is searching for some perfect middle; just when she thinks she's discovered it she finds herself unable to resist a degree of intensification, right or left. What Vera could tell her, but what Samantha will be unable to believe, with those knobs at her disposal, is that reality is a little bit dull; that flesh is only flesh, neither pink nor green. Just an ordinary human middle ground.

"Meaning?"

"Meaning she hates her job, is mad at everybody all the time, and tells all her troubles to me like I'm her best friend. I'm sick of it. I'd like to come here and live with you."

Samantha's last words thrill her, but also make her drop the topic like a hot potato. Kay doesn't know how much Vera is indebted to *her*, for sharing her children all these years. But she also knows how easy it is to be Favorite Auntie, and Kay knows it too.

Vera tires of the cartoons' glaze about the same time it seems the children in Ramblin' Rod's studio audience do; they wave goodbye to the viewers at home with somewhat defeated expressions. Vera spends a moment wondering if the studio children were even able to see the cartoons, decides that they probably did on a television screen like everybody else, and that this, perhaps, is the reason for their inscrutable disappointment, the fact that they never actually pierced the shell of the cartoon world and reached the bright interior where gravity and mortality and other laws do not apply. No one probably told them beforehand that sitting on the bleachers in the studio would be farther from the cartoons, not inside them.

Her niece, too, seems a bit deflated, maybe from the sugary dose of child entertainment she is really too old for, though she'd hugged her stuffed dog and seemed to watch with fixed attention. Now Vera feels the girl's impatience from the way she casts herself back onto the cushions. She can't say she remembers what it's like. Her own childhood left her as soon as the next few babies were born in the family. She simply wasn't allowed to decide when it was time to stop being a child and start being something else.

***

The next morning—another mild, sunny one—stretches out in front of them. There are few entertainments Vera can provide besides her daily rounds, and how much of that can bear repeating now that the girl is older? The very repetition is what moves Vera forward into her day, but what does it feel like to the girl who is used to more action, more novelty, and friends her own age? Yesterday at the store they picked out some cotton yarn; they'll crochet the bag in the afternoon, after their walk. This morning they'll take in the Historical Society, a downtown attraction they've never explored together. Samantha told her she gave an oral report on the Klamath Indians last spring, and Vera thinks they'll find some interesting pioneer and tribal artifacts on display.

As they near the corner of Jefferson and Park, the intersection with the green strip of the Park Blocks, Samantha points to a gathering of people that seem to be headed toward them from the direction of Portland State. The two of them pause on the sidewalk, watching. Is it a parade? Vera doesn't see the flash of instruments, doesn't feel the reverberations of a bass drum. As the group approaches, it becomes a bunch of students with signs, shouting slogans. Vera rests her hand on Samantha's shoulder as a precaution. At first the shouts sound only like *Hunh hunh! Hunh hunh!* but as the faces and beards and dungarees come into focus, so do the words: *Hell no! We won't go!*

Two police cars glide into the loading zone near them, and two others are nosing into position across the street. The officers climb out of their cars and amble to meet at the center of the park strip, conversing as if they only happened to convene there for a morning chat, though each of them crosses his arms in front of his chest and their glances keep sliding sharply toward the direction of the marchers.

When the chanting is thirty yards away, the officers give up their pretense at small talk and turn to face the protesters. There are eight of them, forming an unbroken row. They seem to be suggesting to the marchers that Jefferson Street is the farthest they should consider advancing, beyond which shoppers and secretaries and businessmen have important things to do that must be carried out in an atmosphere of order and quiet.

Vera tenses in reaction to the set of the officers' jaws, their outthrust chests. She thinks Pinkertons. She thinks of Red Lodge's Liberty Committee during the Great War, and their basement interrogations of Socialists and Wobblies. The marchers are close enough now so that she can see their particularity, the fact that they are little more than boys and girls, that growing hair in long and unkempt fashion seems to be one of their main statements, that and the fact of having dirty bare or sandaled feet beneath their dungarees. Their chants have grown more raucous. Like birds obeying an invisible signal to change direction, they have moved from *Hell no! We won't go!* to *One, two, three, four! We don't want your fucking war!*

At this, Vera sucks in her breath and almost cups her hands

over her niece's ears, though it is too late; the word is loose in the air. The two of them should just turn from where they stand and find a roundabout way to the Historical Society. This is not their argument. Vera touches her niece's shoulder to give it a little steer but the girl twitches her hand away. Does not shake it off, exactly, but makes clear that she has no intention of being guided. Her face seems transfixed by the marchers, her mouth a little slack with fascination. There is something excited and happy and terrified in her niece's eyes as she takes their measure.

Vera's hand finds Samantha's arm and stays there. She, too, is a little mesmerized, more by the officers than the students. Their uniforms are different from long ago, these ones navy blue and crisp— the pleats so sharp, in fact, it almost hurts to look at them. But the faces, pink and shaved, are familiar. The shoulders thrown back, the posture of prideful, righteous duty—that is familiar. The guns and batons in holsters hang heavy and glossy at their hips.

"Let's go, Samantha." The air is beginning to change, thickening with a dangerous charge.

"No! I want to see!"

The marchers and the police are face-to-face. The police, if they wanted to inform the marchers of something, explain the regulations, or ask for a parade permit, could not be heard against the chanting—back again to *Hell no!* The students are stalled, milling about in place, feet restless, no order to their movements although their ranks are closer now, shoulder to shoulder. More police have filtered in, there are about a dozen now, to about forty or fifty marchers with their homemade signs.

Her father wrote the messages on paper; the men would ball them up and pass them to other miners during shift changes. Shake hands, pass on a circular: Strike against draft. Strike against militarism. Do not register. Pull another out of your pocket, shake hands, pass on a circular. Right under the noses of the shift bosses, those men standing with arms crossed, enforcing an orderly transfer of workers. Down with war profiteers. Down with invisible government.

Her brother Werner was put on the slacker list for not registering, his name published. The newspaper printed the warnings: Such as do not appear for examination . . . if they fail then to heed the call . . . deserters and if apprehended . . . in time of war . . . punishable by death.

He didn't register—*I've got no beef with those Huns*—and then he did. What else could he do?

Protesters are bunched up against one another, up against the line of police, unbudging. Now their feet are out of step, voices out of chant, shouting, practically spitting, in the officers' faces.

Hell no—don't want your fucking—

Glossy black holsters, arms no longer crossed but hanging down, fingers loose and empty.

Then, like birds obeying an invisible signal, hands go to batons.

She draws Samantha back against the building wall. A dentist's office, she remembers, behind them. Novocaine, laughing gas.

Hell no, hell no.

Like birds, batons raised, batons slicing the air, black arcs, black wings.

The protesters roar out, as if already struck. No chant, no rhymes, no feet in step, nothing linking them together anymore. A collection of kids, uncollected. Just people's children, parents maybe thinking, *He's at class.* Or, *She's at her job,* Or, *That kid needs a goddamn haircut.* Or not thinking at all, just everyone having an ordinary day.

The students haven't been touched, not yet, but their cries sound wounded. They are hurt, they are angry. Wronged.

Both sides are out of order now, movements jagged, shoving. The batons, the signs, swinging, sawing. Police and students not just on the grass of the Park Blocks anymore, like a playing field, like a game, but on the street in front of them. Raging and surging and pushing. She hears Samantha's sharp intake of breath.

They need to leave, now. Kent State. Tear gas. She turns, sees that their immediate way is blocked by a new phalanx of officers approaching, two more squad cars parked at crazy angles in the middle of the street. In the distance, sirens.

While she hesitates, tries to plot their route, the crowd surges closer to their position on the sidewalk. Directly in front of them is a girl, smaller than the rest, maybe someone's younger sister. Vera can't judge age these days, all the children barefoot, all the hair long. The girl trips on someone's dropped sign, goes down to her hands and knees, looks toward Vera and Samantha, her mouth open with surprise. A young man behind her is pushed forward, falls over the fallen girl. Another scuffle in front and someone is pushed backwards, falls.

Samantha tries to jerk her hand free of Vera's clutch.

"Help her, she's on the bottom."

"No, Samantha."

"We need to!"

"*No*, Samantha."

Samantha tries to get loose. And then she does, in one slippery twist, moving off the sidewalk and into the street to offer the girl a hand, a way out. A sign comes see-sawing down on her niece's back. Samantha looks up, annoyed, *ow*, as if her brother has not followed the rules, has tagged her too roughly. She looks mad, she's going to tell.

"Samantha!"

Samantha ignores her, the way these barefoot children have ignored all their parents. The girl has reached for Samantha's hand, taken it, and Samantha is trying to push the men off her with one hand, pull the girl with the other. Vera must help, must end this, must get them out of here. She moves into the scrum, trying to pry Samantha free.

Someone in front of them is shouting *pig fucking pig fucking pig,* his own face red and distorted. A baton swings down, cracks the top of the boy's head. Everyone around cries out except the boy who took the blow, he alone is silent, staggering, falling back. The girl who was on the bottom has managed to rise upright on her knees, until the dazed, now bleeding boy lurches back, topples her like a bowling pin and in the process Samantha, too.

Samantha on the ground, blood on the sky-blue seersucker of her shorts.

Vera can hear the officer's words because they are delivered over a bullhorn—*Disperse NOW! You must disperse NOW!* But she cannot hear her own words, her own voice—tearing, torn—hoarse from shouting something. She makes a guttural noise, her arms push, lift, pull—she tugs at whatever is in between her and her girl—she pushes and pulls.

A hand grips her by the elbow. She tries to resist it, her girl still on the ground, but the hand is insistent, then a voice, equally insistent. "I'll get her. Stay back."

Vera turns her head, sees that it is the drummer boy, the one she's noticed in the neighborhood.

He somehow separates Samantha from the flail of limbs and deposits her, mussed and terrified, at Vera's side. Vera is opening her mouth to thank him when she sees his gaze slide behind her, over her shoulder. He raises a quick hand—to forestall her thanks, or say goodbye—then is gone around the corner of the dentist's office, just as suddenly as he'd appeared. Vera turns to see what made him go: a stone-faced officer approaching, notebook open.

He levels his pen at her: "You wait right here, ma'am. Don't you go anywhere."

Then he turns back to help with the sorting—dazed children, angry and cursing children, crying children, as many as the police can corral being herded into the paddy wagon. Many more are leaving than are being rounded up—the rear guard is either running up the Park Blocks toward the refuge of the college, or slipping sideways into the city streets.

When the officer returns, he demands her name and identification, which she produces for him to scowl at. Can she explain herself, her involvement in all this? Is she aware that he could write her a court summons if he chooses to, for disorderly conduct? That she was endangering this child?

Samantha tries to protest that it was all her fault, her eyes filling with tears. Vera shushes her. She feels her father's tongue wanting to flare; she feels on the verge of offering her opinion of this war and of the officers' batons.

Instead she answers yes to every admonishment, tells him they just got caught in the middle. Sees, in a funny way, that the man just needs to let off steam, calm down. His eyes, close up, are bloodshot and red-rimmed. He has a middle-aged paunch. Too old for this kind of shenanigans. Who knows but that he doesn't have a teenager at home, someone shaggy and disobedient who keeps slipping away before his father can get him into the barber's chair.

By the time he's done lecturing her, telling her to be more careful next time, to avoid these agitators like the plague, he regards Vera kindly, as if she might be his own aunt gone strangely awry for a brief period.

No court summons for her; it is a fact that almost shames her, thinking about how she calculated that politeness was her strongest weapon against the officer's irritation—that and respectability. Also in her arsenal: her two-piece summer suit, a pale green tweed today; her low walking heels. She recalls now that she used her white patent leather pocketbook as a kind of battering tool when she was trying to part the tangle of people between her and Samantha. But no summons, because the officer, when he wound down, came to see her as she wished to be seen: a respectable American.

***

Puhutteko te suomea? Her mother, asking left, asking right, in the immigration line. Please, does anyone speak Finnish? Vera by the hand, Celia in her arms, Kate and Werner and Walter trying to manage the hand baggage. *Puhutteko te suomea?*

One alphabet letter chalked on their back by the health inspectors—just one *L* or *K*, for cough or eye disease or something else—would be enough to send them all back home across the Atlantic.

The inspectors had buttonhooks; they turned up the eyelids to check.

Vera imagined them sent home, not even seeing Dad after all this time, Celia born after he left and now walking and him never even meeting her yet. Him waiting and waiting at Sault Ste. Marie, Michigan, with no way of knowing why they didn't come.

Or what would happen if just one of them got the alphabet letter? Would Mother send that child home alone?

It was June when they boarded their ship at Hanko, the long sun never setting: strangers, well-wishers, milling about on the pier with the departing passengers. They pinned wild roses to the emigrants' cloaks, embracing them with quick, tight hugs. The girl who pinned a blossom to Vera's shawl whispered, "God bless. I'll see you one of these days in the *fri contri.*"

Mrs. Vera Killorn. She enunciated it clearly. The officer had been on the point of writing it down, but something in her firm delivery left his pen hovering. No need to make a fuss about this, she could almost see him thinking. All a misunderstanding that Mrs. Killorn, in her tweed summer suit, was mixed up in this. It was a good Irish name, Killorn, better to have had at a certain point than a Finnish name. There were radical Red Finns and churchgoing, conservative White Finns. In Finland, it became a civil war. In America, the White Finns sometimes translated issues of the worker newspapers such as *Industrialisti* or *Työmies* for those in charge who wanted to know the contents. The Red Finns went to jail and court and deportation parties where they danced and danced and sometimes dropped. Polite or not so polite men in overcoats and short-brimmed hats flashed badges and produced lists. Do you know this man? How about this man? This woman? No? We think you might.

***

They go to rest and gather their wits on a park bench. Samantha sits beside her, still sniffing her last tears away and shivering on this warm day. Someone else's smear of blood, now a drying rust, stains her shorts. At the bench Vera brushes her off, checks her for scrapes, makes the child test her joints. She is all right. Now they sit, stunned, and don't talk.

They remain in silence for some minutes, just breathing, feeling the flicker of sun between leaves. Sparrows have resumed chatter. Finally, Vera straightens her spine and pats her niece's arm, reassuring in its substance. On the ground, a few abandoned signs, a sandal. Like the trampled grass after a carnival has left town. Like the fifth of July.

"Should we go straight to Manning's, dear? Or eat at home? I don't think I'm up to the museum right now."

"Me neither. Whatever you want, Auntie."

The day is too lovely to waste: Picnic warm. Beer-by-the-lake warm. There are days when all you should think about is pleasure. When you should play hooky with your husband and go to Belle Island, feel sand.

As they make their way through the restaurant toward a table, she feels the pressure coming, the silverware glinting up at her at odd angles. The secret is to breathe through the squeezing, try to breathe it away. She lags behind a moment to feel for her pillbox, slip a nitro under her tongue. Simple angina, she tells herself, hasn't she lived with it for years? You don't go through a morning like they just had and not have it rear its head.

The meal is a strange copy of yesterday; they are still quelled, subdued. It's early for lunch and Vera takes only a cup of coffee and a bowl of barley soup, Samantha a square of custard and a glass of milk, foaming from the dispenser. They just need a quiet place to be.

"Will those kids go to jail?" Samantha asks.

"Jail? No, I doubt it. They'll pay some kind of fine, I expect, or their parents will."

"Why are we in the war, anyway?"

Vera stirs her coffee. "I don't think we even know anymore. It started with wanting to stop communism. Do you know what that is?"

"Not really. I hear it on the news."

When the family gets together at the holidays, there are things they never, by unspoken compact, speak of. There are gaps in the stories that the younger generation doesn't notice. It's not Vera's business to fill in these gaps and, anyway, she's used to burying the past. The men in the short-brimmed hats wanted Reds, of which, when Vera began counting the Party membership cards in her brothers' pockets back then, she guessed she knew several.

Do you know this man?

It was simple: She knew nothing.

"Communism is a form of government. Our government thinks it's dangerous and doesn't want to see it spread."

Samantha nods, but looks confused. This won't be the end of her questions. But it's not Vera's fault that the girl saw things, needs answers. They were simply walking down the Park Blocks.

"Who's right?"

"Who's right about the war?" Vera wants to tell her the protesting kids are. But it's different when you say it to a child who belongs to you. She thinks even Carl, with his once-radical politics, would have a hard time saying it to his daughter. And certainly Kay. You want your own child to follow the rules, stay safe.

"Different people have different opinions. Nobody likes war."

Samantha, she sees, could go on probing it all afternoon. Vera feels some responsibility to return more or less the same daughter to Kay and Carl that she received. Do they turn off the news at home? No way to do it completely. Samantha would have seen the film from the jungles of Vietnam, the body bags coming back off the planes. She's grown up with the assassinations, the televised funerals. It's all right there in the living room.

"Let's think about something else. Too much of politics gives me a headache. Shall we go home and make your purse?"

Her apartment has never looked so welcoming—the doilies she crocheted to pin over the shiny spots on the arms of the sofa and rocker, her Royal Doulton balloon lady, the Melmac plates in the slots of the dish dryer. She rummages in a drawer for her crochet hooks, Samantha looking over her shoulder and poking at some World's Fair cards and assorted snapshots that came loose from an album.

"So much junk," Vera says, pushing aside vacation maps and brochures.

"Who's this?" Samantha asks, pulling a small Brownie photo out of the mix. It is of Carl and Ofelia beside the bay in San Francisco when they lived there, Ofelia's cloche pulled low over her dark eyes and fashionable bob. Carl is caught in mid-laugh, holding Ofelia from behind in an embrace, her loose white dress a sinuous curve against his dark suit. Kay let the family know early on that her children were not to be made confused by knowledge of Carl's past wives.

"Hard to tell," Vera says, frowning. Hastily she reaches for a few of the World's Fair cards and spreads them out over the top of an album. "This was a good trip Ernie and I made," she says, adjusting her reading glasses on her nose and peering down. "The Chicago World's Fair. We took a full week, stayed at a nice hotel."

"Can you tell *where* this is?" Samantha holds her snapshot higher.

"Hmm." Vera glances over. "San Francisco maybe?" Vera counters with another World's Fair card. "Look at this. The Scintillator—it cast colored lights out all over the lake. The exhibits were all about advances—they called the fair 'A Century of Progress.' Things you would take for granted now, like television, but when we saw them at the World's Fair no one had seen a television before."

Samantha nods politely at the World's Fair cards. But she can't leave the snapshot: "Dad lived in San Francisco once, right? Is it him?"

Vera takes the snapshot and pretends to study it. It's a photo she knows very well. Ofelia made an enlargement of it and framed it. "It could be."

Samantha looks hard at her. "You know it is, Auntie. Who's the woman?"

Oh, Lord. First the political education and now this. "Your father was very handsome, you know. He had lady friends to go dancing with and so forth. That was way before your mother."

"I know it was way before her. Look how young he is."

"Yes, so young I almost couldn't recognize him."

"Me either." Samantha stares. "I don't even know who he is there. He's not like my dad at all."

Samantha paws through the loose photos and finds another, this one of Carl and their brother Werner smoking pipes, Werner's arm around Sylvia and Carl's around Ofelia. "Look, that's Uncle Werner!" Werner is unmistakable at any age, with his long, dour face. Sylvia, you wouldn't necessarily recognize right away, she's so smiling and blond in her youth. "And that's Dad, and there's that woman again. Look at them. He loved her, didn't he? It's obvious. So were they just boyfriend and girlfriend, or were they more?" Samantha's eyes are boring into her.

"More?"

"Were they married?"

"No, dear, the only wedding of your father's I've ever been to was with your mother." She is grateful for Kay's technical distinction about Carl's common-law unions, very useful now.

"Can I have this?"

"Let's keep it here. If you were your mother, you wouldn't like something like this around, would you?"

"I don't see why it would matter. It's not like Mom even likes him. At least this lady looks like she did. What was her name?"

"I forget. Let's get going on the crocheting before we run out of time. I've got the hooks. I'm going to show you how to make two squares that you can stitch together to make a pocket. Then we can make a loop for a button, and a strap."

"She's pretty."

"So is your mother."

Samantha shrugs and moves to return both photos to the drawer. Then she sees writing on the back of the first, and reads triumphantly, "Carl and Ofelia, June 1925. She's Ofelia!"

"Yes, that's right, she was Ofelia. She was way in the past, you can see the date for yourself. Now pay attention to what I do. I'm going to show you how to make a square that you can make big or small. And once you have these squares, you can stitch them together into anything. You can make a purse, like we're going to do, or a tiny blanket, or a giant blanket. Whatever size blanket you think you're going to need."

By the time Carl rings the buzzer, they're just finishing sewing on the button for the purse's loop. Samantha is delighted with it, and Vera sends home one of the hooks and the leftover cotton yarn so she can make another for a friend. They pack Samantha's things up, and show Carl yesterday's purchases from Meier & Frank—"Sis, you're spoiling her!" Samantha throws her arms around her auntie's neck, and Vera doesn't want her to go. But she is exhausted.

Carl and Samantha will be driving past the Park Blocks on their way out of town, and that will remind Samantha about the protest. Will she tell him about it? Or is this the beginning of an older canniness, deciding to keep some things to herself? Vera can picture how Carl will straighten, look over with concern if Samantha chatters on about the marchers, what they shouted, how the policeman talked to Auntie. And what about Ofelia? Will Samantha grill him? Will he let slip that in their common-law arrangement he considered her his first wife? Nothing Vera can do about any of it.

They'll be crossing Broadway, then past the elk statue that stands guard over Main, then their tires will hum over the metal grate of the Hawthorne Bridge, the waters of the Willamette below them, until they're on a straight street pointed to the outskirts. At least a forty-minute drive this time of day. Kay chose the neighborhood, liked that the schools were big and new.

They're on the other side of the river now, who can say how far? Vera can't picture it anymore.

She puts the remaining crochet hook back in the drawer, sees again the photograph of Carl and Ofelia. The two of them did give off sparks. Also in the drawer is a fob with the key to the Indianapolis apartment, hers and Ernie's, and the key to their last Buick. It seems, given the tangible fact of the keys, that she ought to be able to grab her pocketbook, drive back, unlock a door, and find the leather easy chair and upholstered rocker where the two of them used to sit, feet up, reading the evening paper after work. Only the stubborn fact of the chairs here, in her Jefferson Street apartment, refutes the possibility. If they are here, then they cannot still be there.

She picks up a souvenir wooden nickel and smells it to see if any trace of Ernie's tobacco or suit smell remains. Nothing. It was the prop in a joke they had, whenever one wanted the other to do a favor. The wooden nickel came from a bar in Carson City, Nevada, and they passed it back and forth to each other for twenty-five years.

"Ernie, if you come I'll give you a wooden nickel," she says out loud in the dusk of the apartment. But, of course, she is alone.

They fell in love in a single day, after standing next to each other at the Red Lodge parade on the Fourth of July. He was a stranger, but she liked the things he laughed at, and the things he whistled at under his breath were the same things she admired.

Clapping her gloved hands after the last float, she was afraid that the burly man in the straw boater she'd been eying sideways was about to turn and leave. Instead he waited until she faced him, tipped his hat, and asked if he could buy her a lemonade. They spent the rest of the day watching the townspeople gorge themselves in eating contests, balance on poles, and wrestle each other to the ground. They shared stories, and bites of a sandwich, and bumped elbows. When they strolled, he steadied her arm more than strictly necessary. Finally, they were sitting on a blanket spread over the grass, waiting for dark, and Vera's whole body was alive with nearness to his, just inches away. When the fireworks started, it was a surprise, even though that's what they'd been waiting for. Her face tilted up with all the others, following the rockets that whistled into the sky, shimmying hard against gravity.

Every explosion rocked Vera's chest; there was no getting used to them. Then the sizzle of sparks melted into light that gilded the whole upstretched crowd, all the faces massed together. Each blast was a mini-death as the flesh was shaken, pounded, mortified. Each crackling fanfare of light was a flowering of life given back.

You needed to take a great love when it was offered, and make room in yourself for its immensity. Not everyone was capable of becoming so defenseless. Not everyone could open the door and let the stranger in, and let the stranger stay, until he was no longer strange, but part of you, even after he had to go.

Vegas for
Beginners

t's past midnight and they're sleeping in a rental car in a supermarket parking lot, seats tilted back as far as they go. The windows
are cracked to let a breeze through. Her mother tried to park close
enough to the store so they weren't isolated, but far enough away so
they wouldn't attract attention and be shooed along. The botched
reservation was perhaps not her mother's direct fault. A room will

be ready for them by noon tomorrow. But still. Why are they even in Las Vegas?

Once Samantha dreamed her mother was driving them on a road that suddenly pitched steeply down. Samantha didn't know if the brakes went out, or if her mother simply decided not to apply them, but she woke up right before they plunged into the Willamette. She imagined her mother stuck in the dream without her, the boxy gray Toyota Corona sinking down in the dark water, a fan of bubbles streaming up. Her mother would be alone on the riverbed because Samantha had bailed; she became conscious in time to save herself. Whenever she thinks of the dream she is unspeakably sad. Also furious.

Before the trip she spent the summer working in her high school's office, where she answered the phone at the front desk and typed up dittos for the new school year. The three adult secretaries marveled at her steady accuracy—she rarely had to pull out a razor blade to scrape the waxy purple ink off the ditto master to retype a correction. The job was easy and they liked her. It was a CETA placement, based on her family's income, which meant they had to take her even if they didn't like her. Since it was summer, there wasn't a whole lot the secretaries could find for her to do. She had cleaned and organized all the storage areas in her first week, then typed up the dittos and ran them off while the secretaries spelled one another taking afternoons off and long lunch hours. The smell of the spirit fluid filled the back room as the purple pages rolled off. Samantha straightened the stacks of moist pages, wondering if she were getting high. Getting high wasn't something she was interested in; she had other things on her mind, and she needed her brain to be working straight.

Toward the end of the summer, Mr. Knott, one of the social studies teachers and a football coach, came through the office to check his mail. He favored rugby or golf shirts or a Centennial High sweatshirt, even when he was teaching. "You working here?" he said, flashing his joshing grin. He was famous for being well liked, especially by guys on teams. He assigned easy group projects that allowed the kids to talk among themselves while he looked over the newspaper at his desk.

"Yep." Duh.

In his good-guy confidential manner, he leaned over her desk to see what she was reading. It was a pamphlet she had picked up from the rack at the CETA office: "Emancipated Minors: The Law and You." She hadn't known there was such a thing—a free pass out of purgatory. She immediately started to make budgets. There were apartment complexes on major bus routes a ten-minute walk from the high school. They always had signs advertising cheap studios. She knew from consulting the school handbook, part of the reference collection on her receptionist's desk, that she could take early dismissal in the afternoons if she were accumulating enough credits and had a paid job to go to. The secretaries would recommend her to other employers enthusiastically. Her father, an old father, was retired, and along with his social security check came allowances for her mother and herself. Her brother was already out of the house and so his check was sent to him. She could have her dependent check sent to her, too, if she were emancipated.

"For you?"

She gave a curt nod. Mr. Knott looked so shocked it embarrassed her.

"Listen, Samantha," he said. "Whatever it is can't be that bad."

She kept her eyes down.

"Once you go out there—you know, start supporting yourself—it never ends. How old are you?"

"Sixteen next month."

He shook his head. "You don't want to go to work. You want to go to college."

She was insulted that he thought she wouldn't go to college. "I'm working now."

"Well, sure, but that's different. Right now, you can spend it on clothes and stuff, right?"

She nodded.

"So why do you want to start having to pay rent and food and all that jazz?"

She shrugged. She wasn't about to go into it with him. He made her promise to talk to the school counselors, and she said she would. Anything to get him to move away, looking like an old high school jock in his athletic gear, today a Trail Blazers jersey over a T-shirt and cargo shorts. Mr. Knott seemed most at home in the halls of Centennial, whereas all she wanted to do was move on and start her life.

It sometimes suited her mother to pretend she was grown up, too. Before coming to Las Vegas, her mother tried to age her cosmetically for the casinos so they could pal around together. What they saw in the mirror was a fifteen-year-old in red lipstick and teased hair. Samantha told her *no way*, rubbing the lipstick off with a tissue until all that remained was a faint stain. It was a mystery to her, trained to understand her mother's inner life better than anyone, why she would choose this particular destination, where the gaming laws of the state of Nevada mandated their separation. The thing her mother hated above all was to be alone.

The sun wakes them up, baking through the glass. Samantha takes one look at her mother, drawn and grim, and decides to stop sulking. No one needs to tell her this was a stupid idea, badly managed. It has always been her job to shore her mother up. Fix what can be fixed.

"Let's go eat, Mom."

"We could get something from the store."

"No, we'll go crazy sitting here any longer. There was a Denny's, remember? Let's go back that way and sit in the air-conditioning and have a real breakfast." She wishes she could take the driver's seat, but her Oregon learner's permit isn't legal in the rental. So her mother points the Datsun the way Samantha directs. She seems stunned by where they have landed, and it does resemble the moon's surface, a stark, stripped place. Samantha remembers the way, one long straight mile, then a turn and another straight mile. They go past auto dealerships and pawnshops and massage parlors and strip malls with real estate offices and chiropractors. Then there is the yellow Denny's sign, and with it a weird feeling of home.

Samantha admits she likes seeing the wizened men with cowboy hats and the slot machines in the lobby and the waitress with the piled red hair and the sun-tough skin. All this daylight brightness, combined with the menu, with its splashy photos of pancakes and hash browns, especially after their cramped and fitful night, starts to make her feel like they are on vacation. She says it, to buck her mother up: "Well, we're on vacation. I'm having a waffle."

"Good for you." Her mother's voice is still wan. "I think I'll just have coffee right now."

Their hotel lets them check in by the time they arrive, and because of the mix-up they are given complimentary buffet vouchers. Her mother cheers up quite a bit at this windfall, along with the standard booty of the free drink coupon, the free keno coupon, the double-down blackjack voucher, the free pull on the Big Bertha, and the daily grubstake of twenty nickels in a packet. Samantha doesn't point out that the clerk didn't mistake her for a second adult and give them double casino swag. Even with her retainer in its plastic case.

They are traveling as a pair because her mother filed for divorce from her father, feeling she finally had a steady-enough job at the electric company, one with benefits and vacation time, of which she's now taking a week. For now, her father still lives in the house, sleeping in her brother's old room with its ski posters of Vail and Aspen. Samantha's brother is working a summer job and living in an apartment with roommates before he goes back to college. So it's just her and her mother, six days before school starts, and there is no point anymore in wondering why her mother so persistently needed to go to Las Vegas. Samantha is pretty sure she doesn't know why herself. "We'll be at the pool together," her mother had said. "We can go to the restaurants together. It's just for the couple hours a day when I want to play the slots we'll be apart."

The whole family used to go to Reno and Lake Tahoe for vacations, her father's idea originally. But her mother loved it, and so they all came to like it. They'd drive from Portland to Klamath Falls to Susanville, California, where they'd stop for the night. Susanville air smelled burnt and Susanville water tasted odd, but that was part of what made it a trip. The next day they'd be in Nevada, driving across sagebrush desert until passing under Reno's Biggest Little City arch to spend a couple of nights at their favorite motel with the turquoise pool. While their parents gambled, Samantha and her brother stayed back to cannonball at the pool and loaf in the air-conditioned room, watching reruns of *The Beverly Hillbillies* and *Green Acres*. Then when their parents came back, glamorous in sunglasses, exhilarated in a way Steve and Samantha never saw them at home, everyone rested delicately in a moment of happiness that was unusual for their family. Somehow when gambling with her free nickels their mother usually beat the house, and she'd pour her winnings—three or four or five dollars—on the bedspread, saying "Share the wealth, everybody!"

Their dad would be up or down from playing blackjack. If he were up, he'd peel off a few ones for each of them. Sammy and Steve would sort the winnings, in nickels and ones, into two respective piles to spend at the gift shops. When they swam in the pool in the afternoon, their father read the newspaper under the shaded table. The kids played Marco Polo around their mother doing laps in her pink one-piece suit and flowered rubber swim cap. Her mother was terrified of high blood pressure, and always did fifty laps before she was ready for the buffet with its glistening beef and rows of cake squares.

On the way to Lake Tahoe they'd stop at Virginia City to walk the planks of the wooden sidewalks and look in at the saloons and general stores. Even though Virginia City was just a tourist ghost town, being there made their dad expansive and pleased. He came from a place in Montana that was now a real ghost town, nailed-up buildings and rotting timbers, and though you could visit nearby Red Lodge, he said there was no longer anything to see in Scotch Coulee, where he'd grown up. Over frosty mugs of root beer in the Silver Queen Hotel, he'd tell his stories again: about his horse Betty, his dog Shep, being a trap boy in the coal mine, catching rabbits instead of going to school, making his own skis out of chokecherry limbs. The *Silver Queen* was a ceiling-high portrait of a lady with an interesting smirk whose strapless dress was made up of thousands of silver dollars minted in Carson City. Every year Samantha took a picture of her on her Kodak, though the lady never changed.

In Lake Tahoe, they'd take the tram up the mountain to Heavenly Valley or swim in the glass-clear waters of the lake. They'd make an excursion to the Ponderosa Ranch and go horseback riding and eat a chuck wagon supper and drink orange pop out of tin cups they'd get to take home. All of this had been repeated yearly, and rather than do it again as half a family, her mother had decided that she and Samantha should fly to Las Vegas, something new.

That first afternoon, they nap in their cool, gold-and-ivory hotel room. Her mother appreciates the small soaps and shampoo and shower cap; she loves anything that's free. Samantha isn't used to hotels with interior hallways and high-rise floors. They've always stayed in motels with their own front door to the outside. Always there would be kids running around in the parking lot and family cars loaded with pool toys. Here they are on the twelfth floor, with a window that doesn't open, looking out to a parking garage and some hazy mountains in a shimmer of heat. The pool is on a rooftop on the sixth floor. This is where Samantha will establish base, reading and plotting her future, working on her tan for the first day of school.

It's not so bad being in Las Vegas with her mother. The next day they breakfast in the casino downstairs, watching the gamblers over the partition as if observing the wildlife on safari. In the slot machine area, at ten in the morning, it's just the retirees with their eyeshades—the men with striped polo shirts over big stomachs, the women in pastel shell-and-slacks ensembles, with silver perms and low, white dressy sandals. At Samantha's age, she can only observe this perimeter, can't penetrate the real Las Vegas with the green gaming tables and the back rooms. She would have loved to have watched her father play blackjack, see what he'd show on his face when calling for cards and flipping over busted hands.

Samantha marks her mother's free keno card of the day, imagining the clothes she will buy with the cash, but it doesn't win. Everyone here is dreaming of just one jackpot. The thing about her mother is that her discipline—risking little to none of her own money, stopping when she is ahead by five dollars, never playing anything but the nickel machines—guarantees that the most she'd ever walk away with would be a twenty-dollar jackpot. Which she did win once, legendary now in her memory, and which she kept in a carefully separate envelope until she found just the right bathing suit on sale. The jackpot suit.

At the pool that afternoon there is a boy her age who watches her. She pretends not to notice him as she strolls to the coffee urn in her yellow two-piece and makes herself a cup with three sugars and a lot of cream. She doesn't really like coffee, but likes the mixing of it, especially here by the pool where it gives her the opportunity to move into the shade, survey the scene, and show off her newly dieted body, ready for dance team season. If she shows up in the fall above last year's weight, she'll be fined a quarter a pound at every Monday weigh-in. She has big sunglasses on, so she doesn't think the boy can catch her looking. From this distance, he looks cute.

She brings the coffee back to her lounge chair where her book, *The Bell Jar*, and her bag have marked her territory, and arranges herself on her stomach so she can equalize her tan.

She feels him approaching, a pair of furred shins presenting themselves in front of her. She looks up over her sunglasses.

"You didn't offer me a cup," he says, adjusting the adjacent lounge chair and sitting on it, elbows on knees.

He's not bad, his brown hair wavy, his body bronzed and lean, but his eyes are not what she would have wished—spaced too closely together and the gaze somehow flat. Also, the smug tone. And the accent: Russian?

"No," she says.

"Well, I might like some. Especially, to drink it with you."

"It's over there."

"So I see. Thank you for the invitation."

He crosses the pool deck to mix his own foam cup.

After a chubby childhood wearing glasses and suffering through her mother's haircuts and home permanents, she was surprised to gradually realize that she had some potential with boys. The summer before sixth grade she had grown faster than she had eaten and was suddenly slim. In seventh grade, she had insisted on growing her hair long and straight. In eighth grade, she had fought her mother to get contact lenses and paid for them herself with babysitting money saved over many months. The summer before high school, after a day working in the berry fields, she climbed on the rattletrap field bus, twenty crumpled and juice-stained dollars in the pocket of her cutoffs, and a boy she didn't know said, "Hey, Blondie, sit here." She didn't, she followed her friend Kathleen to sit where they always sat, but she marveled silently on the ride back to their neighborhood: Blondie! And she wasn't! She was sure she had brown hair—light brown, yes—but maybe the summer sun had done something, changed something. Maybe she was changed?

Then the braces her mother had scrimped and saved for came off. At high school dances, the boys, warm and damp in their collared shirts, gave off soap and deodorant odors in the dark. One boy carried on shy conversations with her at her locker, and thrust a ribboned package at her before Christmas vacation freshman year, his face twisted with embarrassment. Then, sophomore year, she had her first real date with a boy who could drive and took her to the Organ Grinder, a pizza restaurant where a player piano tinkled all night while silent movies played on a big screen, giving them something to look at when they ran out of things to talk about.

This boy's name is Yuri, and his family did emigrate from Russia a few years ago, and he is neither shy nor at a lack for things to say. He is traveling with his father on business, from L.A., and he talks fast and with a confident sharpness, like she imagines a father in business might.

"Ever been there?"

"Disneyland, once, with my family."

"Of course!" His laugh is mocking. "You Americans go to Disneyland and think you have been to a real place."

"Wherever people go is a real place," she says with irritation. She could have added how parents are more likely to fight about money at an expensive place like Disneyland. How whole vacations are poisoned by angry silence, and how that feels especially unbearable on Main Street, where every themed character wears a fixed smile. How some kids who have been brought to Disneyland actually just want to go home.

"You are a philosopher."

"No."

"Observer, then."

She shrugs.

He picks up her book and reads the back cover. "She is a poet?"

"Yeah." She doesn't want to talk about Sylvia Plath with him.

"And you?"

"I don't know. Not really. Sometimes. For fun."

"In my country—my old country—we honor poets. But poets don't make money, you know."

"So no writing poetry for you."

"Money interests me."

"Well, most of us."

He waves this away. "There are those who do something about it, and those who don't."

"How are you going to make it?'

He exhales thoughtfully, seeming to appreciate the question.

"Ultimately? Real estate. That is where the killing can be made." His eyes narrow on the word *killing*.

He tells her about the Mercedes he will own, the particular model and its features, and she begins to think it's not worth her time to keep listening. She's been gratified by his interest, but she isn't required to be bored. She shifts a little, making a motion to gather her things.

"What are you doing?"

"I think I'm getting too much sun," she says. This much is true. She normally tans just fine, but the sun here is fierce, ready to destroy you.

"No, no, you just need some lotion. Here, I will do it for you." Without asking he picks up her bottle of Coppertone and squirts some on his palm. He waits for her to lie back down.

"No, really. I'm going to meet my mother for lunch."

"Lunch? It is only eleven thirty. Not time for lunch. Stay fifteen more minutes. We are having such a good chat together."

His hand in the air with its dollop of suntan lotion is waiting for her to comply.

She can do whatever she wants here. She'll never see him again. It's not like the minefield of school hallways where you have to be careful who you hang out with because of the talk.

She flattens back down on her stomach and pulls her long hair out of the way, leaving him her back.

"Is a very good thing I'm here. You didn't cover all spots properly before. There is pink by the straps."

Gingerly he slides the straps off her shoulders. She tenses, then relaxes under the circles he is rubbing, small ones, then larger. His hand moves to the strap encircling her back, and hesitates.

"You want that I undo this? To have no line?"

"No!"

"Okay, relax. Some girls, they hate the lines."

He puts more on his hand and moves it over her ribs, the small of her back, around the upper edge of her swimsuit bottom.

"You want that I do your legs?"

She is a mix of sleepy and tingling. It feels so good she would gladly have him do her legs, her arms, everywhere, except she knows where this is intended to lead. And she doesn't even feel particularly attracted to him. And it seems wrong that a boy she knows nothing about and will never see again be the one to touch the back of her legs when no other boy has. Not the arrogant trumpet player she had had a crush on whose house she detoured by on walks to school last year, hoping to see him. Not the sweet speechless one she didn't have a crush on who had given her the necklace at Christmas with the tiny pearl hanging from a gold-filled chain.

"No, thanks. I already did that. I can reach there."

"Okay, done."

Now she thinks he is mad at her, and even though she doesn't want to care, she cares a little.

"Thank you."

"It was my pleasure," he says, with a courtly tone that makes her giggle a little. Is she being stuck up? A prude?

"Tomorrow I go," he says sadly.

Even though she'd been wondering, she dared not ask, in case it would make him think she was interested.

"Which means tonight we should go do something," he says.

"Like what? Everything here is for adults. I don't even know why I came here with my mother."

"No, no, there are clubs where we can dance. I know about them. One is even run by a friend of my father, and he will let us in."

"My mother would never let me do that," she says.

"Bring your mother! My father's friend will give her a drink on the house. We'll just dance. Who knows, maybe your mother will dance too. *I* will dance with her," he declares.

Samantha is too aghast to laugh. Her mother at a club! Her mother who is still married to her father! But she wonders; is that what her mother's life will be after the divorce? Going out, having a drink bought for her? She is okay-looking for a mother: trim figure, dark-rimmed rectangular glasses. Short dark hair with a little pouf on top. She's an exercise fanatic because *her* mother, Samantha's grandmother, died of a stroke when she was fifty-two. Her mother is fifty-three now. She drinks, sometimes, one cocktail or glass of wine in an evening. Rarely two, and never three. When a casino gives her a drink coupon, or comes around offering a house drink when she's playing the slots, she orders orange juice. Or if it's the end of the day, and she has swum her laps and is having dinner and not driving, a single whiskey sour.

"My mother is married."

"Why is she here, then?" At her silence, he says, "No, never mind, that was rude of me. Listen. Better idea, I will come to your room at nine, meet your mother. She will not be able to say no to me, I guarantee."

Samantha laughed. "You think."

"I know."

"You give me *your* room number. I'll call if we'll do it."

He pouts. "You won't call."

"You never know."

"You won't."

He is wrong to count her out, Samantha thinks. She doesn't know what she might do. She has, in her bureau drawer at home, two pads of dismissal notes that she stamped with the office approval when she was working this summer. She and her best friend, June, will fill them in separately—dentist appointments, doctor appointments—and show them to teachers. June is class president and Samantha runs the literary magazine. They get straight A's. The teachers won't look twice at their slips when they tell them they have to leave early. June will borrow her brother's car. They might go to the mall, or to the lake. But they have in mind other things, too—downtown things—like going to lunch at Hamburger Mary's, where they've heard some of the waiters serve in drag and the creamers are baby bottles with the nipples cut off. Or they might go see an afternoon matinee of *Deep Throat* at the Blue Mouse theater, where it has been running for four years. There's no telling, really.

Back in her room she has vicious stripes from the sun. Her front, her face, is bright red; she wonders if Yuri noticed, outside in the bright light. She showers in cool water, the spray needling her painfully, then rubs Noxzema into the redness. What a disaster if she peels. School ID pictures will be taken on the first day. And now what is she to do with herself during the rest of the vacation?

She lies on her back on the made bed, not even bothering to turn on the television or pick up her book. She's still like that when her mother lets herself in a few minutes later, and gasps at the sight of her.

"I know," she says.

"Didn't you feel it?"

"No."

"Did you put lotion on?"

"*Yes.*" But really, she thinks she didn't. She dived in the pool after breakfast and was pleasantly wet and cool and must have dozed on her back for a couple of hours.

"Well, you can't go back out there today."

"Duh."

Her mother goes to the bathroom to wash her hands and doesn't speak. That last bit of sarcasm could set off a silence that will last two days if she doesn't remedy it immediately.

"Sorry," Samantha says.

Her mother looks at her coldly.

"I'm just mad at myself," Samantha says. That will do the trick, she thinks, self-blame, and she's right. Her mother comes over and sits on the side of the bed.

"You poor thing."

Over lunch downstairs in the coffee shop, Samantha tells her about Yuri's invitation.

"Is the boy nice?"

"Really? That's what you want to know?"

The waitress sets down Samantha's Tab and her mother's ice water.

"It's not strange that a boy invited you out."

"No! It's strange that he invited *you* out. I told him you were married."

"Not really."

"What do you mean? You're really married until you're not married. That's the way it works."

"I mean it's not a marriage anymore, and it's about to be finished in every sense. Get used to that idea. Anyway, what do you think I'd do? I'd be there to look after you."

"I don't need my mother on a date."

"Well, you're not going on your own."

"Who said I wanted to go? I don't want to go! And especially not with my mother."

They sit in silence until their food comes, a salad for Samantha and a tuna sandwich for her mother.

"How come *now*?"

Her mother puts down her sandwich and waits.

"Why now, when he's old?"

"Samantha, he's always been old," her mother said wearily.

"Apparently not too old to marry in the first place."

"I shouldn't have."

"You can't just say that."

"Don't tell me what I can say," her mother says, picking up her sandwich but not biting into it. "I made a mistake. For years I didn't have enough money to leave him. I still don't. But I can't stand it anymore."

"Because he can't work anymore? Because he lost his marbles?" It's true her father went crazy last year. He had hallucinations, movies he said they shone through the windows at night. Their mother had taken Samantha and Steve to visit him at the mental hospital, where he was drugged and groggy. Men were shouting obscenities from their rooms. His eyes were wet when he kissed them goodbye. He told Steve and Samantha not to visit anymore; he didn't want them to see him here. When he came home he had a long lineup of pill bottles. He's quieter now during the day instead of restless. He has a sweet, tired smile for her when she enters the bedroom that was Steve's, but is his now. He rocks in his chair and reads *The Labor Press*, the same issue over and over. It only comes out once a week.

"You know it hasn't been a proper marriage for years. His family should be rallying around him now, but they look at me like I'm the crazy one when I try to get their help. They act like I'm causing it."

Samantha closes her ears. She had loved Auntie—her aunt Vera—who died of a heart attack last summer. And she loves her aunt Celia. When Aunt Celia and Uncle Matt still had the farm she loved how different it was from her house: the rag rugs her aunt made on a loom; the fields of berries and beans; the musty smell of the farmhouse and the animal smells of the henhouse and barn; the sauna where all the women sat together in the steam that hissed a white cloud with each ladle of water they drew from the wooden bucket and splashed over the rocks. She liked it when they sometimes talked Finnish around her, and liked it when they tried to teach her words. Her mother never took the sauna with them—said she was all clean and dry and didn't want to get undressed. Now the farm is gone and Matt is dead and Aunt Celia lives in a little house in southeast Portland where she still grows blueberries and plums.

Samantha and her mother are on the edge of the argument that will do them in for the rest of the vacation. Usually Samantha backpedals from these edges as fast as she can, wanting to preserve some shred of normalcy so she doesn't have to face the fact that she lives in a total freak show. She is tempted, though, so tempted, to say something to make the chasm between her and her mother split wide and irreparably. Maybe she'll mention the two wives, say Dad should have stayed married to one or the other. It really wouldn't have mattered which—neither would have tortured him the way her mother did. Yelled at him, demeaned him.

"Look, I don't want to speak ill of his family. I know they love you. They've just hurt my feelings so many times . . ."

Or here, Samantha could say, "Who *hasn't* hurt your feelings with some invisible slight? Who in the world has been spared your paranoia and bitterness?" She has so many grenades in her pack. So many pins her fingers are itching to pull.

"We could go to Hoover Dam tomorrow," her mother says, fishing a brochure out of her purse.

The idea is so ridiculously boring that Samantha can't help but snort.

"So you want to sunbathe instead?"

Samantha looks at the photos of the huge white concrete shell, the towers, the turquoise basin, the rock outcroppings and rim of mountains. She doesn't want to sunbathe tomorrow.

She shrugs. "Why not?"

They stop at the front desk and buy the excursion tickets.

"You ladies will love this!" the woman at the desk in the ruffled blouse chirps, stamping their vouchers. "Make sure you take in the buffet at the Gold Strike in Boulder City. The motor coach will stop there, and you've got a coupon here for two dollars off each meal."

They finish the day avoiding talk of her father, her father's family, the divorce that will become final in two months, whether her mother will be able to keep the house, and where her father will live. She can't imagine living alone with her mother, who will want to go on as if life has just gotten better, as if her father has not just been cast away to fend for himself in confusion. Her "Emancipated Minor" pamphlet is buried in the same bureau drawer as the pads of permission slips. It is her wild card; she'll play it if she has to. Her mother goes to the pool to swim and Samantha stays back in the room, reading her novel. She wonders if Yuri is still there. She knows her mother will be scanning every young male, trying to pick him out.

That night they stroll up and down the Strip, cooled now to eighty degrees from the broil of the afternoon. Samantha feels dwarfed by the lights and the giant marquees and the waves of people. Her mother has, uncharacteristically, decided to spend her small winnings each day in hopes of a bigger win. Her purse holds a plastic cup with fifteen or so nickels, her last profits of the day. Going for broke still doesn't mean using her own cash.

When they get back to the open-air entrance of their own ho-tel's casino, the big dollar machine out front has no line. Her mother still has the token for today's free pull. The machine is taller than she is; she has to reach up for the arm and then lean into it to bring it down. They can hear the mechanical workings of the reels as they spin. The first reel stops, with a little bounce, on a cherry cluster. Her mother squeals—already a winner. Luck stays with her: The second, then the third reel bounce into place, cherries across the payline. The bell trills. Her mother is clapping, and others are smil-ing at her, more in amusement than anything—*Lady, it's ten dol-lars.* The dollar coins clank down with a heavy sound. Her mother scoops them up; she'll go to the cashier's cage and trade them in immediately for a ten-dollar bill. It will find its special envelope.

Indisputably minor, Samantha waits for her over the cooling vents, lounging under the fizz of neon. Night never falls here. It sneaks in at the street corner off the main drag, a little darkness muffled by the alarms of winners. It will be run out of town. Her mother disappears into the bright thicket of slot machines, her cup blackened by coins she hates to give away. What she likes is the illusion of risk. Meanwhile, a man in a white suit stands too close, compliments Samantha on her tan, which is really a burn, a skin she is about to shed.

INTERSTATE

Her father moves to an apartment on 122nd Avenue, a soulless boulevard of fast-food outlets, discount stores, and rivers of moving traffic. The divorce sharpens his wits temporarily—meetings with his lawyer, papers to sign, property to squabble over, though there is not much property to fight about, just the ranch house with its corner lot. Carl got his lump sum for half of the house, took his collection of big-band LPs, his television set, the bureau Steve had abandoned when he moved out, a twin bed, a lamp, and some linens his sister Celia pitched in.

Her brother, Steve, is working in L.A., so it falls to Samantha to keep tabs. When she visits, she notes that her father seems to be eating only peppermint ice cream. Ants have established cloverleaf traffic patterns around the soaked bottoms of the grocery bags he uses as trash receptacles, and the bags themselves hold only empty cartons sticky with pink. She takes out the trash, wipes at the spot on the floor, buys ant traps. She doesn't go so far as to do his laundry, though once she scrubs his bathroom in a whirlwind of disgust and vigorous intention, not breathing. She doesn't want to take care of him. She is eighteen, he is seventy-two. The balance of who is caring for whom is tilting too fast. She's used to his being old, he's always been old, but she isn't yet willing to admit that he's become her charge, her mother having washed her hands. Her own life appears before her like a stretch of wide-open highway, and she has no intention of narrowing it to the cluttered junk of 122nd Avenue. He is still her father, and she still needs one. He has his lump sum. He can take her to lunch if she drives, she can count on him to still reach for the check.

For the few months before she starts college she has taken a receptionist's job in a medical office. They appreciate her for her good spelling and proficient typing, and she doesn't make mistakes on the check deposit form. She isn't scared of old people or medical smells. She likes her co-workers because they are kind, because they are to be in her life so briefly, a wayside stop. She can afford them anything. She has an old used car she bought herself, small paychecks, lunch hours to visit her father. She'll find him shadow dancing to Benny Goodman or Artie Shaw. When he sees her, he stretches his arms open wide and she allows herself to be folded into them. The foxtrot is as familiar to her as Road Runner cartoons, as Partridge Family songs. Hasn't she grown up to all of it? Undoubtedly her first foxtrots were in his arms when she was still an infant. She doesn't remember those. She does remember standing in socks on his polished shoes, trying not to slide off as the dance moved under her. She still doesn't have to know the steps. He leads with imperceptible tightenings of his arms; she frankly doesn't know how he leads. But it is easy to foxtrot with him, or rumba or waltz. You don't have to know much to do it.

He told her early on that she was a natural. Her mother must not have been; they never danced together that Samantha could recall.

She doesn't blame her mother for not being a natural, and she is trying to stop blaming her for not sticking it out. If you are the third wife, if you are much younger and had to be talked into the marriage in the first place, if the marriage never seemed the way marriages were supposed to, like green islands of laughter and camaraderie (the image she has of her mother's wishful thinking), are you to be blamed for jettisoning the thing when the children are older? Though the jettisoned partner is elderly and showing signs of losing his faculties? More than signs. Things Samantha has become adept at shunting to one side of her brain, a small drawer for them.

Even after she goes to college and lives downtown, they keep up their routines. She stops by, checks on the ants, does a bit of cleaning and washing (who else, now?), and then they drive out for lunch, usually a little batter-fried fish-and-chips place where the owners yell your number when the food is ready. Her father never allows her to pay a tab, even when she has money; this is like his always walking on the outside of the sidewalk and his no-nonsense leading on the dance floor. This is her father. The one who, when already retired, idled outside the school waiting to give her and her friends rides home, who only needed to hear that she lacked for something before his wallet was out, his fingers plucking through his thin supply of ones and fives.

When the pictures of starlets from *People* magazine start appearing taped to his walls, their eyes scratched out with pins, their lips gone white in some kind of rubbing, she wants no part of it.

"You don't need these," she says firmly, taking them down, tossing them on top of the empty ice cream cartons. "Why did you do that?"

"They were watching," he tells her. "Like the movies that they shine at night."

Tweaking the psychotropic meds stops the movies, but they make other things impossible, too. He still listens to the big bands, but now rarely dances. His checkbook unfurls streams of white adding machine tape where the teller has sorted out his balance for him, though he used to do the math okay. He sleeps away afternoons in his chair.

Samantha and her brother discuss places he could go next, how far the lump sum might be stretched. His older sister offers to take him in: Celia on her own after Matt died, her mind intact, but legs and hearing weak; Carl's body sound, but mind unpredictable.

It is done. The new roommates have comic spells; it would make a good sitcom if you just had to live through half an hour of it—Aunt Celia sending Carl down to the cellar for a jar of plum preserves. She has a bum knee, so no sense risking those dim, uneven stairs. He descends nimbly, then wanders for a while in the dark, forgetting where the string is to snap on the bulb, forgetting in the search for the string what his errand is. He shouts up to ask, but Celia is deaf; she doesn't hear. He trots back up the stairs, empty-handed, she asks where the preserves are, he slaps the side of his head—What a dummy—then trots back down, only to lose himself again in the dark.

But in general, living with Celia is the happiest place he could have found himself. Their youngest sister, Nora, brings them groceries, and takes Carl dancing at the Eagles Lodge. Five of the brothers and sisters in the family have died. The new order starts from Celia, now oldest; then Carl; then Emil, off in Eugene; then Nora. The baby of them all, Hank, died ten years earlier, of a mysterious and lingering illness that Samantha will later learn was AIDS. The three of them who still live in Portland, widowed and divorced, huddle together as if on a lifeboat. They speak both Finnish and

English, they rock in rocking chairs and pass the time with television. They go on like this for months, then years.

Eventually Carl begins losing his way in the neighborhood, going out for a walk and not coming back until his retired nephew Bill locates him by trolling with the car after Celia has sounded the alarm. If Samantha is not ready to admit that things are bad, neither is her aunt. They conspire to send him on a little Amtrak trip up to Seattle, where Samantha has just begun graduate school. If there is anything he loves, it's trains, cities, restaurants, visits.

Samantha has the schedule, she knows when the train is due. What is she doing that morning before its arrival? Probably nothing important, probably puttering in her studio apartment. It takes two buses to reach King Street Station from her studio in the U District. Two buses, plus the time waiting for the connection. She knows that, should have factored it all in. The first bus is not late, nor does it cover its route any more slowly than usual. The second bus is just a trip down the transit mall, down Third and across the streets someone taught her the mnemonic for when she first moved there: Jesus Christ Made Seattle Under Protest. Two for each letter: Jefferson, James, Cherry, Columbia, Marion, Madison, Spring, Seneca, University, Union, Pike, Pine—only ticked off in reverse to get to the train station. The transit mall is clogged. Suddenly it's become rush hour, although the way Seattle is heading, it's almost always rush hour.

Six or half a dozen: Should she get off the bus and jog along the streets? Would that beat the bus? Ultimately, she does, so she is not only late, but sweaty and breathless. She finds him wandering there in the marble vastness of the grand public architecture of another age, his one small suitcase in hand, the train having arrived ten minutes ago.

She sees immediately what the waiting, the dizzy pattern of the mosaic tiles, the whiteness and coldness of the marble, has done to him. What she has done to him.

"You should have been here," he says.

"I know, I'm sorry, traffic on the transit mall, bus took forever, ended up jogging."

You should have been here. It is a remarkable statement from him, considering. Though his eyes are stretched wide, his pupils, pinpoints—she can see him slipping away through them—he is able to correctly assess the situation and affix responsibility. You should have been here—from him, who had never blamed her for anything, that she could remember, her entire life. Who never once raised his voice at her—could that be right? Or is she mythologizing? She thinks it's right.

She should have been there; no excusing it away. What act of passive aggression, or perhaps of grad student depression, left her doing nothing much in her apartment all morning when she knew her father was at that moment on the train coming to visit her? Why did she not leave hours early, so that she is sitting on the wooden bench reading Virginia Woolf, drinking a coffee, ready to spring up immediately when the announcement comes that the *Cascades* train is pulling into the station? Why was she not outside on the platform scanning all the doors the minute a conductor opened them and put down his step stool, ready to assist frail passengers?

Years will pass and she will forgive herself many things, but never this. Her boys will be at birthday parties and sports practices, and her forever gesture of redemption, heart pounding from an old contrition, will be to be there always ten minutes early to claim them—never, *never*, ten minutes late.

What must ten minutes have felt like to him? It is the age before cell phones, but he is already losing memory of how to dial, or even which end of the receiver is up. In an earlier version of the two of them he would be found pacing outside the station, checking his watch, worrying about *her*.

But in this version, he is lost in a marble tomb that stretches on either side higher and wider than he can comfortably contain within his perceptions. The strangers clicking heels across that endless patterned floor know exactly where they need to be, their motions fluid with destination. He has, over the years, driven a Model T across the country, worked in Henry Ford's automobile plant, been a hired hand on an Arizona ranch, played alto sax in a San Francisco speakeasy, mucked coal in a Montana mine, and devoted much of his adult life to balancing on girders, hammering ventilation shafts. He possessed skills, grace, and agility. All of these gifts vaporous now. He still has the compact muscular body but he is losing the ability to steer it. He stands in the middle of a great hall, wandering a few steps first in this direction, then that.

She comes, she is very, truly, sorry, she tries to take his bag (he won't let her, he's the man), she gets them onto the bus in the transit mall. With his daughter beside him, the two of them safely ensconced in a bus above the squawking traffic in one of the west coast cities he helped shape with skyscrapers, his pupils begin to gradually expand to a normal diameter.

He finds lucid moments again during his first day, but he is always on the edge of that marble vastness she nearly abandoned him to. She finds the place where peppermint ice cream cones can be procured on University Way, takes him to her favorite bakery for a Danish, buys him a cup of black coffee from the country's second Starbucks, and orders him foods she knows he'll like at the restaurant where she waitresses part-time. The other waitresses all make a fuss over him and of course he likes that. He likes women, he likes restaurants, all that is fine.

Aunt Celia packed carefully laundered pajamas and undergarments in the small suitcase, and with a fresh shirt he'll be all set for the weekend in the sage-colored leisure suit he wore for the journey, an unfortunate purchase he made on his own shortly after the divorce. The suits he was born to wear, had always worn on Sundays, are a deep navy serge. Growing up, she thought he looked like a movie star in them, a cross between Rock Hudson and Gregory Peck, though the suits came off the rack at Penney's. But he likes to keep up-to-date, no moss growing on him, so now it is the leisure suit, shirt collar open, and he also wears his still-dark hair a little longer in back, touching the collar.

Her studio is tiny; they will manage by taking turns in the bathroom tiled in small black-and-white diamonds from the twenties—his heyday. The apartment's one luxurious feature is the roomy walk-in closet. She regrets that she has only a futon to offer him—a man of his age should have more comfortable arrangements—but he doesn't complain. For herself, she sets up a foam pad and sleeping bag on the floor beside him. Not only has she never had enough money to buy more than the futon, desk, and metal bistro table, she knows that Seattle is but one stopping point on her forward trajectory, and sees no reason to accumulate unnecessary objects she will only have to tow after her.

The day has been full, he has been rescued once and not lost sight of after that, and they are due for a good night's sleep. No special itinerary needs to be planned for the next day: He is so easy, really, a man satisfied with walks, frequent coffees, newspapers, and a hot meal. The point, as she sees it, is simply to be together.

The bedtime routine goes smoothly at first. If his pupils are contracting, she doesn't see. If the meds haven't been swallowed, she forgets to check. It's true, and she might have made a note to remember, that nighttime is a sticking point, the time of voices, etc.

Lights are out, neighbors are not mumbling through walls, no shadows or headlights are insinuating themselves through the vinyl shades. What precipitates his agitation, then, is wholly internal, an avatar, perhaps, of the self lost in the wide marble hall.

"It's not really hard yet," he says to her, sitting up, his Cary Grant wagon-wheel pajamas buttoned neatly to the top button.

"What?"

"Not really hard. Not yet." His tone is rueful, apologetic.

It takes her a moment to understand that he is talking about his penis, held semierect in his hand, as he pulls back the covers to show her.

"Dad, it's me."

She comes to understand that he can't understand that it *is* her, not one of the wives, or girlfriends, or even, she begins to suspect he thinks, a prostitute into whose lair he's stumbled. He told a boyfriend of hers once, man to man, about the cathouses. There were out-of-town jobs, opportunities.

"Dad, it's me"—the only girl who had a working model of the solar system in seventh-grade science because you went to the hardware store and got the crank, the gear, the dowels for the Styrofoam balls. Knew how to make it work.

He doesn't move from his futon, doesn't protest when she covers him up. Blinks at her. Lets a small, embarrassed, lascivious smile play about his lips while he watches her pace the length of her twelve-foot apartment.

Who can she call? Not deaf, lame Aunt Celia in Portland, obviously. Not her mother, who will only get angry and hysterical, until Samantha will have to take care of *her* on top of this.

She dials Steve in Los Angeles. Explains the inconceivable. Hands her father the phone.

"Hello?" He is puzzled. Who does this hooker want him to chat with?

Carl listens for some seconds. The pupils may have widened a millimeter. Then he looks at her. Sees her. Hits his open palm to his forehead. Again. Not the sitcom slap of the plum preserves—*What a dummy*—but really hits. As if he is trying to hurt, maybe kill, the pale, jellylike brain inside.

"Dad, stop. It's okay now."

He can't reply to this remark, can't look at her after that single moment of recognition. Can only pound and pound his unrelenting skull.

Earlier that day she thought, as they strolled University Way, that the next stop after Aunt Celia's might be to live with her. An apartment with two bedrooms, his social security check to cover things, some square meals for the two of them. She'll fix oatmeal, fry up little cutlets, nothing complicated, but things he likes. He'll read the paper, doze, take short walks when she's in classes. She pictures him riding sidecar with her as she zooms down the interstate of her future—goggles firmly attached, silk scarf flying. He loves road trips.

In fact, the stops after his sister's detail a sadder litany. First, foster care, though who even knew that they *have* this in reverse, for the elderly. Foster care, by definition, makes her and her brother the failed or incompetent guardians who relinquished responsibility, but she manages to put that thought away in the little mental drawer she keeps for the purpose. Romanian immigrants, favoring plastic flowers and clear, crackling slipcovers over the furniture, make him one of their family in exchange for a not unreasonable monthly stipend, the whole of his social security check. They feed him nourishing meals, accomplish the dressing and the grooming, see to the meds, accompany him on walks, hand him the channel changer and sit beside him for the evening news. Their big, strapping adult son seems genuinely fond of her father, seems not to be lying when he grinningly puts his arm around the old man's shoulders and squeezes. *The grandfather we were missing!* It is harder to tell if her father likes him back. He bears the arrangement. Eats seconds of the home-cooked meals. Doesn't confuse his surroundings with a brothel.

Then one day, after taking a roundhouse swing at the strapping son's pregnant wife, her father is dispatched to a Senior Living Environment, but has trouble remembering which buttons to push in the elevator to find the dining hall. After he is discovered in another resident's apartment donning a strange hat and unfamiliar trousers, he is shuttled to his next stop, the nursing home. When Samantha flies in to visit from Boston, where she now lives and has a job, it embarrasses her that none of the nurses or aides ever know her. She isn't there often enough to be known, though it is true that they experience high staff turnover. Since her father doesn't recognize her, either, she makes repeated trips to a place where she has to introduce herself again and again. Still, he grows fond of her on every visit, expresses regret that they didn't meet sooner.

Once, she brings a cassette player with a tape she's mixed of his big-band favorites. She doesn't know what she expected. A little jitterbugging, maybe? He sits in a wheelchair, though she is pretty sure he doesn't have to. It's the meds; they make him feel like not using his legs.

Inexplicably, the sound of Count Basie enrages him to the point of shouting. The nurses, who do not know her, do not know what she might be inflicting on the old man confined to the wheelchair, look on with stern attention as she shushes him up, presses the STOP button, stashes the player and tape in her tote bag. Evidently, there is to be no more "Jumpin' at the Woodside."

But before they pass through these stages of his disappearance, he is still a traveler on a weekend visit to Seattle. Has tired himself out walking up and down University Way. He lies still and abashed on her futon, perhaps staring at movies on the ceiling, she doesn't know. She moved her sleeping bag into the walk-in closet, where she has hours until morning to play through scenes of her childhood, review the many competent repairs her father made to the house, whose leaky faucets and leaning fences her mother had to hire someone to fix after the divorce. There is time before morning to mentally rearrange her possessions on the wide shelves he built and varnished for her, time to wax skis on the worktable he made and set up in the garage. Time even, before dusk takes over the backyard, to attempt the always tricky cartwheel on the balance beam he constructed, and on which she was good at doing forward and backward rolls, letting her individual vertebrae search for the beam, though for the cartwheels she was always too tentative, always afraid of a heel slipping off, even knowing that there was grass below to catch her.

Curled up in the walk-in closet with all that time, she takes herself point by point through her floor and beam routines, repeating them if she misses an element. She actually hated gymnastics, though it took her years to realize it. A tenth of a point off for the slightest insufficient or incorrect gesture. Unrelenting disapproval of the unpointed toe, the crooked arm. You could do everything else right and then not stick the dismount, sway a bit as you internally scanned for the center. A further deduction for not smiling as they judged you.

She lies awake, forced to relive the impossibility of it all, while her father, who went to sleep knowing her name, who wished her a good night, breathes steadily in the next room, then snores. She doesn't know how much she sleeps; whatever dreams she has are an uneasy mix of heels slipping and landings unstuck—though in her father's backyard, falling off her father's honed and sanded beam, there is always the forgiveness of his tended grass. She lies perfectly still, waiting for morning to bring a modicum of gray to her closet, surrounded by her entire dark hanging wardrobe, beheaded flat figures that resemble her.

GRAVITY

T he summer before the Millennium, Samantha is worried about the city's recommended list of things to assemble for the crash. She has not yet collected jugs of water, canned goods, flashlights, firewood, sterno cells, first-aid kit, or stores of cash in small bills. But she and Mark and the boys do have, only half-jokingly, a "Y2K" room to put it all in when she does: a fifteen-by-fifteen concrete space added on to the basement when they constructed a family room upstairs. They hadn't yet figured out what to do with its bleak, prison-like interior—model train table?

arts and crafts? treadmill?—when Mark jokingly dubbed it the Y2K room and that's what it became. It has small windows at the top that can be easily sheeted with plastic and duct-taped, should there be a need for that. Her mind fails to supply her with the scenario that would require living in a bunker—missiles firing themselves? neighbors fighting in the street over cans of baked beans?—but the city has sent a list and she has always been a person to follow instructions.

That is one preoccupation. Another is the coming baby, which she knows, without sonogram documentation, will be a boy. She and Mark only make boys. The baby is due, unnervingly and momentously, on January 2, which could also mean a bunch of other days including January 1, the day of the four-digit changeover. Michael and Christopher were each relatively punctual in their arrivals, one two days early, the other two days late. She worries more about the city list because of this.

But on the July day that JFK Jr.'s plane disappears into the sea, Samantha stops thinking about all of that. Mark is the one to tell her about the plane disappearing—Samantha never learns important things before he does. He reads the two papers in the morning that come to the house, sometimes buys a third on his train commute to work, and now carries a pager that feeds him continuous headlines from CNN at the touch of a button. She'll come upon him standing in the middle of a room huddled over the pager's miniature green screen, as if warming himself at a tiny campfire.

Samantha hasn't thought of John-John since his wedding to that impossibly gorgeous woman he married in secret on some island off the Georgia coast. The wife was in the plane that went down. It shouldn't matter to her that those two were so stunningly beautiful together. It shouldn't make her any more sad for their loss, their disappeared plane.

But it does. When the boys are down for naps, Samantha lies on the bed upstairs with Mark, watching the divers hunt. It is like watching nothing, because the divers are under the sea, and there are only the stationary rescue and coast guard ships to stare at. The reporters have to do something with this space of nothing, so they fill it by making up social theories about John's "generation," and although they are just blathering, Samantha is one of the people they are talking about, she and Mark. She was only four, but she can remember watching her mother get that November phone call, the one that shattered her into strange and sudden weeping. Thereafter the commemorative issue of *Life* occupied a center position on the coffee table. Many afternoons Samantha would sprawl on her stomach on the rug, browsing pictures she soon memorized: the pink suit, the convertible in blinding, metallic sunlight, then the pages and pages of people in black. There he was, the boy younger than she, but looking like a small grown-up standing there on the curb, saluting. His father's funeral was on his third birthday, one of the facts that made young Samantha feel the sorriest for him.

It's hard to turn off the television, even after they've heard the same few sketchy reports recited over and over. They click through all the networks and are soon so boned-up on the coverage that they catch the reporters making careless mistakes—one reports John's age as thirty-nine, instead of thirty-eight. Another keeps mispronouncing his wife, Carolyn's name for his sister, Caroline's. Some are still reporting Carolyn's father as the doctor in Greenwich, Connecticut. She and Mark know better—that's the stepfather. They know that the Cessna on which John got his pilot's license was N529JK (for his father's birthday). What Samantha doesn't know is why she's unable to turn away. It's pretty certain that they're all dead—John, Carolyn, the wife's sister who was flying with them. Searchers have recovered a luggage tag, a woman's shoe, a prescription bottle. They're down there, all right.

She should get up, but it feels good to have a reason to take to her bed. She has just entered her second trimester, the one with all the supposed extra energy to facilitate the nesting instinct, but she is bone tired. This is her chance to get ready, to get organized, since the boys' three days of care continue through the summer, her time off from teaching college. She has a short story that she's working on, of a mother-daughter pair with a Demeter and Persephone undercurrent. She can't seem to end it—the mother's unending lament of abandonment, all the ways the daughter tries to shake her mother off but can't, even from the arms of the ultimate bad boyfriend. She should put it aside and move on, but that one story line has her by the throat.

It's very nice just to lie here in the heat, not trying to get through a checklist during the boys' naps, letting Mark make sandwiches for them and bring them upstairs for lazy eating in bed.

By now the networks all have a signature "Tragedy at Sea" graphic and soundtrack to cut away to when they take their station or commercial breaks, and she is appalled by the way the plane crash has been immediately packaged into a made-for-TV movie. In the last few hours, stations have also edited the film clips of JFK Jr.'s childhood into a smoothly repeating loop that keeps insisting on a certain, fixed narrative, a pressing inevitability that begins like a wholesome pastel dream and ends with the crack of an unseen rifle.

John Kennedy Jr. is speaking now from the television, on a tape of course, saying that he remembers barely anything of those White House years apart from the pictures themselves, which are not actual memories, but became the memories he has. Samantha knows what he means. How does anyone know what happened to him, to her, at the beginning, apart from a story you've been told? The only memories you can be sure you own completely are the ones that come from a place so inner that no one else has ever had access to them, like the mysterious little grains lining the bottoms of pockets.

She is two or three, sitting on her knees on the bathroom counter, which she reached by climbing from a step stool. It is the time before the new Formica. She is about to look for the orange baby aspirin in the medicine chest, which, she remembers, tastes good. She is suddenly transfixed by her image in the cabinet mirror, inches away, making her forget the orange pills. There is only the swooning collapse and then the expanding distance between the outside Samantha and the inside Samantha. That is perhaps her first wholly owned memory, the discovery of herself.

Michael bounds in after waking up and snuggles between them, liking the boats on the television and not paying attention to the announcer's words. After the boats disappoint by failing to move, he wants to play a game they do when they're all in the big bed: Let's Be Wolves in a Den (plunge down beneath the covers and growl); Let's Be Mice in a Tunnel (plunge down beneath the covers and squeak). Sometimes they are manatees, or lizards, or crows, but they are always creatures in a family, and it always ends with a plunge into togetherness and shelter. Soon Christopher wanders in with his blanket. He's just gotten his real bed and now can release himself at will from naps just like his brother. They all have a few more rounds of Let's Be Bunnies, Let's Be Dolphins, Let's Be Ladybugs, then Samantha gets up. They barely all fit anymore, the boys are getting so rangy and long.

She remembers a crying jag a few weeks after Michael was born because every day, every hour, he looked different and was turning into someone new, but at the cost of losing a previous version of himself—the little starfish hands of the startle reflex, the grimaces and fantastic expressions as he tried to focus his early gazing. It was hormone-suffused grief, and had nothing to do with her gratitude that he was healthy and growing, but it was grief nonetheless. At weigh-ins she would ridiculously keep track of whether he could still be carried within her. It comforted her in an odd way that at nine and a half pounds it was still imaginatively possible to tuck him inside herself. Also, barely, at eleven pounds. By, say, thirteen pounds, her body mourned that her son belonged utterly to the outside world.

There had been a time when she'd been afraid she wouldn't

be able to do it: carry him. The doctor told her early in the second trimester—the point she is at now, actually—that the ultrasound showed she was slightly dilated. He suspected a slight anatomical abnormality because she was a DES daughter; her mother remembered taking—or thought she took, she knew she took it for Steve—diethylstilbestrol when Samantha was in utero because they thought then it was an effective prevention against miscarriage.

He recommended a procedure called cerclage. Even before he explained it, she didn't like the sound of the word, deceptively buttery and soft on the tongue, except for that one hard "c" in the middle. He described how they could stitch up the *os*, the way one might truss a turkey, to keep it closed until the fetus was full term. Of course, he admitted, there would be some risk to the pregnancy. Perhaps a ten percent chance of miscarriage caused by the cerclage itself. But most of the time, he said, the cerclage did its job.

They said no to the cerclage. She'd been sent to her bed for a week, which felt like a punishment, but when nothing changed for the worse she was given permission to move about gingerly. The whole time she carried Michael it was with nervousness that he would fall from her too soon. He didn't. Neither did Christopher, in spite of the pneumonia she'd had with him, and the early labor that they'd stopped with drugs.

She's been waiting for the quickening moment when this baby will move from idea to being. She pictures the fetal curl, like a translucent shrimp, or a small, moon-faced alien inside. It still feels improbable that he could go from such watery form to a big-footed boy like the ones jostling her for space in the cave of the covers.

"Okay, time to move," she announces.

"Again, again," the boys chant. So they do a last round.

"Let's be dinos," Michael says.

"What kind?"

"Pterodactyls."

So they plunge beneath the covers one last time, roaring from their buried nest.

The afternoon leaves no time for thinking about checklists, her writing, or anything else. Mark escapes to the supermarket—and that is exactly what it is, escape—and Samantha tries to fold laundry in the family room while helping the boys manage their train setup. She's learned to let them create tracks that drift off onto carpet or dead-end into each other, because those scenarios of ending without purpose don't bother them, but there are bound to be skirmishes over whether a piece should curve out or curve in, and she needs to be there to shore up Christopher's side of the argument, so that Michael doesn't get to call all the shots.

As she folds, she sees Carolyn Bessette-Kennedy's blond hair float up like a silvery sea plant, John strapped into his seat, his hands still gripping the controls. Does the salt water smooth away the expressions? She's read that Carolyn didn't want to fly with him. He claimed she did, though, joked about it with reporters when he was interviewed around the time he was getting his pilot's license. *My wife is the only one who will go up with me*, he said. But other articles reported that she did all she could to avoid it. Did she have time to feel angry with him when the plane began its dive?

Because Samantha has myths on her mind, her Demeter story that doesn't want to be finished, her mind turns to Icarus, the prideful glee of a boy who just wanted to fly, no matter who said no. Maybe she should write one based on that.

When Mark returns with the groceries and takes the boys to the park, Samantha settles herself at the kitchen table to call her mother. At first, the distance between them, the width of the whole country, didn't seem too much. With every step Samantha took into her life—out of the house, then out of town, then to the other coast—her mother turned against her, fell silent and cold until she finally had to realize that the coldness wasn't bringing Samantha any closer. They eventually achieved a kind of détente, visiting and calling. But things warmed beyond détente when she and Mark began having children. Her mother adored the little boys; the boys adored their grandmother. Just like that, there was nothing more Samantha could hold against Kathryn. She began to miss her.

She usually calls her just once on the weekend because when her mother gets to talking she can't quit. If Samantha could count on quick, five- or ten-minute chats—wedged in between work, the boys, the house—she'd call her several times a week. She'd actually like to.

"Are you watching?"

"Such a shame. That poor family." Her mother starts detailing the whole Kennedy saga, from Joe to JFK to Rosemary to Kathleen and onward, leaving no space to make it a conversation. Samantha says "Yes" and "Uh-huh" and "I know," and this is perfectly satisfactory. She has enough leftover mental space to flip through the baby-naming book she left out. It's too early, but she can't resist. And even though everything in her assumes boy, she starts with the girl pages, just to see. Abaranne, Abebi, Abelia, Abellona, Abia, Abigail—the first six entries. Abebi (Nigerian) means "she came after asking." Abelia (Hebrew) simply means "sigh."

They have been through this before, of course, all the improbable choices before settling on the solid and familiar. But she likes the freedom of this moment, the becoming-before-the-became. Her mother doesn't know about the baby yet, no one besides Mark does, and Samantha toys with the idea of telling her now. She doubts it will be a girl, but she likes the name Kathryn, maybe shortened to Kate. Her father used to call her mother "Kay," but after the divorce, she became mostly Kathryn again, whenever she introduced herself to someone new.

"Remember?" her mother asks.

Samantha's lost the thread. She plays back her auditory memory; her mother was up to Bobby's assassination.

"I do."

"You were so grown up; even people who wanted to shut the door in our faces would take a leaflet from you."

"It was fun." Until it wasn't. Their whole family had canvassed, then gone to a rally at some hot, downtown hotel. Samantha remembers Robert Kennedy's rabbitty grin, the limp forelock of hair. They stood in line to shake his hand. He had to adjust his gaze downward to smile at her, and she didn't have time to tell him that she helped with the leafleting before she was pressed forward by the crowd. Then he was on to California.

"The Realtor came by today," her mother says. "She thinks the house will sell quickly."

"That's good, right?"

"Except I'm not ready; well, I'm more than ready, I can't cope with the upkeep anymore. But I'll never be able to pack all this up."

"Yes, you will. I'll help."

"Really?"

"Of course I will. I've told you."

"But you won't be able to stay very long."

"Then we'll have to be efficient."

"I don't think I can do it."

"We'll do it." Although Samantha is thinking about the baby, teaching, the fact that she lives more than three thousand miles away, and the extra work for Mark with the boys while she's gone.

"And I'm not sure about the place in Tacoma. It doesn't have any green space."

Samantha waits. They've covered this ground several times. The Tacoma retirement apartment is just two miles from Samantha's brother and his family. When Samantha and Kathryn priced places in Boston, it was clear her mother would never be able to afford one near her.

"When it comes right down to it, I don't want to go anywhere."

"I know."

"But I just can't handle all this on my own."

"Yes. That's what you've got to remember."

Mark and the boys come in trailing sand out of Tonka trucks. "Out on the patio with those," she tells them. "You can keep playing for five more minutes."

"Mom, Mark and the boys are home from the park. I should finish getting dinner."

"It's so wonderful, the help you get from your husband. He's a good man."

"Yes."

"Still, I don't see how you do all you do. Of course, I did work, when I had to. We could never make ends meet on what your father earned. I never wanted to be away from you kids, though."

"I know. Mom, I've got to—"

"Is that Grandma?" Michael asks.

Samantha covers the receiver. "You want to say hi?" she asks him.

"Tell her to come visit." He races off behind Christopher.

"Mom, Michael says you need to come visit soon."

"Oh, the little sweetheart. Tell him I love him. And Christopher, too."

"I will. I'll call you soon. Let's get you on a plane before I go back to school."

"I wish I could."

"You can! Nothing to it. Next time we talk we'll plan a date and then I'll send you a ticket."

"I couldn't let you do that."

"Yes, you can. Okay, my spaghetti sauce is ready. Mark says hi."

Mark looks up from his pager and waves.

Her mother lavishes unstinting and unconditional love on her boys. It takes Samantha's breath away sometimes, how they respond, want to be by her, listen to her read stories in silly animal voices. But it shouldn't. That was the mother she had, too, when she was little.

She leaves the table to stir the spaghetti sauce.

Mark has picked up the naming book and is paging through. "Where do they come up with these? Viridis, Vida, Viveca? Walburga, Walda, Wanetta?"

She returns to look over his shoulder. "You skipped Virginia and Vivian."

"Still." He flips over to the boy's side. "First page I open: Dearborn, Decimus, Declan, Deems, Delaney." He tosses it aside. "We need a new book."

"Or a narrowing principle. Like only considering family names."

"How about waiting until we see him?"

"Him?"

"Or her."

They've already said no to the amnio. A nod at fate or God or nature. Whoever comes is theirs. She'll be forty when this baby is born; the Down syndrome risk is one in one hundred.

Some nights she wakes up with a nameless feeling of dread, the same dream or vision she had when she was in the ICU with pneumonia, eight months pregnant with Christopher. She is at the bottom of a canyon surrounded by high, sheer walls, with no footholds to help her climb out. The sky and rocks are both a merciless, depthless gray. She doesn't know how she got there, or why she is so alone, or why this landscape has no sound, like a mute button has been pushed.

Then she'll become aware of Mark breathing by her side, and see that the gray is really the gray of before-dawn light, and that everything is about to be bright and loud. She is glad when the day explodes into alarms and small-boy voices with urgent needs.

By the third day, the operation changes from rescue to salvage. They winch up the fuselage, the seawater pouring out, and then it is over. Everyone knew it was over from the beginning; it was a game they all colluded in, that it wasn't over. The networks keep doing their best to make good viewing out of what remains, namely grief, keeping their cameras as close as they can to the faces of the bereaved. Samantha turns it off.

Meanwhile, there are the lists. Michael's day-care group is taking the T downtown to the aquarium, and for once Samantha kept her name off the chaperone list. She is tired. She is paying money to the day care to get rest. But she ticks off the items of the packing list for his knapsack—his lunch with disposable wrappings, his sunblock (applied, and in the bag), his windbreaker (they will be down near the wharf), and his hat, which she is certain he will lose. That's okay, but they have a brief tussle over which hat it will be, his favorite with the truck logo, or one he'll never miss if it's left on the train. She wins by distracting him, drawing him into a conversation over whether he thinks the scuba diver at the Aquarium will be feeding the fish in the giant tank when he's there, and why doesn't the shark ever eat him up?

Michael is knowledgeable about this, as he is about all things having to do with the aquarium.

"They're not hungry, Mom," he explains patiently. "They feed them so much that they don't need to eat the divers. They don't need to eat the other fish, either."

"I find that remarkable," Samantha says, and she does. That a little nourishment can lull the predator into a torporous calm, content to circle and circle, but never strike.

Christopher is jealous of Michael's field trip, so she reminds him that the teachers have made this a wading-pool day for the younger kids, and he cheers up a little. But he is slow to separate this morning, sticking close to her while they watch the big kids line up with their chaperones, two kids to each parent or teacher. She holds hands with Christopher, the two of them waving to Michael as the line troops off, around the corner to the T station. She stays with him for the morning free play outside in the yard, where the teachers have set up an activity table with cans of shaving cream for the kids to squirt. She likes these stray moments alone with Christopher, who soon will be the boy in the middle, likes watching him forget all about her in his concentration, tunneling his little truck through the shaving-cream mountain.

When he is fine and doesn't need her, running off to rinse his mentholated hands, which make him smell, oddly, like his six-foot father, she heads home to the glow and the trial of an empty morning. Where to start? The kitchen, as usual, with its jumble of dishes and cereal boxes. As she loads the dishwasher, she realizes that the thing she's been keeping at bay on some barely conscious level now wants to be acknowledged. The low cramping, the backache, which she has been pushing out of focus because of breakfast, lunches, sunscreen, swimming suit, and towel. But now there it is, not just incidental, but real. And not just in the background, but—as if it realizes that she can finally pay attention—insistent.

She lies down on the couch, her feet up. She is thinking of gravity, of her sudden fear of it. Then thinking: If bed rest, how? How to get the kids home from day care, how to get through the day tomorrow when they don't have it, how to do anything? She can't do anything at the moment but think these questions, because the cramps are mounting, not going away; because she knows her calls need to be first to the doctor, then to Mark.

The phone is across the room, which means becoming vertical. Right now, she is a woman putting her feet up to rest. Once she gets up, anything about that story could change. She pictures Michael, off the train now, and walking through the aquarium. It is always crowded there, no matter when you go. What if he dashes ahead or dawdles behind? What if his teacher doesn't notice until he's run headlong down the spiraling ramp, past the eels and angelfish, lionfish and jellyfish, God forbid out the front doors? He's only four; he'd be looking for her. Even though he came with his teachers, he'd forget that. She'd be the one he'd call for.

Unmistakably, now, come tight waves of contraction. *Little one,* she thinks. *Let's be manatees. Let's be ladybugs. Let's play possum.* She is not prepared for this threat coming in under the radar when what she expected were ATMs that wouldn't accept her card, lines at the gasoline pump, cash registers everywhere refusing to open their drawers, or even, if it came to that, a failing hospital generator. The executive list-makers would have thought of backup generators, and backups for those. She has been mentally readying herself for a digital global predicament that could be managed with a stockpile of canned goods and duct tape and small bills. Not this slippage in the corner when nobody is looking.

She dials 911; it's the first time she ever has had to. Her first public declaration of unambiguous need.

The voice that answers is brisk with challenge: What is her emergency?

Her emergency is gravity. Melting states of matter. Her one heart beating through the separate, adventuring hearts of her sons, the smallest of them at this moment being pulled from her by a tide too strong, too deep, and too wide, leaving before she can even call him back by name.

Inside Passage

From Seattle, 2007

Day 1.

When Steve and his wife, Peggy, arrive at the agreed-upon time to take them from Tacoma to the dock in Seattle, her mother is still buck-naked in the bathroom from her shower but at least packed (she'll discover she forgot arch supports and her best walking shoes, though she has a pair she didn't intend to bring.

Steve, in turn, forgot to bring her Steinbeck's *Pearl*). Kathryn finishes the last ten pages of *The Grapes of Wrath* in the car on the way,
headed to Pier 66.

Steve finds Bell Street in Seattle, heads downhill. There, visible
in glimpses through buildings, almost two city blocks long, is the
vast and shining cruise ship.

Samantha can't stop fingering their passports and embarkation papers. This has been too long in preparation and feels too
irrevocable—probably the only cruise of her mother's lifetime, just
one sailing with their names on the manifest. It took six months
and a congressman's office to help Kathryn get a passport—no birth
certificate from the hospital in Nainital—but finally someone in
the State Department found her parents' passport applications
from the twenties with the children's names listed.

They snake through the line to load luggage. Samantha remembers that Mark warned her not to board first, but she has no
idea why; she made him turn off the cruising infomercial before it
ended so they could go to bed. In any case, they're far from first, her
mother just stepping out of the shower when they were supposed
to be heading north on I-5, but they made it. Her mother's eighty-
fifth-birthday cruise.

Samantha and Kathryn hand over their luggage, render their
credit cards for onboard purchases, show their passports, and have
their pictures snapped for cruising IDs. They give hugs goodbye
to Steve and Peggy, then follow lines on the terminal floor to the
gangplank, turning down the opportunity to purchase discount
field glasses and the "best price" Alaska hat. They are required to
stop and pose for a celebratory Embarkation Portrait.

Finally, they are actually on board after swiping their new
IDs, and are immediately greeted by smiling stewards proffering
trays of complimentary champagne and orange juice. Samantha
thinks this is more like it, though it will be the last free drink of
the cruise.

Her mother is entranced by their mini-suite: balcony, fancy

bathroom amenities, a safe, a captain's log of activities thick as a paperback, and a welcoming note from their cabin stewards, Alphonso and Julian. Their luggage is already in the room. The second bed unfolds from a sofa near their sliding glass door to the balcony. Samantha will take it, leaving her mother the bed closest to the bathroom. Everything is snug and ingenious.

Time for lunch—their first experience of the buffet. In recent weeks, her mother has complained of nausea, merely pecks at food. An X-ray found a shadow on her lung, a mass, and the surgeon's appointment to biopsy it will be two days after their return. She says she can't possibly eat a meal, but opts to attempt a little snack after viewing the gleaming line of offerings. When they finish, all that remains on her plate is a large pile of clean chicken bones.

They are not yet under way. Samantha settles her mother on one of their balcony chairs, then goes to scout out the ship's library. She finds hundreds of pristine hardbacks. No Steinbeck, her mother's current kick, but she selects a stack for her inspection. Underfoot, she detects the slightest motion. She returns to join her mother on the balcony, watching as Seattle stretches away, then shrinks to a vanishing point.

While her mother naps, Samantha continues her exploration of the gym and spa, listening to the white-jacketed attendant's explanation of toxin-ridding treatments and Embarkation Specials, four yoga classes for the price of three. She figures out how to read the restaurant screens displayed around ship, colored bars indicating the number of open tables; she acquaints herself with the key to the surcharge venues, which they will avoid. Even if Samantha pays, her mother won't enjoy it if it's a surcharge restaurant.

After dinner, they catch the last five minutes of a comic's routine consisting of two bald jokes plus one poking fun of his mother that her mother doesn't get. Looking in through the casino on their walk back, Kathryn is disappointed to see that all play is for paper scrip. Slots to her mean a shower of nickels in the stainless-steel well, real wealth that blackens the fingers.

Day 2.

Samantha is up before six thirty, while her mother still sleeps soundly. Samantha's three sons at home—twelve, ten, and the youngest that they kept trying for past a miscarriage, now seven—are currently under Mark's watch; she feels astonished to wake with time on her hands. She ventures off alone to the buffet with her novel; they have agreed on this plan since her mother is not a breakfast eater. Samantha waits at the buffet entrance for the velvet rope to be drawn back. She stands behind a man from Texas with his wife, whom he met in Tokyo, the two of them now living in Alabama. She learns through chitchat that he is a Korea vet, air force; that he once lived at a base in the northwest and doesn't like rain; and that they cruise frequently because "Life is like a roll of toilet paper: The closer you get to the end, the faster it goes."

Samantha uses her graduate school waitress skills to transport her dishes of oatmeal, berries, omelet, and coffee, Dos Passos's fat trilogy, *U.S.A.*, tucked under her arm. She is happy to sit by the window for an hour alone after breakfast, reading and watching the sea, gray and tossed, and the smudges of islands on the horizon. She is already wearing her yoga pants and goes straight to class at eight, where she is bemused by the gently rolling sensation beneath her feet in Mountain pose, and the inverted view of sea and sky outside the floor-to-ceiling windows during Down Dog.

Her mother is awake when she returns, so they review the multipage list of shore excursions, dozens upon dozens. Samantha points out the Level One activities with easy walking. Her mother favors the helicopter ride to the mushing camp where she can pet the husky puppies, until she sees the price.

They begin shipboard rounds, stopping first for her mother's coffee, then pause at a table in the lounge so Samantha can enter the drawing for the Picasso linotype. Her mother thinks the linotype stinks, wouldn't want it if she won it. The day passes in a pleasant tedium of rambling and watching the sea and reading their books and dozing and visiting the radiant buffet.

Samantha awakens in the middle of the night to a decidedly pitching ship. Her mother gets out of bed to pee, and Samantha springs up to steady her against the rolling. The creaking of the brand-new ship dispels the hotel-at-sea illusion. It's a vessel, without doubt. Being tossed.

Day 3.

When Samantha opens her eyes again, the sky is clear, sea calm. Berries and oatmeal and omelet and coffee and novel. Yoga in the middle of the ocean.

They take their first shore excursion: Mendenhall Glacier and Salmon Bake. Her mother adores all—the storytelling bus driver, the gentle hiking paths around the glacier she manages well with her walking stick, the views of Juneau. For dinner, they sit at a picnic table overlooking a creek, piney and damp, and are serenaded by a cheerful folk singer. They have two hours on their own. Instead of taking the tour bus back to dock, Samantha proposes a short walk in town, then a walk to the ship. Her mother also hankers to shop and loves to walk, so agrees.

The walk back turns out to be farther than Samantha thought, a misleading bend in the road revealing at least another half-mile. The embarkation deadline looms in thirty minutes, and the ship hovers in the distance, a smooth, ivory toy. Her mother is seriously flagging, her face drawn and grim. Could this have been Samantha's major life error, ruining the birthday cruise and perhaps sending her mother to the emergency room? Her mother says she needs to sit, but there is no place to sit, and no time to sit if there were a place.

Of the little traffic on the road, all of it is coming toward them; the wrong direction for hitching a ride. Then Samantha sees a taxi headed opposite and waves it down. At first the driver passes them and she thinks he didn't see, but he drives just far enough to do a U-turn at a wider place in the road. He deposits them directly in front of the gangplank with twenty-five minutes to spare. Samantha thinks he probably saved their cruise, and maybe even her mother's life, and wonders how big she should make the tip for that.

Day 4.

Skagway: a two-hour streetcar tour. Their guide, Jeannie, reports on the 5:1 single men to single woman ratio in Alaska: "The odds are good but the goods are odd."

Later, riding the narrow-gauge White Pass train, waterfalls flash by the windows, with views of the cliffs around curves where they can see the tail end of the train winding after them. Her mother fusses, trying to get her camera, a birthday gift from Steve, set in time for the changing scene. Each missed waterfall represents failure: "If I were nimble there's no end to the beautiful pictures I could be taking," she moans. Riding down, the passengers are instructed to change sides to receive the benefit of the opposite view. Her mother is downcast about missing a particular waterfall, now on the opposite side. It's all she can talk about for the rest of the ride.

The only way Samantha can stay patient with her is to remember how relatively little time is left, with or without the mass in her chest, so that enjoying and appreciating her mother becomes inextricably bound to losing her. But this does work, so it's the technique she uses.

Returning to their mini-suite they find that either Alphonso or Julian has spent considerable effort shaping a towel into a bunny with Andes mints for eyes. Her mother snaps photos of the towel art resting on the crisply made bed. A photographic subject that can't elude her, she takes pictures of it from every angle. Neither of them can figure out how the artist got the towel to stay in place so perfectly. Starch?

Samantha thinks they should rehearse "Sentimental Journey," the duet they sang when she was child, for the passenger talent show and the chance to win two free cruises. Her mother gets uncontrollable giggles at the thought. Samantha doesn't know why Kathryn can't find the harmony after a lifetime of hitting it like a professional. She finally figures out that her mother can't hear her, so she sings louder and aims at her ear. Her mother locates the notes. They polish up "Moon River" and others for possible encores.

Day 5.

Her mother says please, no talent show. Samantha has already privately given it up. Cruising day in Glacier Bay: They watch the creamy icebergs glide by their stateroom balcony. Her mother has her camera strap looped around her wrist for extra security. Samantha sits mesmerized by the glowing white against the uncannily blue water. Her mother contentedly snaps away, gobbling up the whole landscape to digest it at a later date.

Samantha knows this is her mother's nirvana: a trip with just the two of them, although she loves Samantha's family and is a spectacular grandmother. But somehow, as early as Samantha can remember, she's been the one entrusted with her mother's inner life—the confidences, confessions, complaints—all of it expressing a grievous sense of lack. Samantha has figured out she can't fill it. Even if it were her job, which it's not, it's unfillable. But this is what Samantha can afford to give her mother for this birthday: one week of all of her, every scintilla, though the calendar counts down on their charmed shipboard bubble. Kathryn takes picture after picture after picture.

Day 6.

Ketchikan: Samantha has been here before, during a summer in graduate school, cleaning fish in a cannery; she didn't remember cruise ships docking then.

Together they spend shore time in the giant souvenir emporiums. Cruise-destination Ketchikan bears no resemblance to the cannery town Samantha lived in. She slept in a tent city with other workers and ate pancakes cooked over a fire grate for supper every night. At first the fish weren't running and she hung around the streets in town with the others. She'd while away the day in the diner with a book while it rained, hamburgers and homemade pie, or loiter in the dusty drugstore she'd invent errands to go to. She was reading Pynchon's *V* that summer, all summer, so in addition to rain and salmon-bloody gloves and hair nets and long rubber aprons and sliming spoons at the ends of thin hoses, she was gripped by the feel of an impenetrable story across time and geography full of characters she continually lost track of.

Then her mother's missing finger. Back home in Portland while Samantha was cleaning fish, Kathryn had felt only the nick as she reached in to clean the chute of the running lawnmower. People don't usually ask about her mother's healed finger stump, but the salesgirl at the souvenir emporium surprisingly does, and Kathryn tells the story, which always includes the bit about living alone in the house and taking care of a big yard all by herself, the reason she had to sell, though she still misses it terribly, even the yard work. The story contains equal and opposite complaints: having the house and not having the house. Samantha remembers the phone call from Steve she got in Ketchikan—word gotten to her through the fish company, no cell phones then—and how she returned home on the next ferry when the salmon were just hitting the peak of their run. That's when the overtime pay started, fish cannery gold.

Of course, you don't blame someone for having such a terrible accident. But Samantha can't help picturing her mother, shoving the mower to and fro with irritation as she managed a difficult corner. She could afford to hire someone, but insisted that the exercise was good for her. Always angry, though, as she pitted her slight weight against the machine. She'd be angry at a clogged chute, angry she was alone to deal with it, angry that the backyard—missing its swing set, its wading pool, its balance beam—was all her job. So angry she wouldn't think to turn the mower off. So angry her motions would be sudden, fury fueling them.

Night after night for the rest of that summer the two of them stared at the red, angry stump, stitched and oozing, as Samantha daubed, padded, bandaged. When it happened, Kathryn had screamed for help and the next-door neighbor, the one she had feuded with for years about Princess the barking dog, came to her aid. The neighbor found the finger part and wrapped it in ice. The neighbor called 911 and Steve. The doctors said if they reattached the top joint, the finger would be stiff and unfeeling and useless. It would get in her way. So she came home from the hospital with the bandaged stump, and when people asked with concern what happened, she told about taking care of the house, all by herself, with that big yard.

They reboard and retreat to their stateroom with their emporium gifts for Samantha's family and Steve's family: sweatshirts and T-shirts and fossils and antique trading beads. When they emerge for dinner, people are breaking up from clusters of whale spotting. Apparently, a pod of thirty or so whales spouted and cavorted on both sides of ship and neither Kathryn nor Samantha looked up from their books to note the spectacle off their mini-suite balcony. Samantha fetches her field glasses and Kathryn her coat. No sign of them.

It's the optional Dress Like You Mean It night, which means sequins and shiny shoes and many roaming shipboard photographers, offering portraits. Samantha continues in jeans and sandals and a black long-sleeved T-shirt, but regrets the lack of something more silky. Her mother has given up her yellow shirt with a picture of a yawning puppy and humorous caption about not doing mornings, but still wears a T-shirt with writing, this time a map of the Oregon coast. So it's for the best Samantha did not bring dressier clothes.

They are greeted warmly by the Filipina hostess who always secures them an immediate window seat in the Royal Court, and are led to the table by the tall Indian maître'd who says it's nice to see them again. Kathryn is in love with the maître'd, who spoke to them in a formally gracious manner on their first night until Kathryn tried a few words of her childhood Hindi on him and his surprise broke through the corporate mask to ask, how did Madam come to know Hindi? They swapped locations—her missionary Dhamtari and Mussoorie for his Bangalore, and though they didn't overlap in India's vastness, it was enough for Kathryn to stake her claim of affiliation.

Samantha forces herself to accompany her mother to "Legs, Legs, Legs," the evening's showgirl feature. She reminds herself it is not a true sacrifice if she says even one sarcastic thing or rolls her eyes or even discreetly falls asleep, so she the watches the entire glittery spectacle. She has to admit that the gymnast couple hanging from suspended scarves is pretty good. She watches the kick line with a critical eye, having been a member of a state champion dance team in high school, coached by a woman who was all about synchronization.

They skip Vegas night, but head to the Chocolate Paradise buffet. There are many jokes in the elevator on the way to the dessert party about death by chocolate being a good way to go—jokes made mostly by elderly people who know a thing or two about death. Choco partygoers are greeted by waiters carrying champagne on trays; Samantha withdraws her reaching hand after learning the price per glass that will be swiped to her ID card. There is a giant ice sculpture of a whale, also an enormous chocolate sculpture of a cruise ship amid chocolate waves. Low romantic lighting. The crowds streaming in from the Palace Theater, having just watched seminude showgirls, help themselves to platefuls of desserts from a boggling expanse. Samantha wonders—a kind of sexual release? Her mother selects an array, later marveling that the indigestion that prevented her from ordering an entrée at dinner is unaffected by an infusion of chocolate raspberry cake, mousse, macaroon, profiterole, and éclair.

Their nightly bulletin has instructions for debarkation. Kathryn and Samantha will opt for gray luggage tags, which will put them among the last ones to leave the ship. Her mother would like to stay for another loop if they could, do it all again.

Day 7.

Victoria Day, last full sail day.

At breakfast, diners to the left and right of Samantha point simultaneously to a whale spouting on the port side. She looks up from her book just in time to miss it.

She completes her yoga series of four classes, resolving to begin a newly mindful way of life at home.

The children of the Buccaneer Club are sometimes paraded through the decks and lounges wearing their pirate bandannas. Their keepers lead them in their signature chant: *Yo ho ho and a yo ho ho! From stem to stern we'll go Go GO!* The spiky-haired Aussie art auctioneer in the Diamond Atrium, listing the important features of the limited-edition linotypes for sale, interrupts his flood of impassioned pedagogy to smile insincerely at the shouting children on the atrium balcony overhead. Elderly passersby comment, "How sweet!" and "Aren't they having fun!" But there is something enraged and manic in the children's shouting. They know they have been penned away from the adults for the entire voyage, the parents having more fun without them, so for once the exhortations of their keepers make sense: Shout in faces of adults and force adults to smile back. The keepers must enjoy this, too, having been required to invent amusements for the children for a solid week while the parents sipped the Daily Cocktail ("Octopus Hug," "Endless Sunset," "Full Fathom Five") in souvenir glasses, while lying on lounge chairs that are really beds. There are beds everywhere on the ship with adults sprawled on them, mouths open.

Kathryn wears her new Inside Passage map T-shirt, so Samantha can consult their current position by gazing at her mother's flattened chest. Her mother had some years ago stopped wearing a brassiere. One day she said, enough of that. Most of the passengers seem to be sporting their port purchases, so that they have become a vast, place-labeled herd, as if no one can remember their location unless wearing it.

Samantha pops her head into the hall to listen each time the ding-dong signals the cruise director's instructions. These will invariably be news of a jackpot bingo round or a shopping talk by Harry (diamonds, tanzanite, alexandrite, white quartz, ammolite, and watches). They are told never to be in port without Harry's mobile number; he will use his clout to intercede with shopkeepers not discounting items deeply enough for the VIP status the cruisers should rightfully enjoy. Samantha wishes the ding-dong announcements would just once contain a timely suggestion to look out the port or starboard deck for spouting whales, but all suggestions lead to jewelry, jugglers, and the Jackpot Jumbo Wheel. Kathryn and Samantha have, on the last cruising day, discovered a most beautiful lounge on the top floor at the most forward part of the deck, and spend some hopeful time on watch with Samantha's field glasses, but the sea will yield them no whale.

Later in the day, after Kathryn has showered, she bends to apply a pain patch to her lower back. Samantha is about to ask if she needs help, but her mother's movements are practiced in the application of the pain patch. Samantha takes the opportunity to stare, unobserved, at her mother's body, not unlike the Picasso etchings going up for Final Auction at 1:30. If Picasso were to draw Kathryn he could make use of the wobbled etching line, what her mother's silhouetted flesh has become, a series of ripples and blurred edges.

At the photo gallery wall Kathryn and Samantha find portraits of themselves—at embarkation, in the Tropical Café (with plushly costumed seagull), in the Summer Palace (with plushly costumed dolphin). In every shot, they look happy and relaxed, well lit, eyes open, smiles broad. Even she is tempted to pay the $19.99 for the 5-by-7 embossed leatherette folio. But it is Kathryn who splurges on it, won't let Samantha buy it for her as a gift. She picks a lovely one of the two of them—no plush characters involved—their heads tilted toward each other. For an extra dollar they get a copy, one for Samantha to take home to Boston. The leatherette folio will sit open for display on Kathryn's bookcase in Tacoma, displacing the carved plaster Buddha that Samantha made in art class in seventh grade.

Samantha and Kathryn have not sampled the Thai, Chinese, French, or Italian cuisine in the surcharge restaurants. They had no interest in the Cultured Pearl Seminar, nor did they bother to obtain raffle tickets for Parisian diamond jewelry. They attended no dance parties.

Samantha sampled one open-air Jacuzzi (not hot enough to suit her), but did not venture down a water slide. She read carefully about, but did not book an appointment for, the many spa offerings.

They finally visited the bridge, but the officers had the shades of the observation window lowered. They stumbled upon the Friends of Bill W. meeting in the chapel right off the bar, forward on the fifteenth deck.

Karaoke. Samantha needs to cross this item off her life list. She searches the master book for the Stevie Nicks song she has forgotten the title to, hums a few bars to people nearby, until one woman reminds her of its name, "Landslide." Samantha gets dry mouth waiting; wine makes it worse. Kathryn situates herself for multiple snaps. Samantha stands through the opening instrumental notes, which are strangely unrecognizable to her. What key to come in on? Wrong guess. She straightens out the key, but has the feeling she's inaudible (Kathryn will later confirm this, though her hearing is not to be trusted). She does have some stretches where her voice seems to fill up the song. She dares not look at individuals in the audience, but couldn't really see them anyway, so bright is the glare from the spotlight. She waits through another instrumental passage with no patter or interesting moves. She decides karaoke is harder than it looks, and vows to give full credit to all comers from now on.

The song ends and Samantha feels undeservedly triumphant; people are clapping. Kathryn took two pictures of a brass rail, none of Samantha. She is heartbroken, wants Samantha to sing more. But Samantha has crossed this item off her life list, doesn't need to sing more, at least until her sons are by her side. The woman who knew the "Landslide" title performs "Play That Funky Music" with *her* mother. Brilliant choice. Her mother stands comically blank like Letterman's mother, and *that* daughter is bright in a sexy flowered dress and pouffy hair and *does* move during the instrumental section. But she has a sidekick, the pleasantly blank mother, so Samantha gives herself credit for going it alone.

THE BIG GOOMBAH

Tacoma, 2007

The big goombah is gone from where it had been sitting on her chest, and what is there instead is nothing. You can spare half a lung, the surgeon told her, after he described a mass the size of tennis ball. Benign. He'd been so sure it would be otherwise that he had tossed it in formalin, ruining it for purposes of culture, so that they are unable to determine what spore or bacterium latched on to Kathryn's lung, blooming there like cauliflower. I was wrong, he said, grinning in his lavishly colorful scrub cap, inviting her into the joke: His being wrong was rare. But you wanted that big goombah out of there anyway, he assures her. Did she? She probably did.

When she came back to life, the boys' choir was singing away. No one else heard it. It's coming from above me, she said. Next floor up. It's faint, but they never stop rehearsing. What do you think they're rehearsing for? That one song, over and over.

You've had a lot of anesthesia, Samantha pointed out. And don't forget the morphine. There's no boys' choir.

Kathryn just closed her eyes, discussion over.

In every other respect, she's herself again and the fog has cleared. She follows the presidential debates—Obama versus that other guy—from her rehab bed. Reads mysteries. Rehab itself consists of reaching for things in a pretend pantry, going bowling with a pretend ball, dressing and washing. Rehab, in other words, consists of practicing life, in the cocoon of the facility where falls are caught and accidents prevented. With her therapist chirping prompts, Kathryn makes rehab chocolate chip cookies and serves them to her son, visiting that night. He isn't a rehab pretend son. He's her real son, Steve.

I wish they'd call off the singing, she says.

There's no singing, Mom. None whatsoever. These cookies are good.

Take them home to the girls, she says. I certainly don't need any. She isn't a grandma who bakes much; she's done with that, after a lifetime of baking. First, everything from scratch, the way her mother taught her, then mixes—everyone used them. But her rehab cookies are from scratch and she might as well get the credit.

Great, her son says, wrapping them in napkins.

Just leave me a few, she says, so he unwraps one of the bundles.

She starts going places with her walker, and the singing follows. When she rolls as far as the rec room without needing a chaperone, it's sometimes difficult to hear it over the babble of the television and the mumbling of patients overlaid with the bright tones of therapists. But the singing never completely goes away—filaments of human longing braided to celestial hopes so lovely, she sometimes has to pause in the hall, head cocked, waiting for a particular swell. She is—was—a soprano herself; she tries to figure out the song: Handel? Schubert? It's both familiar and unknown, but as fine as you'd hear in a big cathedral, not like the hearty congregational singing of her youth.

The week after surgery, when her surgeon comes to the rehab wing on rounds, he tells her she's ready to go home. Pain flares from the empty hole in her chest. The choir reaches its highest note and holds it.

I'm still practicing, she tells him.

He laughs, this time wearing a scrub cap with giraffe print. Has he just come from removing parts of children? Or does he think giraffes are generally consoling to all age groups?

What are you practicing? he asks.

Life.

This is it. You're alive. Go home and get back to mischief.

Samantha is on hand to help, but the physical therapist recommends that Kathryn pack up her own things. When the therapist leaves the room, her daughter helps anyway, folding Kathryn's robe, stacking the library books. Kathryn's given up asking Samantha if she hears the choir, and she has, as well, learned to turn it up or down, depending on whether she needs to hear someone talk or whether she no longer wants to. But when she's alone she doesn't seem to have any control over the volume knob: The music simply fills her up, and while at first the single choice of song annoyed her, now it's a sequence of notes that feels deeply tuned to her cells, and somehow a known set of words, which she's decided are in German, a language she doesn't speak, though it was her mother's mother's mother tongue. Her own parents spoke snippets of Pennsylvania Dutch to each other when they didn't want the children to understand, and Kathryn knows only *Ach, du lieber Gott im Himmel.* Dear God in heaven.

When the choir follows her home, she has to admit that they

are not musicians in residence at the rehab center. Though no less real for that fact. She has the presence of mind not to mention the singing when she goes to see her favorite doctor, the pulmonologist. She tells him other news instead: that she practiced putting five pounds of flour up on a shelf in a pretend pantry, and is now home putting real groceries away in her own pantry. Nothing she buys in real life approaches the practice five-pound weight, so the flour bag was overtraining. Her retirement complex, which her children have dubbed the Home, provides the evening meal, and all she needs otherwise is a little coffee, a little oatmeal, a few cans of soup, and some Egg Beaters. Her doctor compliments her on her recovery and especially on the results of her lung function test, blowing into the tube. She thanks him.

You're not going to miss the lobe, he says.

That's what that smart-aleck surgeon said.

Dr. Singh laughs. He has an easy laugh and she likes to say starchy things to provoke it. He wears a different color turban every time she visits him, always in deep, jewel tones, and she always compliments him on the way they match his shirt or tie. He tells her his wife does that, the matching. His dark beard is very neat and she wonders if his wife does that, too. When he first found out she'd been born in India to missionary parents he took a great interest in the fact, not only because of their shared nativity, but because it made her medical case very interesting. The first thing he thought of was a latent tuberculosis biding its time in the childish pink tissue of her lung and coming to life as her immune system weakened with age. But because her know-it-all surgeon tossed her goombah into the formalin fixative, they will never know exactly what it was.

What about the rest of your life? he asks.

She has a moment of confusion; does he mean until she dies? Then he elaborates: Are you getting out, doing things?

She drives to her son's when his busy family has time, looks forward to her daughter's visits when her busy family can spare her for a plane trip. She supposes, to an outside view, she does not look very occupied. Her only regular engagements are with her physicians and her tablemates at dinner. Impossible to explain to Dr. Singh, kind as he is, about the many steps of her day, the time it takes to do the simplest thing—make a bed, for instance. To her great disgrace, she doesn't always do that anymore. Or dusting: She has many magazines stacked up in the particular order in which she intends to read them. They must all be dusted individually and dusted around. When she does her laundry in the machines downstairs, she loads up her wheeled cart with the wet clothes to bring back upstairs and drape on her wooden drying frame. The fact that the wooden drying frame is getting old and rickety and that she can't find a replacement at Target or Fred Myers worries her. Will she outlast it? She absolutely doesn't trust the cleanliness of the dryers at the Home after once she saw another resident put unwashed wet tarps in one. When Samantha pointed out that the hot air has a sterilizing effect, Kathryn holds her peace, knowing her daughter can supply endless counterarguments to many things Kathryn holds as true. When Samantha further suggested that a high school girl might come in and do these chores for twenty dollars, Kathryn had two thoughts: Twenty dollars was a lot of money, and the high school girl wouldn't know how to do things the way Kathryn needs them to be done.

I'm busy all the time, she tells Dr. Singh.

Because volunteer work can be a wonderful way to stay healthy and active, he says.

She blinks at him. She's worked all her life and feels like she is working still. Before children, she was a bookkeeper at Mixer-Mobile, then when they were in school, she got a part-time job as receptionist at the County Mental Health Department. By the time they were old enough, she moved into a full-time secretarial job at Portland General Electric, taking the bus downtown. Even before the kids were grown, she did temp work whenever Carl was on strike or laid off. Then she retired, and had housework and yard work to do. Now she only looks after a small apartment a young person could clean in an hour, but it takes her days, attacking it in small shifts. And then there are her checkbook and bills.

I'm plenty busy, she tells him. She is so hurt he might think her lazy that she can't even inject the feisty note to make him laugh. She thinks, with shame, of all the hours she spends reading, how she lets herself finish a book before she does the week's laundry.

That's good, he says. That's why you're so young.

She forgives him, because he has the best intentions, and because she has a soft spot for him. When she first moved to the retirement complex in Tacoma she thought of it as full of old people, and of herself as something else. But the thing about living there is that you lose folks, at least one a month, and sometimes even at a once-a-week clip. The oldest ones from when she moved in are gone now, some to assisted living or nursing homes, and some just gone. Found dead in their apartments. Ambulances come and go. She sees them through her window that looks out to the back parking lot, and then she hears what happened at dinner. Every evening she puts out her *Good Night* door tag, and every morning she removes it before ten, or her neighbor Vivian will worry and start making calls. If she's running water and doesn't hear the phone or the knock, Glen will unlock the door with his master key, Vivian at his heels. It is both startling and reassuring to see them bursting in. She feels the same worry and zeal if Vivian forgets her door tag and she's the one who needs to make a call. Everyone, she knows, will die someday. But she inhabits a world where someday could be this day, this very one, and an empty chair at the dining table doesn't automatically mean that someone is out to dinner.

One day, a week or so after she got home and returned to her routines of scrambled egg, morning hygiene, book, nap, book, dusting, dinner, television, and door tag, the boys' choir leaves her flat. Her head fills with an unaccountable silence, the way ear pressure can change suddenly during a cold or on a flight. Alarmed, she takes her walker and ranges up and down the halls, trying to pick up the frequency. All she hears are televisions barking behind doors, the distant rumble of elevator machinery, and the greetings of residents shouting at each other as they congregate near the dining hall or community room. The return to unsung, unaccompanied life is almost unbearable. *No*, she protests—to herself or to someone else, she no longer knows which. Her religion, or lack of it, is confused these days: long since transformed from her Mennonite roots, and having passed through many stages in between, including, oddly, a seventies-infused return to the idea of reincarnation that her missionary parents had traveled halfway around the world to set straight. But, anyway, to whomever: *No, no, no.* And then— *Why has thou forsaken me?*

When she makes the mistake of mourning the vanished choir to Samantha during a phone call, her daughter irritatingly insists that it was never there in the first place, an auditory hallucination, hangover from the anesthesia, but as Kathryn points out to her tartly, Samantha wasn't the one to hear it, was she? So she has only ordinary reality to consider, whereas Kathryn had the unearthly beauty of the choir itself.

How could she make up music like that? It was utterly complete, with words she knew were words but that somehow never reached her as distinct and comprehensible. She was going to have to come closer, the singing seemed to say, if she wanted to hear all of it. And now she's ready to, the hole in the middle of her widening like an aperture—bigger, brighter, everything she can let in. Maybe she'll hear it again just beyond the walls of the Home. Maybe it will come back to her in the garden at the side of the building, where there's a little plastic bench she can sit on, amid the tulips with their splitting sides. She dresses in spring yellow and green for the excursion, and because there's still a nip in the air, loads her fleece into the walker basket.

Got a date? a resident asks her in the elevator, a lady whose name slips her mind. People come and go, and the whole process lately seems speeded up, the changeovers happening too often. But it doesn't matter which lady it is, because all residents, whoever they are, use the same script if someone looks about to leave the premises. Sometimes the saucy *Running away?* or *Going out to cause trouble?* But most often a wink, a smirk, a knowing tone: *Got a date?*

And the correct answer, the only answer you are allowed to give, is yes.

CENTENNIAL

Boston, 2013

Kathryn stands still, not changing face. She watches the adults fix their gaze on the ground beneath them, picking their way among the stones and roots.

She watches her mother in the dandie, or rather, glimpses her as the dandie pivots and dips between the Indian bearers on the trail. She can see the backs of the other missionaries, bobbing in the dimness, going down, seeming to sink into something—she knows it is the trail descending to the lower part of the mountain where the cars are parked that will take them to the train, but it looks simply like the mothers and fathers are sinking into the earth. Kathryn fixes her eyes on the bearers' white shirts, the pair of parentheses around the darkness that is becoming her mother. If her mother turns back to look, there is time for one more wave, one more flare of her face. But then the white shirts of the dandie bearers round the bend and she is gone.

She could catch her. She could break away from the line of children and run quicker than the teachers, be gone before they know it. She could weave through the other mothers and fathers until she is even with the dandie. She would slow to a walk and slip her hand up to her mother's, and they would remain clasped like that down to the car, and she would climb in and lean against her mother's warm side during the winding curves and have to be woken up when it was time to walk to the station. Every year before has been like that; Kathryn turning back and waving and waving to her brother Paul as he stood in the Woodstock line just as she is standing now.

She almost bolts for it, but then she happens to look down the row and catches Paul's eye; he's nine years older than she, about to begin his last year at Woodstock. He is grinningly his tall, tanned, belted self, and gives her a wink and then goes cross-eyed on purpose to make her smile, and though she doesn't smile back, he has had his effect. He has changed the moment, and it no longer seems possible to break free.

***

After dinner she finds her apartment, the one with the KATHRYN AVENUE sign her grandsons bought her at Seaside, Oregon, from the Pig 'N Pancake restaurant gift shop. It has made the move to Boston with her. Her new place is four doors down from the dining hall; sometimes she is off by one door. But this is her door and her sign, although someone has filled her studio apartment with all new things, furniture that doesn't belong to her. Someone has moved her out while she was at dinner eating beef stew and pear crisp. She sits in the not-her-chair, feeling her chest go shallow. They have disposed of all the things her daughter bought her after moving her across the country. Someone has decided she needs to go.

Her grandson Michael, who drives, comes for his visit. He times them after her meals because he dislikes sitting in the dining room with her tablemates. She doesn't blame him. Whenever a new person, a young person, joins them, the tablemates huddle in like vultures. They clamp their beaks around the young life and pull and tear for shreds of the world. Her grandson takes his place on the couch and puts on the animal videos they watch together. An old blind horse led around by his friend the goat. A mother deer licking spikes from the fur of an orphaned Labrador puppy. They usually fill her heart with tenderness. Michael tells her he hopes she will feel better soon, his way of saying that no one is taking and replacing her furniture. His mother must have warned him. Kathryn stares at the screen that she begins to see is her own television by her own table and her grandson plies the remote from where he is stretched out on her own sofa, asking her if she prefers *Animal Odd Couples* to videos of sea turtles. She does not prefer. She does not. She does. She is disappearing, just as they have decided that she must, moving her furniture out in an hour's time, then back again so her grandson will suspect nothing. If he found out he would help her, so they keep him from finding out. He just wants to know if sea turtles are better than—what. What. *What* are they better than?

Samantha arrives later and explains again how the furniture heist was real to her, Kathryn, but was not real. Her daughter is calm about this and so is her grandson flicking the channels, spelling p-u-p-p-i-e-s one letter at a time into the bar that says *search*. She doesn't know how he does that. When he's not around and she tries getting the puppy channel she always winds up with the news or the Catholics. They are mostly Catholic at her new building. They have lived in the neighborhood all their lives and gone to grammar school with some of the people they now eat with in the dining room. They went to Mass and drank from the same cup.

Yesterday Samantha took her to Shaw's and they picked out two cards, one for a tablemate who hasn't been well, and one for her brother Paul, who is about to turn one hundred. She and Michael and Samantha are going to go to his birthday party next week in Ohio.

"Only I shouldn't go anymore," Kathryn tells Samantha.

"Why not?"

"Because of all this."

"What's this?"

"This cracking up." And she means it. She should not ruin anybody's hundredth-birthday party by cracking up in the middle of it.

"But this is it. You won't see him again. He won't travel and you can barely travel. This is your last chance."

To see him alive, Kathryn adds for her. Her tall, belted, buckled, always smarter-than-she brother. Who teased and teased.

Though he did bring her egg custard when she was lying in the infirmary at Woodstock, her fingernail pressing moons in the pads of her thumbs, her throat full of razor blades. Her mother always made egg custard when she had a cold. "This will slip right down," she'd say.

***

"Eat your pudding," says Miss Smithson after supper, when everyone else has been excused.

"It makes me gag, miss."

"Children are going hungry in this country, children are mere skeletons, and you will not waste a good pudding."

Kathryn sits alone at the table in the commons, the light left burning for her alone. The chocolate pudding has a skin on the top of it that is like the skin on the milk when they boil it to get out the germs. That's the part she gags on. Her mother doesn't make her eat what she says she can't eat. Her mother is so far away at the mission in Dhamtari that a letter takes more than a week, sometimes two. They talk to each other in an echo chamber, Kathryn telling about things that are over and disappeared before her mother hears about them. Then her mother answers back about something Kathryn can barely remember.

But she gets news of her thirty-two rabbits. They are all living in the row of pens the groundskeeper built. They are all being fed and send their love.

Alone in the commons the shadows are uncommonly long. She knows they are just shadows, not ghosts. She doesn't know a single dead person and thinks that the old British ghosts in this school would not bother with a new American girl who doesn't like the skins on puddings. She rolls up the skin on her spoon and tries to scrape it on the lip of the dish so that the spoon is clean enough to try the pudding. She tells herself this is boring to ghosts, a girl scraping a spoon, making small clinks in the silence.

***

Kathryn acknowledges that the shower curtain is her shower curtain and not the shower curtain of the new person they tried to move into her apartment when she was at dinner. Samantha picked out the attractive aqua-patterned print just as she picked out the other new things the apartment needed. She comes every day and tidies up the circulars Kathryn picks up in the lobby and makes herself coffee and washes the cup.

At the hospital last week, they told her she hadn't had a real stroke, just a mini-stroke, and they didn't see any damage to the brain. Back at the apartment Kathryn had gone to every corner, reacquainting herself with the things Samantha had brought in big Target bags. Everything looked nice. Everything went together, bought as it was in one fell swoop, and her daughter kept tight control over clutter. Her old apartment in Tacoma had piles of things she was meaning to get to, like the letters from disabled veterans, Native American students who needed funds for college, and children with cleft palates. She had tried to help them all, taking turns, sending one twenty-five-dollar check a month, and saving the rest of the letters in a stack to work through. She wrote in block letters on the check memo lines, NO GIFTS BACK, because she wanted all twenty-five dollars to go to the children and Native Americans and veterans, but they sent them anyway, the address labels, the key chains, the Christmas cards, dream catchers, and plastic crucifixes—*With our thanks to you.* Then there were the stacks of old bills for shredding, and the stacks of circulars she meant to read. Her daughter pitched it all before the move. As Samantha filled trash bag after trash bag, Kathryn had wanted to grab her wrists and say *Stop it right there*, but when it was all gone and the tables and counters were clear she couldn't remember what it was she felt so attached to. It was like being given back time. The circulars and mail and papers represented hours and hours she owed people, and Samantha had wiped away the debt in ten minutes.

"The place looks nice," Kathryn tells her.

"Does it look like home?" Samantha asks.

Kathryn makes the face that she uses to mean, *Not really.* Samantha turns away and finds a balled-up tissue and puts it in the garbage, though Kathryn had intended to use it again. She replaces rolls of tissue on the shelf in the bathroom from her grocery bag. Samantha is always refilling, replenishing. Kathryn is always saying thank you.

Before the hospital, Samantha had come to visit her in the apartment as usual. Kathryn woke up in her armchair and was glad to see her. She tried to say that—*I'm glad to see you.* It had come out as if someone took her sentences and snipped them into syllables and shook them in a bag. And Samantha said, let's take it slower, and asked if she could understand her. And Kathryn said *yes*, and it was a sound that attached itself to a real word and had a meaning. Then Samantha asked her what she had for lunch and Kathryn said, *ar loo rum ta de.* They looked at each other, and Samantha said, let's give it a minute. And then Kathryn wanted to ask her if she had come from work, and said, *od him bay see foo*—and shook her head and tried to start over—*sa zeh eh ra meh nug.* And that's when Samantha said, let's go to the emergency room.

But it wasn't a stroke. It wasn't the event Kathryn had been waiting for every day since turning forty-nine, her mother's age when first paralyzed. Sometimes when Kathryn walked, one side suddenly drooped, a little curtsey. It lasted a second. That wasn't a stroke, either.

***

When Kathryn's mother was dead, and her father was dead, and her oldest brother, Russell, was dead, Russell's widow, Bertha, sent her a letter, wrapped in a sheet of paper blank except for Bert's careful handwriting, *I think you should have this.*

The letter was from her father, written to Russell and Bertha the day after her mother died. It chronicled the events in careful detail—her father was an expert record keeper. He always logged which sermon he had preached on a given Sunday in the small notebook he kept in his breast pocket. He made lists of congregation members absent, and whether they had good reason or no reason. He added salient facts about the service—who had complimented the sermon, whether a visiting dignitary of the church had come to share their fellowship, or a returning missionary had made a presentation of maps and slides and artifacts.

In this methodical way, he began the letter by noting that he and Mamma had had a nice lunch talking about Paul and Beulah's upcoming wedding, only a week away. Mamma had been awfully excited about the prospect of seeing everyone. Many hands were taking part in the preparations. Mamma could no longer prepare a dish, but she went over the lists of things her sisters were bringing to Beulah's family home in Elida. Mamma expressed the hope that her cold would be entirely gone by then. They decided that she should nap, to speed this recovery. He helped her from the wheelchair to the bed and made sure she was comfortable. He worked a crossword puzzle from the living room couch and looked in from time to time. Her sleep was more restless than usual, but he attributed this to the fact that she'd been poorly all week—her chest congested, her sinuses filled. At four o'clock a visitor had come to the door, Mrs. Yoder from the congregation, saying her husband had been taken to the hospital for chest pains. She was in a state. He saw nothing for it but to offer to drive her to the hospital. He looked in on Mamma; she was breathing in a labored fashion. He roused her enough to tell her he'd be back shortly, and to ask if he could do anything for her before he left. He couldn't make out her reply, her voice thick with sleep and congestion, but he thought it better to let her drift back to sleep than to wake her more. He returned two hours later to find Mamma's eyes half open and her breathing shallow and rattled. The doctor came immediately and said she'd had another paralytic stroke. She never focused her eyes properly after that moment or said another word to him. Dr. Heller said there was nothing either of them could have done even if they'd been at her side when it happened. He was stunned that he hadn't been, that he'd been at Mr. Yoder's bedside instead, who was believed to be suffering from indigestion. But, of course, he'd had no way of knowing. His dear companion of thirty-two years and their own Mamma had been returned to her Christ that night. Kathryn came home from Goshen College the next day, and he found it difficult to describe to them the extent of her shock. He tried to comfort her, though she didn't seem to want him, and he listened for her movements everywhere in the house because the depth of her silence worried him. But together they were bearing up and taking comfort in the Lord. He was, as ever, their loving father, etc.

The letter Bertha turned over came as a shock. Kathryn remembered those days and she didn't. The wedding had gone forward the day after the funeral. For Kathryn, it was a sleepwalking affair; the service for one melting into the service for the other, the organ and hymns for both one long dirge. She had chosen the dress her mother was buried in because no one else knew which was her favorite, and she had kissed her cold face as many times as she could before they pulled her off.

Now Bertha, who had sent her the letter, is dead, beside Kathryn's buried brother, Russell. Paul's wife Beulah is dead. And his second wife, Carol. Paul is not dead, and is waiting for his birthday card from the president. He plans to play golf on his one hundredth birthday. He took up French tapes and workbooks in his nineties to keep his brain fresh, and every day he jogs one slow lap around his apartment complex in Liberty, Ohio, when there is no snow on the ground. When there is snow he marches in place in the living room, a man of disciplined habits like their father. He was married again three years ago to a slightly younger widow in his Bible study group (a woman Kathryn has never met, and who, she understands, is not doing too well) and cooks for her and makes sure she takes her pills.

***

In Oregon, all the men grew Centennial beards timed for the day the state turned one hundred, also the year Samantha was born. It was an extraordinary thing to see the husbands transform into lumberjacks over the course of a few weeks, even the ones who wore suits to work.

Carl's beard made him look a little like an Old Order Mennonite. The beard and the hearkening back to her unsmiling great-uncles and grandfather in Johnstown, Pennsylvania, made Kathryn nervous. She'd married Carl for his unlikeness to all that, for the fact that her father couldn't size him up, or make sense of his union politics and Finnish socialism and cheerful good humor. Apart from the Mennonite overtones, Carl looked good in a beard, but she didn't like the way it felt against her skin when he crossed the divide of their twin beds to embrace her. After the divorce, she missed him sometimes.

When he died, she took him back, as if the divorce gap of fourteen years after the marriage of twenty-eight years had never happened, so that these days she feels more widow than divorcee. They chat once in a while. He takes a seat in her apartment, looking the way he did when he first took a seat at the counter where she waitressed. He chides her for not having loved him, and she says she did, sometimes. She asks if he stayed faithful when he worked out of town, and he shifts his eyes and almost disappears. He sharpens back into himself on her couch, and accuses her of never wanting him in that way. She says that's not one hundred percent true. She asks why he let himself get old, a passive lump. He says he couldn't help it; he *was* old. And so on.

Now she is six years older than he lived to be, so she guesses he has the last laugh about who's old and who's not. Paul is undeniably old but still belts and buckles and marches in place. The birthday card Kathryn picked for him has a satisfying 100 right in the middle, so round and full. When they talk by phone he goes on about his many wholesome habits, but Kathryn has no time for sibling irritation anymore. He is the last one who knew her when she had thirty-two rabbits, the last who knew their mother's sadness and their father's righteousness, the last who knew that as a child she gagged on the boiled milk and her arms crawled with eczema. They can sit side by side and hear the same notes of the Indian cuckoo, smell the same damp Woodstock dormitories, fear the same piano teacher, feel the same burning rap across the knuckles when they miss a note.

She dreads getting on the plane and her apartment vanishing when she turns her back on it, but her daughter and grandson will be with her and her son, Steve, will fly from the other coast and meet them. She hasn't seen her son for four months, and she likes it better when he is real and not just an idea in her head. Just like she likes Samantha being real. She knows Samantha tries hard to stay that way, but also needs to be at work or home with her family, which adds up to more than ninety percent of every day. It's always when she's gone that they replace Kathryn's furniture. They will not stop until they have her out on the curb, and Samantha will be nowhere to be found when it happens, which is their plan.

***

In the days ahead, Samantha comes and goes many more times than usual, and Kathryn likes this, but she doesn't like the way her daughter looks so worried all the time, or the arguments they have about the attendants here—Samantha so trusting, so willing to be duped. And though she likes it that Samantha decides one night to sleep over on her couch, she doesn't like it that after deciding to do this, she puts her head between her hands and begins to cry. The air goes out of Kathryn, witnessing this. She goes to the couch to sit by her child and stroke her long hair and put her arms around her. She knows to hold on patiently, waiting for her daughter to say what's the matter. Samantha crumples over sideways, sniffling, and Kathryn hands her a tissue from the supply she always keeps in her pocket. Could it be a teacher who scolded her? Trouble with a friend at school?

"What is it, Sammy?" She pats her shoulder.

Her daughter says nothing, and Kathryn presses again, still patting. It's something, all right. Something is worrying her.

Samantha raises a tear-stained face. "Everything's okay."

"But it's not. I can see."

"It's just work. I'm a little behind. But it'll be fine." Samantha straightens and blows her nose.

Something sharp jabs at Kathryn as her daughter flashes from child to adult—unemployment always Kathryn's worst fear, after all the layoffs, the strikes. All the times the household budgeting envelopes were empty and they still owed the orthodontist, the gas bill, the piano teacher.

"Are you going to lose your job?" she asks.

Samantha blows her nose again, harder, and says, "No, Mom, don't worry. Everything's fine. I'm going to call the boys before they go to bed."

Kathryn remains beside her on the couch while Samantha talks to each of the two younger boys in turn, asking if they did their homework, if Christopher worked on his sophomore speech, Matty, his Spanish. She says to one that she doesn't think she'll make it to the soccer game. Did Dad wash his uniform? Make sure he throws it in tonight if he didn't. She says to the other, text me if you want to go anywhere after school tomorrow. Just because I'm not around doesn't mean you don't have to ask.

"Because I need to," she says into the phone. "Because I just do," she says again. Then, "I'm sorry. We'll figure it out."

It dawns on Kathryn that she is the problem. The boys are asking for their mother, and she's here, not home with them.

She tries to rise abruptly, but hovers in midair. Samantha gives her the boost up and rises too, keeping a steadying arm around her. "Where's your walker?" she asks.

Kathryn doesn't retort that when her daughter needed her because she was crying on the couch, Kathryn didn't need her walker to cross the room to get to her.

"Don't walk without it, Mom, okay?"

"Stop telling me what to do."

"Fine."

"I'm not a child."

"Fine."

Samantha stands by while she pulls one leg after the other into her bed. Then Samantha retrieves the walker from where Kathryn stranded it and parks it pointedly alongside the bed. From Kathryn's view at eye level, it's like a little cage; if she wants to get out of bed, she has to step right into its box. Samantha turns out the all the lights, leaving the little night-light in the bathroom to glow.

She, Kathryn, is the problem, and it's not her fault. She told

Samantha that she was fine in her apartment in Tacoma. She had her car, the social security that covered her rent, and there were no attendants to bully her and plot to make her homeless on the street. Sometimes she has dreams she is sleeping under a bridge, and then she wakes up, and Samantha is not there, and even though Kathryn is not under a bridge it still takes her a very long time to figure out where she actually *is*. She lies very still while she does this, so that when a woman charges in, all loud and fake-happy, saying, "Time for breakfast, Miss Kathryn! Do you want some help getting up?" she tries to play possum for as long as possible, because she *does not know* that person.

There is a strange light coming from the other side of the studio. At first she tries to ignore it so it will go away, and then, as surreptitiously as possible, she raises her head enough to see what it might be.

It is one of them, a dark figure crouching, but before she can cry out, her eyes adjust slightly and she sees that it is Samantha sitting at Kathryn's small table, tapping away on her laptop, her face glowing as she leans toward its screen.

As the problem, she knows she is the one who needs to go, though where, she can't say yet. They will have won, those people here who mean to put her out, but she'll have won, too, being away from their clutches. She'll bring her pocketbook, her charge plate. She's left home before, taken a train, gone west.

Samantha does her best, but she has her hands full. And she needn't have upset the applecart in the first place—Kathryn was fine in her apartment in Tacoma, driving herself to Fred Meyers or Safeway, buying her milk and eggs and cans of soup. Kathryn liked it that way and she'll get things back to normal as soon as possible. She will have to go it alone, but she's prepared for that—the way she was alone in the narrow bed at Woodstock, and the narrow bed of her marriage, and that of her divorce-become-widowhood, and is alone now in the new twin bed Samantha bought for her here.

Aloneness has been her constant companion: The children left, didn't they? And before they actually left, they always wanted to be away, doing this or that with other people. Carl didn't leave, she made him go, but the aloneness after amounted to the same thing. She left her father, too, but only because she was a superfluity to him, a person warming the teakettle, someone who didn't quite fit into his routine. He actually marked her absent in his little book when she stayed home from church after her mother's death. As soon as he left the house, she'd go lie down on her mother's bed and cover herself with her mother's winter coat, curling up as small as she could under its woolen weight. Morbid, he called it, when he found her sleeping there.

But by then aloneness was already her special friend, slipping its cold arm around her when she was a girl left behind at school, watching her mother's white-shirted bearers disappear down the trail like the last flickers of candles before unseen fingers pinched them out.

Coda

Boston, 2015

The winter shadows lengthen, and the sun flares orange and goes out. Samantha draws the blinds against her reflection in the windows. Kathryn occasionally stirs, mostly without talking, but sometimes she'll stare and murmur things to the place she has business with, a place beyond Samantha. And sometimes she'll look straight at Samantha and say, almost unintelligibly, but Samantha can make it out, *I love you, baby.*

Kathryn sleeps during Samantha's meals on trays and during Mark's calls and the family's visits. She sleeps when Samantha and the aide give her a sponge bath, rubbing lotion on her limbs and dressing her in a fresh flowered housecoat, worn backward like a hospital gown. She sleeps when Samantha raises or lowers the head of the bed or tilts her slightly one way or another, rolling towels as wedges to keep her angled and not flat on her back. Samantha reads and does yoga, looks out at the frozen trees, returns cups and trays to the dining room, and keeps a chart of the morphine drops.

In the days to come, only one of Kathryn's eyes will open—and that just a thin crescent. It gleams in the dark and seems to hold Samantha's, but she knows this is not really true. Her mother's eye is fixed and unseeing. Kathryn's body, always small, is now, without food or water for two weeks, so flat that it scarcely makes a shape in the covers. By miraculous luck of the calendar, Samantha has been able to accompany her mother this whole final part of the journey; it's as if Kathryn purposely picked the time between semesters to die, knowing it was when they could be together day and night without interruption. The boys come over some evenings to do their homework, and they text her, but no one is suggesting that Samantha come home.

The shadows lengthen, the sun flares orange and goes out. On the fifteenth day, her mother's breathing comes in little fish gasps, her mouth ajar. Samantha angles her toward the window to catch every flash of birdwing, every thin ray of winter light. She sits on the edge of the bed and holds her mother's hand, silky warm. The good eye is open its slit. Once in a while Samantha says something, some commentary on the still and unchanging world outside, or some encouragement that her mother can go when she is ready, follow whatever new thing is revealing itself. She also says ordinary things like, the boys will be coming home from school now, they'll be letting the dog out. She tries to conjure the running dog for her mother to see.

ACKNOWLEDGMENTS

My thanks go to the editors of publications in which some of these chapters first appeared: "Your Best Yet," at *Harvard Review*; "Pie," as a *Solo* for *Ploughshares*; "The Big Goombah" (under the title "Boys' Choir"), at *The Carolina Quarterly*; and "Ultraviolet," at *MussoorieWriters.com*.

I appreciate, more than I can say, the generosity of Suzanne Berne, Paul Doherty, and Elizabeth Graver, who indefatigably read and commented on multiple drafts of this shape-shifting project. I am grateful to the National Endowment of the Arts for a fellowship that allowed me time to write, for a grant from the American-Scandinavian Foundation that supported travel to Finland, and to Boston College for providing, through several channels, both writing time and resources for research. Finally, it's been a gift and a privilege to be represented by Emily Forland and edited by Pat Strachan.